Praise for *The Happiest Girl in the World*

"A brilliant and often heartbreaking novel. Following a young girl striving to live a complicated dream, *The Happiest Girl in the World* probes the tragedy of the at-all-costs mentality that fuels Olympic performances."

—Blythe Lawrence, coauthor of Aly Raisman's
Fierce: How Competing for Myself Changed Everything

"*The Happiest Girl in the World* is a searing look at elite gymnastics and the lengths an athlete will go to reach her goal. Dillon writes a harrowing story about how hope can be saddled with burdens and how sacrifice can wear down the soul. It's timely and spirited. I devoured this book."

—Elissa R. Sloan, author of
The Unraveling of Cassidy Holmes

Praise for *Mercy House*

"A life-altering debut featuring fierce, funny, and irreverent women who battle the most powerful institution in the world. This is the book we've all been waiting for."

—Amy Schumer

"Never underestimate the power of a group of women. Fierce, thoughtful, and dramatic—this is a story of true courage."

—Susan Wiggs, *New York Times* bestselling author

"In *Mercy House,* Alena Dillon gives us one of fiction's more unlikely lovable heroines: elderly, dynamic Sister Evelyn, whose tale—and that of her housemates—is as unexpected as it is moving. This is a thoughtful, accomplished debut."

—Therese Anne Fowler, *New York Times* bestselling author of *Z, A Well-Behaved Woman,* and *A Good Neighborhood*

"[A] stirring, fiery debut. . . . Dillon balances her protagonist's righteous anger with an earnest exploration of Evie's faith and devotion to justice and community service. This uncompromising story will light up book clubs."

—*Publishers Weekly*

"Dillon's debut novel is heartwarming to its core. With a widely diverse cast of supporting characters, author Dillon brings Bed-Stuy to life. Realistic in scope and pious without being preachy, *Mercy House* will appeal to fans of Naomi Ragen's *The Devil in Jerusalem* (2015) and Autumn J. Bright's *Lovely* (2017)."

—*Booklist*

"Dillon's debut novel is heartwarming and easy to read, [and] it never glosses over the history of abuse and sexism in the Catholic Church. . . . Those interested in religious fiction will also appreciate a simple narrative tackling complex church events. Perfect for reading groups."

—*Library Journal*

The
HAPPIEST
GIRL
in the
WORLD

Also by Alena Dillon

Mercy House

The HAPPIEST GIRL in the WORLD

A Novel

ALENA DILLON

WILLIAM MORROW
An Imprint of HarperCollinsPublishers

P.S.™ is a trademark of HarperCollins Publishers.

HarperCollins books may be purchased for educational, business, or sales promotional use. For information, please email the Special Markets Department at SPsales@harpercollins.com.

FIRST EDITION

Designed by Diahann Sturge

Library of Congress Cataloging-in-Publication Data has been applied for.

ISBN 978-0-06-301904-1

21 22 23 24 25 LSC 10 9 8 7 6 5 4 3 2 1

For survivors, the athletes who inspire us, and
those who are one and the same

AUTHOR'S NOTE

This is the part where we explain that this novel is a work of fiction. References to real people, events, organizations, or locations are not harbingers of fact, but only a tool to provide a sense of authenticity. Everything else—characters, places, establishments—is the product of the author's imagination.

And yes, yes. That is correct. This story is my creation. It came from my brain. But it also came from what we've seen in the news—all that was admitted, and all that was denied. It was informed by the suffering of actual people, at the hands of actual people.

The story in this book is not real, but it may, in fact, speak truth.

PROLOGUE

The Olympic Trials

zero in on the spot across the floor, the exact spot—my launching pad. Nothing outside that spot matters. Not the white noise of the crowd, not my family in the stands, not my coach and what he did. It all fades into the background. And I run. I need to cover only fifty feet, but I put all my body's strength into crossing that distance as fast as I can. I go to that spot like a cheetah goes for a gazelle. My senses are heightened and I feel the give of the carpet and the send-off of the spring, and it's as if the mat wants me to stay put but knows I must go, like a good mother, the kind mine intends to be. The road to hell is paved with good intentions, and this: a spring floor.

As I sprint, I breathe deliberately in and out through pursed lips. My shoulders round forward to make my body aerodynamic, to slice through the air—a human imitating a rocket—and my arms are straight and swinging. Now I *am* a rocket, courageous and unstoppable. Maybe even a little dangerous.

I can't think of that now. I'm not allowed to feel on the gym floor.

I bolt toward that spot, toward the gold, toward the end of my gymnastics career and freedom and womanhood and a new identity.

My arms outstretch and reach for the rest of my life. I hurdle off one leg, dive forward onto one hand and then the other, skimming over them. This part is child's play. I've been doing roundoffs since I was six years old. I'm building momentum I'll eventually need. Back when I had time for anything other than training and my dad didn't look at me like I scared him, I used to play Super Mario Bros. with him and my twin brother, Joe, in our unfinished basement. It took three jumps to make Mario fly. The roundoff is my first jump.

When I'm inverted, I swing my legs together and my heels hammer into the floor as one.

Jump two: I bend my knees and throw myself backward. It goes against every survival instinct to jump without first looking where you're going—especially when leading with your head. So much about this life has meant working against every survival instinct. More than that. It's meant letting one self die so another could be born, over and over, reincarnating at every training stage. I've already died at least six times to get to this moment.

If I speak now, maybe I'll remember who I was at the beginning. Maybe I'll realize who I'm meant to become.

I land upside down on my hands and push back to my feet. This motion is effortless. I'm functioning on autopilot, muscle memory. I've been doing back handsprings since I was seven.

First the sprint, then the roundoff, and now a back handspring. I've gathered the speed of a locomotive. My wheels are whirring, my pistons are pumping. Hear that whistle? It's telling you that I can't stop now, so you better get out of my way.

Jump three: I land on the mat and hurl myself backward again, but this time all the gathered energy catapults me more vertically. I've trained so hard and so long, I've defied all reason, even gravity. I've learned to do what no one else can. I've uncovered an impossible secret. I'm flying.

Nobody achieves these heights without stepping on a few heads.

Midair, I cross my arms over my chest—like a corpse, but never more alive. I tense my core and swivel. Now I'm not just flying, I'm spinning too, a planet both rotating on its axis and orbiting the sun. When my dad first saw this move, he called me a spandex-wrapped football. He used to speak only the language of team sports—not uneven bars and vaults and beams. The day he called me that, I laughed hard and he looked relieved. We shared an understanding and, for an instant, something opened inside each of us and light passed through.

My feet, bound together as if by rope, pass over my head and return to their rightful position below me, but they're still hovering eight feet above the ground. I continue revolving.

My name means "winged," and in this moment, I am. I'm the Angel Gabriel, here to proclaim to everyone in this packed arena and everyone watching at home, holding their breath until my feet land, that there is more than the ordinary—there is another way. It takes sweat and blood. It takes failure and sacrifice. It takes a small lifetime. But at the end of all that, there is this. There's no shame in greatness.

I keep spiraling and circling and soaring.

One year, my training paused after a wrist fracture, and I went to my town's annual county fair. There was a ride called Gravitron, and it looked like a flying saucer. It spun, and when it reached a certain speed, the floor dropped out, but centripetal force kept you plastered against the wall. That's what this feels like. I am a self-contained Gravitron. I am a centripetal force.

I've hardened in the air. I'm as compact as I can be. When matter is compressed into a small space it creates a black hole. I'm a black hole. I've sucked out souls. What will happen when I land?

I'm too old and tired to come back. I'll never again be the

object of a crowd's awe. I'll never again be what the whole world is looking at. A black hole sometimes occurs when a star is dying. (Am I dying?) And because light can't escape from black holes, they are invisible.

I might soon be invisible. Will my success matter when no one sees me? Or will I be alone and haunted by the memory of what it cost to be special for an instant?

I'm careening back to earth now. A back handspring and double twisting double layout are almost behind me. That's a lot of velocity to diffuse and convert. I have to stomp this energy out like a fire.

My feet punch into the mat. The impact rushes up my ankles, into the contracted muscles of my calves and thighs, through my hip bones and abdomen, rattles across my rib cage like a xylophone, and vibrates into my raised arms before settling, as a pulse, in my fingertips.

I stuck the standard layout at nine years old and the double at twelve. It took another two years before I performed the full twist, and another after that before it became a double twisting double layout.

I'm not done, and the next move is the hardest. After the physical exhaustion of that series, I have to take all the impetus garnered from the run and flips in this direction and reverse its thrust into a front tuck. It's often more horsepower than I can handle. It wants to fuel a larger movement, and I sometimes have to contain it with a stutter step forward. But that single step—one step in a lifetime of many million steps—could cost me fifteen years of work. That step cannot be undone. I know that, my coach knows that, my mom knows that, my entire town knows that. They've been discussing this crucial moment for months.

And I imagine they're watching me now, those small-town people with their nine-to-fives, household chores, and favorite sitcoms, their clear notions of right and wrong—what simple pleasures. I haven't had time to know them as more than people in cars I passed on the way to the gym in the next state. But they know me. One form of me, at least. I don't even know the real me.

My dad wanted to name me Sarah, a typical, everyday name. He never cared about being somebody. He had my mom and his house and his kids and that was enough for him. My mom hoped I'd be more than her, a housewife without a college degree, and my father, a used-car salesman who was too honest to be successful in his trade. More than Waynesville, Indiana. More than just another girl. She wanted me to be a fiery winged thing. My dad got his name, but my mother got hers too, in what was perhaps their last real compromise.

I am Sera. And this is my truth.

PART I

CHAPTER 1

In the beginning, we flitted around the gym like dandelion seeds in the wind. Skipping. Cartwheeling. Somersaulting. Leaping. Arching our spines the wrong way and tumbling through a back walkover. Our bodies were lean and limber. Generous and forgiving. They didn't know limitations, only what they couldn't do yet. They didn't know injury, only elasticity, amusement, and wonder. They didn't know starvation, only hunger. They didn't know the wrong kind of touch, only the guidance of a spotter. The pull of being hoisted up after a fall. A celebratory high five. This was before our voices were stripped. We'd spend decades restoring our diaphragms, larynxes, lips, tongues, and teeth.

Back then, when we felt whimsical, we pranced the mats like nymphs. When we were dogged, we strutted the perimeter as if we owned the place. Like we were child queens, the fantastical kind that jointly, harmoniously ruled over the same land. But instead of from robes, our long legs stemmed from sweaty leotards that were sometimes too small. Instead of crowns, we wore buns and barrettes, our hair secured with pins and enough hair spray to light up the place. The gym was our kingdom, our playground, our altar. The sport was our discipline and our ministry. It was how we rejoiced, Lucy and I.

We loved gymnastics in a way other girls didn't. This arrogance, combined with the sheer amount of time we spent at the facility, afforded us authority over those who considered gymnastics an after-school activity, not a lifestyle. We called them pretend gymnasts. We were the real things.

Only *we* knew where Coach Jennifer stored the extra chalk. Only *we* knew the exact spot on the vending machine to pound when the Gatorade stuck. Only *we* knew 2008 Olympian Shawn Johnson's middle name (Machel).

Shawn Johnson. Peanut. America's Sweetheart. Adorable but powerful. Approachable but accomplished. She soared higher and spun tighter than we thought possible. But when she exhaled through pursed lips before a routine, and when her face broke into a smile after she nailed it, we imagined her as a normal girl, drumming a pencil as she worked through a math equation or chatting with her family in a Dairy Queen booth.

When it wasn't our turn on the equipment, we re-created the wrap-up interview with Shawn Johnson after she made the Olympic team, alternating who got to be Peanut. As the journalist, I stuck an empty toilet paper roll near Lucy's mouth and asked, "What's it like to be Shawn Johnson right now?"

Lucy bit her lip the way we'd practiced in front of the bathroom mirror. "It's amazing. I feel like the luckiest girl in the world."

"Happiest," I corrected.

It was important, as two future Olympians ourselves, that we got it right. We were young dreamers who thought it possible, if we just believed strongly enough, if we just worked hard enough, that we could both triumph in an arena where so few did. Where so few survived at all.

After I landed my first back handspring on the beam, Lucy's knees popped in and out as if she were doing the Charleston while her fists punched the air. Her face opened with delight and turned up toward the rafters, like she was Snoopy from *Peanuts*. She was maybe nine years old at the time, almost a year older than me, as our birthdays bookended 1999. Her hair was the color of fox fur, her freckles prominent, and her teeth banded in patriotic braces. It's one of my memory's most genuine examples of bliss, even all these years later.

From that point on, we performed her dance whenever we progressed onto a more challenging movement. I did it when she stuck a layout stepout on the high beam. She did it when I perfected a front aerial. I did it when she was first invited to the Talent Opportunity Program camp, known as

TOPs, down at the Balogh Ranch, and she did it when I was accepted the following year.

At Elite Gymnastics in Indianapolis, a city home to the headquarters of USA Gymnastics, we were among the few girls Coach Jennifer believed had that special quality. She knew if girls, even at six years old, had what it took by the way they held themselves, the fearlessness with which they bounded into new movements, and the grace with which they leapt. Either you had it or you didn't, and Lucy and I had it.

Since we both lived an hour from Indianapolis in opposite directions, we had gymnastics to thank for our friendship. The girls at school were poor fools who weren't in our secret, who hadn't found what we'd found, who didn't speak our language. Lucy and I were soul sisters, pure and simple.

But in an unclean world, nothing pure remains that way for long.

July 2010

The Balogh Ranch was the epicenter of our country's gymnastics. It was a mecca. The mother ship calling us home. Smack-dab in the middle of the Texas wilderness, the ranch was an autonomous world of gymnastics, made up of training facilities, forest trails, fields populated with animals (goats, miniature horses, chickens, peacocks—even a camel), and log bunkhouses named for host cities of the summer Olympics: Athens Motel, Sydney Inn, Atlanta House, Barcelona Resort. There wasn't anything within an hour's drive. Not a grocery store, a gas station, a hotel—nothing. The place was devoted to gymnastics and gymnasts alone, and the ideals of those inside were enclosed within a chain-link fence. The rest of the world was not welcome. Parents weren't allowed to stay, and with no cell service, they were nearly impossible to contact at all.

In addition to being the official USA Gymnastics National Team Training Center, it also hosted camps for younger girls. They accepted only fifty in each age group, and Lucy and I, against all odds (although it was no surprise to us), were both in. The ranch was going to advance our skills, expose us to new coaches and, of course, Rudi and Vanda Balogh, the husband-and-wife duo who owned the ranch and were two of the most influential personalities of USA Gymnastics. Vanda was the United States national team coordinator and head of the Olympic team selection committee. She decided who made it and who didn't. Impressing her and staying in her good favor was the difference between a dream crushed and a dream realized. It was everything.

What a story Lucy and I would become, the 2016 Olympians the media fawned over: two best friends from small Indiana towns competing for it all on the world stage in Rio de Janeiro. We'd be on the covers of *Seventeen, Time,* and *Sports*

Illustrated, arms looped around each other's necks, grinning into the camera. They'd put us on cereal boxes. We'd advertise women's razors and flavored Greek yogurt. And in interviews, we'd tell journalists, "We feel like the happiest girls in the world."

LUCY AND I requested matching gear each birthday and Christmas, so our ranch dorm had the symmetry of an open-winged butterfly. There were the backpacks screen-printed with a girl bent into a bridge and block lettering that read "Warning: I may flip out." There were the white metal water bottles stamped with "Hear Me Roar" in pink cursive. And on our wrists, there were our rubber friendship bracelets, mine imprinted with "She believed she could," and Lucy's completing the phrase with "So she did."

We recapped the day beat by beat, filed down each other's foot calluses with a special pumice stone, massaged each other's hands with a mint and eucalyptus cream, and snapped pictures of the other doing everyday tasks in the midst of gymnastics poses: brushing our teeth in a handstand, picking our noses in an arabesque, reading a book in an elbow stand, or eating an apple in a straddle jump.

We were often overtaken by whopping bouts of laughter, the kind that lasted well beyond the reasonable bounds of the joke. When one gained control, the other reignited the spell, and it was like we were daughters of Zeus passing thunder back and forth. We laughed until our chiseled abdomens ached and someone pounded on our shared wall and shouted, "It's midnight. Shut the hell up."

One night, Lucy sat cross-legged on her bed, flossing her teeth using a plastic tool to weave through her braces. Her words garbled around her fingers. "I bet you'll have your double tuck dismount by the end of the week."

"If I do, you can buy me a cookie." I said, using a phrase we'd coined; because of our strict diet, baked goods were sacred currency.

The double tuck dismount was my current itch. In that way, gymnastics was like a pox. The more I scratched, the more it spread.

That afternoon, one of the beam coaches had directed me to drive my heels into the ground on my roundoff connecting skill, and I was already jumping higher. My family hadn't eaten red meat for a year to afford new leos, the trip to Texas, and extra training at the gym in Indiana—we were up to twenty hours a week now. Every additional skill on my roster was something tangible to legitimize their sacrifices.

I was treating hand rips from working the uneven bars. I'd trimmed back the dead skin with sterilized nail clippers, dabbed the raw flesh with bacitracin, placed a saturated black tea bag on the tear, and was wrapping my hand with gauze and tape. All gymnasts' palms were wounded. When our rips were gory, we showed them off. I'd taken pictures and would post them to Facebook as soon as I had access to the internet, but for now taped them with arrogant flair.

"Think the Baloghs will come to practice tomorrow?" I asked.

The attention of the famous duo was reserved for national team members, but they'd greeted the campers at our arrival. Rudi had a bushy white mustache like a long toothbrush head. He commanded the room with his flailing arms and thick Romanian accent. Vanda was more reserved. Her hair was dyed the same shade as her tan skin and she spoke through a tight smile with her chin jutted toward the ceiling. Vanda said that if we were good, she'd have Shawn Johnson demonstrate her gold medal skills.

Peanut was on the grounds. Her fingers gripped the same uneven bars I gripped. She was coached by the very people who critiqued me. I was quite literally following in her footsteps, sharing her road to greatness. It didn't matter that the ranch gym was sweltering in the heat of a Texas July, relieved only by oscillating fans that puffed hot air like a dragon's exhale onto my neck. It didn't matter that my training tank was drenched with sweat, and the hair on my nape dripped. It didn't matter that I was dizzy with weariness, that my muscles were spent, that exhaustion radiated from me after a morning of conditioning and an afternoon of routines.

Shawn Johnson had been weary. Her sweat had dripped onto the mats at my feet. Working hard was just part of the deal. Becoming an Olympian hurt. Peanut had done it. Lucy was doing it. I could suck it up or get out. I was only ten, but I'd already learned to suck it up.

"I hope they come when I'm on floor. I feel like that's my strength right now," Lucy said.

"You are rocking floor."

Lucy's hand fell from where it was flossing and her lips waxed, as if she'd tasted something acrid.

"Is it the pulled muscle in your back? I'll go plug in our heating pad."

"No, I keep having these weird stomach pains. And they're getting worse."

"Want me to rub it?"

"That's okay."

The ranch was quiet at night but for the occasional chirp of cicadas and hoot of owls. "Do you think you're gonna . . . puke?"

"It doesn't feel like that. It more, like, hurts." She shook her head and hunched over, cradling her belly. Her lips bulged around her braces. "It's bad. Like, really bad. Can you get Jennifer?"

Our coach's cabin was across the facility, a long dark walk away. Going out would be like falling down a well with only the liquid moon as my rope. It'd offer just enough light to see the faces of the coyotes. Or worse, Rudi's guard dog.

Lucy knew what she was asking. Tears collected in her eyes. "I'm sorry."

Even when she released the high bar and fell onto her chest, breaking her collarbone, Lucy hadn't cried.

"Oh, jeez," I said, because she was scaring me. "I'll be right back."

Her head dropped against the wall behind her and she squeezed her eyes shut. "Thanks."

As I shoved my feet into Lucy's sneakers—they were larger and easier to slip on—I noticed the ranch's welcome letters on top of the dresser, the ones that had been resting on our pillows when we arrived. I thought of that long walk. The blackness. A foreboding howl. I grabbed the paper and handed it to Lucy.

"Actually, we aren't supposed to get Jennifer. Remember? They said if we have a problem at night, we shouldn't call our coaches. We should call the doctor."

Lucy opened her eyes long enough to squint at the paper. "Dr. Levett."

Our cell phones didn't get service at the ranch, but each room was equipped with a landline for on-campus calls. I gestured to it. "Should I call him?"

"Can you just call Jennifer then?"

"Okay," I said, happy for the compromise, and lifted the handset. "What's her number?"

Lucy's lip trembled. "I don't know." She moaned and held her belly. "It really hurts. Call the doctor, I guess."

"Okay. Good idea," I said brightly. "We don't want to get in trouble with the Baloghs. They'd remember if we disobeyed. Besides, Dr. Levett is famous. He treated Kerri Strug in Atlanta and basically every Olympian since. It'll be cool to meet him."

While we waited for the doctor to arrive, I crawled into bed beside Lucy and read to her from *International Gymnast Quarterly* using different voices until I landed on a Cookie Monster impersonation that made her laugh.

Dr. Levett knocked, but I didn't have to get up from bed; he let himself in. He had hair so dark it looked drawn in, a round face, rimless glasses, and a shirt tucked into pants that were hiked around his waist. He was pleasantly rodent-like; if he were to be made into a cartoon, he would have been a kindly chipmunk dad, but with a stethoscope hanging around his neck.

"Hello, girls. So sorry to hear someone isn't feeling good." He smiled at me and then his attention shifted to Lucy. "I'm guessing you're the patient?" When Lucy nodded, he said, "I'm sure it's just indigestion. Sometimes when we eat new foods in a new place, it makes us feel funny. But let's take a look just to be sure."

He was friendlier than the ranch coaches and the Baloghs, who were stern, especially in the severe way they wracked us, pushing us further and further into overextended splits. But this doctor didn't even seem annoyed that we'd pulled him out of bed so late.

"Mind if I borrow your seat?" he asked. I scooted off Lucy's bed and onto mine. He nestled the stethoscope tips into his ears and, before he dipped the tiny dish below the collar of her nightgown, asked, "May I?" With Lucy's consent, he listened to her lungs and heart. Then his fingers, meaty with a spattering of black hair and well-kempt nails filed straight across, palpitated her throat.

He asked Lucy to lie flat on the bed. While he waited for her to get into position, he looked over his shoulder and asked me, "Are you girls having a nice time at the camp?"

"Yes."

He pressed his fingers into the top of her stomach, over her nightshirt. "It's such a wonderful opportunity for you." He shifted his fingers two inches and pressed again. "The Baloghs are some of the greatest coaches in the world. You're so lucky to be able to learn from them and the rest of the staff." He tried one more spot and smiled back at me, sort of mischievously, like we might be in on a shared joke. "You know Shawn Johnson?"

Duh. I nodded.

"I've been Shawn's doctor for years. She's really sweet, just like you girls seem to be." Then he regarded Lucy with the kind of paternal tone a doctor uses before he administers a shot, one that communicates, *There is about to be some degree of unpleasantness, but it's for your own good.* "You have a little bowel upset. New diet, new routine, probably not enough water. I see it all the time. But don't worry. A little adjustment here will clear it right up. This might feel uncomfortable, but it'll be over before you know it, and you won't have to miss a day of training. I know how precious your time here is." He laid one hand flat on Lucy's stomach. The other drifted down her legs and slid under the hem of her nightshirt.

My stuffed basset hound, Petunia, which my parents bought me after our dog of the same name died, was on the pillow beside me. I tugged her ear.

Dr. Levett continued speaking to me. "I probably started working with Shawn when she was around your age, actually. I've worked with a lot of gymnasts I'm sure you've seen on TV. Name the gymnast, and I bet you an ice cream sundae that I'm her doctor. What's your name? I can tell Shawn you said hello."

After the innumerable times I'd said her name, Shawn would now hear mine? I sat up taller. "Sera Wheeler."

"It's nice to meet you, Sera. Who knows? Maybe you'll be on the Olympic team in a few years, and I'll be telling another little lady at this camp that I worked with you too. Wouldn't that be fun?" He removed his arm from beneath Lucy's dress, dipped his fingers into the shirt pocket of his polo, and pulled out two purple discs. "Chew these and have a glass of water." When she extended her little palm, he deposited the tablets onto it. "It's always smart to have a thorough check, so kudos to you both for calling. That was very responsible. Your parents would be proud."

"Thank you, Dr. Levett," Lucy said, and carried the pills obediently to her mouth.

"Please. I'm Eddie to you. And it was my pleasure. You

can call me anytime. I know training can get rough some-times. I'm here to help you gymnasts. I want you to succeed. My motto is 'Gymnasts first,' and I mean it." At the door, he paused and jutted his chin toward my stuffed animal. "When I was a boy, I had a dog just like that. I think you and I have a lot in common."

"Are you feeling better?" I asked Lucy when the door closed behind him.

The hem of her nightshirt was still gathered from her exam. She pulled it down. "Not yet."

I reached for the lamp and twisted the knob to send us into darkness. Light from the moon spilled as if from a tipped cup into our cabin, illuminating Lucy's pale profile as she stared, entirely awake, at the ceiling.

"It'll get better soon."

It was two years before I spoke to Eddie again. In the meantime, I graduated from elementary school; a tsunami struck Japan; USA Gymnastics received a detailed complaint about a celebrated coach touching minors inappropriately and filed it away; Lucy's teeth were freed from their me-tallic chains; the United States killed Osama bin Laden; I launched an Instagram account to share Lucy's and my silly photos; McKayla Maroney's report of Eddie sexually abus-ing her was ignored by a top USA Gymnastics coach; and we trained and we trained and we trained.

CHAPTER 2

May 2012

The morning of the Secret Classic, poison ivy swelled below my left eye, swooped down my cheekbone, and roped up my neck like a strangling vine. I stared at my reflection in the bathroom mirror and screamed.

My father had assigned me to weed the fence line the day before, after hearing how much my mother and I spent on my performance leo.

The leo I'd worn to the state and regional championships was getting tight; its seams cut into my neck and groin and my shoulders tried to break through as wings. This new leo was deep purple, like a ripe plum, almost black and shimmering with a constellation of Swarovski crystals scattered over the front. It stretched over me like a second skin. It also cost three hundred dollars.

"For something she won't wear more than once?" my

father sputtered when he found the receipt in the kitchen garbage. "What is this, her wedding dress?"

"It is a tad expensive. You might be right about that," my mother said, which was her way of communicating that he was absolutely dead wrong. "But this leo is more important than a wedding dress. Judges deduct points if uniforms aren't up to snuff. Plus, you don't get a medal for getting married," she said, and then added an almost undetectable eye roll, the kind Midwestern women spend a lifetime sharpening. "Believe me."

He spoke directly to the receipt, like it might offer a better explanation. "Three hundred dollars for something that doesn't even come with pants?"

I knew it was a lot to spend, especially when my family had already swapped our Chinese takeout night for packages of dried ramen. There were less expensive leotards that were also perfectly nice and conformed to the International Gymnastics Federation's regulation for propriety and elegance. But when my mom saw this particular leo in a catalogue, her eyes glassed over as if she were already picturing her twelve-year-old daughter wearing it on a podium.

When my parents argued about my gym's increase in rates, my father stormed out of the house and returned hours later, smelling sour and sharp. I suspect he drove to a nearby abandoned airfield—he'd read every book in the World War II section of our town's library, and took particular pride in this historical landmark—and swigged from the fifth of

Wild Turkey he stowed in the spare tire cavity while he pictured American soldiers training on great big bombers right around the corner from where, seventy years later, he sold used Kia Fortes. He didn't wear his hangovers gracefully, so our finances suffered when his tie knot hung loose, his feet dragged through the lot, and he closed the blinds in the office that stunk of cheap air fresheners and mediocrity.

I envisioned the Great Leo Dispute of 2012 escalating similarly, and I couldn't have him slumped over at the competition like a pile of coats, so when my father's mouth opened around his next retort, I interrupted.

"I'll do chores to pay you back." He paused in his position and turned to me. "I really do love the leo. It's so pretty," I said, and his lips drifted closed.

My twin brother ended up weeding beside me, not to work off a debt, but as a punishment. When my mother told Joe he couldn't attend his friend's go-kart birthday party because we were traveling to the Classic in Chicago, he hurled his backpack across the living room, knocking a lamp to the floor. It didn't break, so perhaps he would have gotten off scot-free had he not punctuated the outburst by screaming, "I hate Sera, but I really hate you!" with such red-faced rancor, tears sprung to my mother's eyes.

My father was with us, digging out shrubs and whistling "Don't Fence Me In." Gardening was his responsibility, and one he relished. He liked the monotony of the tasks—weed, plant, water; weed, plant, water—and the accessibility of it.

It didn't take much skill or know-how to keep the beds tidy, and they were always in the back, waiting for him. Plus, there was satisfaction in the bloom. When it came to fruits of labor, not everything in his life was so available, so visible. In fact, sometimes there weren't results at all, no matter how hard he tried.

I suspect he selected this activity for my payment and Joe's atonement so we could all be together. I rarely spent time with anyone but my mother, who chauffeured me to practice and stayed to watch. While I waited for the sun to set and Joe slapped at invisible mosquitoes and flexed his hands as if his fingers were plagued by arthritis, my father was so pleased to be with us, he paused just to take in the sight.

"What an evening," he said, shaking out his legs before lowering beside a boxwood shrub. "Cool but not cold. Bright but not blinding. Just perfect."

Joe, who was positioned so my father couldn't see his face, mocked him, and I coughed so as not to laugh.

My brother wore a red Indiana Hoosiers T-shirt whose neck was stretched from his nervous habit of dipping his nose into his collar and pulling it up like a bandit without a bandanna. His chest protruded as two small humps beneath the fabric, sweat stained beneath his armpits and down his back, and his cheeks were flushed, as if rashed. As I burrowed my fingers into the soil, I compared our arms. His were beefy. Mine were sinewy. His hands were soft and fleshy. Mine were blistered and hard. In gymnastics, the smaller you were, the higher you flew. I was at an age susceptible to a growth spurt. In addition to a strict diet and exercise regimen, I'd begun sneaking half of my mother's coffee in the morning, hoping the caffeine would stunt my maturity. I felt satisfied seeing the contrast between my twin and me.

I yanked crabgrass by its root and tossed it in the pile. My mother would have to repaint my nails that night. I could already hear her say, "For the amount of work I do, it's almost like *I* should get a medal. Dontcha think?"

"So, Ser," my dad said. "You nervous about tomorrow?"

I'd competed at countless Junior Olympics competitions, often securing the title of all-around Indiana state champion in my age group, but this was the first national-level competition, the first time I'd be pitted against Junior Olympians from around the country for seats on the national team. The first time I'd be assessed by the USA Gymnastics board, the people who might one day decide whether or not I was Olympic material. And it was the first time I'd perform in the same room as members of the senior national team, my heroes who were seeking to qualify for the Olympic Trials that year. I wanted to impress the Olympic hopefuls, Vanda Balogh, Coach Jennifer, Lucy, my parents, Joe. All the strangers in the stands. Everybody.

"A little," I said.

My father stabbed his spade into the soil and stomped on the corner to drive it deeper. "I don't know how you do it, getting up in front of all those people."

Joe spoke into the ground, "She's a big fat show-off."

I snapped off a blade of grass. "Am not."

He crossed his arms over his full chest. "Maybe you aren't fat, but you are an attention hog."

I said more emphatically, "Am not."

"You're great. You deserve attention," my father said, hedging our argument the way he hedged the backyard. "Just remember there are other things you might be good at too. There's a whole world out there. Give other opportunities a fair shake."

My brother turned his attention to the earth. "Like she needs something else to be good at."

"Joseph," my father said.

"What? If Perfect Sera picks up another hobby, we won't have money to eat at all."

I didn't bother explaining that there was no such thing as perfect in gymnastics. There was no high score at all. It was part of what made greatness so difficult to explain or defend.

WHEN JOE'S REFLECTION appeared above mine in the bathroom mirror the morning of the Classic, his expression lifted from alarm to delight.

"Oh man," he said, his words trilling. "That's bad."

My mother's voice carried up from downstairs. "Sera? Did you chip your fingernails again? I knew you shoulda worn mittens overnight."

This wasn't a face for *Seventeen* or *Sports Illustrated*. This was a face for a medical journal.

"Don't cry," Joe said, pleased with the way the morning was progressing; now both our Saturdays had been ruined. "It'll make it worse."

In a moment, my mother was standing behind Joe. She was always concerned with her image, but in anticipation of seeing other gymnastics moms, and maybe hopeful there'd be photo opportunities, she'd paid special attention that morning. She still wore her hair in the style of Rachel Green, nearly twenty years after the debut of *Friends,* and that day it was especially poofy. Her makeup, a bit overdone as was my mother's tendency, was carefully applied, save for a glob of mascara in her right lashes. She wore the Not Your Daughter's Jeans she had scored at Goodwill and a tangerine fitted shirt with the collar opened one button too many.

My mother took my face in and said, "Okay." Then she pressed her lips together and nodded. "Hmm." Indiana lexicon for "holy shit."

"It's all over," I wailed. "I can't compete like this."

"Like heck you can't, little miss." She propped her hands on her hips. "You're competing today if I have to fling you over the vault myself."

I shoved past her and slammed the door of my bedroom behind me. There, I was surrounded by posters of Olympians—Shawn Johnson, Nastia Liukin, and, the mother of them all, Mary Lou Retton—and inspirational quotes poised over photographs of leaping ladies: "Remember that gymnast who gave up? Neither does anyone else," and "I am strong, I am brave, I am dedicated. I am a WINNER." If my bedroom was my cave, these were the drawings archaeologists would study. My dresser, crowded with trophies wearing medals, reinforced the values of my civilization.

I texted Lucy. Poison ivy. All over my face. I'm a monster.

Her reply vibrated back almost instantly. Nobody will care about your face when they see your Gienger.

THE GIENGER, A release skill on the bars into a half-twisting layout grabbing the high bar in the opposite direction on the way down, wasn't the most difficult part of my routine—the most challenging element was the triple back dismount—but it needed tightening.

I entered the Gienger with a handstand on the high bar and a giant swing. In anticipation of all that was to come, I rushed the handstand. This—something so technical—was far more frustrating than a fall, even one that landed like a dead body flipped out of a coffin. I was used to pain. Pain was a good sign. This mistake was simple, and worse, preventable.

My mother had begun paying closer attention to my training sessions. Whereas before she gossiped with other moms or traded hacks about taming flyaways with a toothbrush or converting old leos into grip bags, now she roosted in the front row of the viewing area a floor above the equipment, the only space a parent was allowed to occupy, and scoped us like a mama eagle, occasionally jotting in a journal she called her little black book.

The week before Chicago, I hung from the low bar, panting. I'd already swung ten mistakes. Jennifer stood on the other side of the high bar. Blond hair had loosened from her ponytail and roped around her face. When we first started training together, she was twenty-four and could demonstrate many of the skills. Now she was thirty, still fit but a little weary, the notch between her eyebrows becoming more pronounced. She was engaged and had a life of her own. All I had was this. There were damp stains beneath her armpits from spotting me. I was worried she was about to call it. But then she stepped up.

"Don't clip the handstand. Go."

I rocked my legs for momentum and pulled my feet up and onto the bar. In a squat, I stood, stretched forward, and hopped to grab the high bar. *Don't screw this up again.* My palms ached with the too-familiar grip. *Don't disappoint everyone.* I swung forward, carried my pointed toes up toward the bar and pushed my feet down to lift my body above it. *Hold that handstand.* I rode the forward thrust upside down. When I was almost vertical, I parted my legs, and only when I was at full height did I draw them back together. At the top, I felt beyond the influence of gravity. I sensed Jennifer below me but I didn't look for her. I lived in that moment, that weightless moment, a lifetime inside a half breath. When my body had enough, I fell back toward reality, around the bar a full rotation—the giant swing. The bar gave a bit, a nod to acknowledge the force of my pull. On my second revolution, I straddled my legs once again and, on my ascent, drove them back together to catapult me upward. When my toes hit two o'clock, I released the bar, bowed my left shoulder to the ceiling, twisted, and fell back to earth, the high bar in front of me, Jennifer below with her guiding hand. The bar caught me like a net.

"Yes!" Jennifer said when it was clear my grip would hold. "Did you feel that? That was it."

Lucy rocked her knees, my skin tingled, and a small flame of satisfaction kindled inside me. It was this feeling, this endorphin release, that kept me coming back for more. These rare but potent bursts of joy overshadowed the falls and blisters and burns, the stress of time, money, and attention. The pressure and the pain. Progress was small and scrupulous, but I was addicted to it. It was a drug available only to the few.

"That was nice," my mother called from the balcony, but there was a pulse beneath her words that revealed the hollowness of her enthusiasm. In the Midwest, insults weren't spoken. They were delivered in hesitations, lukewarm affirmations, and silences. From the sound of her voice, this one was going to be a doozy. I dug my toes into the mat while she continued, "I hope I'm not overstepping here. You're the expert, Jen. But I just wonder if maybe Sera isn't getting enough height."

Jennifer patted my upper back and steered me aside. Parents were not supposed to interrupt. In gymnastics, *they* were the ones seen but not heard. My mother had just committed a mortal sin. She and Jennifer were about to engage in an Indiana showdown.

My coach fixed a smile on her face, like straightening a bow tie, and aimed her coldness to the rafters. "Right now we're focusing on form and consistency."

"The competition is this weekend. Wouldn't it be strategic to focus on all aspects?"

My hands were scarlet, like they should be bleeding but my skin wouldn't let them. Lucy slipped hers into mine and squeezed. Our matching bracelets knocked, and our severed phrase was made whole.

"Chicago isn't about ranking. It's about exposure. Getting used to pressure."

"So you think it's best to treat the Classic as practice?"

That rhetorical tactic was Great Lakes for: It's about as wasteful an idea as tossing a Lotto ticket before the numbers were announced. We could be winners, and Sera should go high enough to get a nosebleed.

Jennifer's mouth tightened. "I didn't mean to imply it's practice. Sorry if I gave that impression."

"I know what you meant." My mother used the balcony

bar to hoist herself to her feet and leaned over it; she looked like a gymnast at a perilous height. "But if Sera won't rank as is, dontcha think we should push her a little harder? Practice more and for longer? Money isn't an issue. Don't you worry about that. That's for Bob and me to fuss over."

Jennifer broadened that fake smile. "There's only so much a young body should take, and we are pushing our girl to the max." Then she checked her wrist, even though she wasn't wearing a watch. "It's getting late. I better let you all go."

That night, while I massaged a hamstring, my mother delivered a glass of water and three Advil and then knelt down to wrap my sprained ankle.

"I just feel terrible about that little dustup with Jennifer," she said, working her thumb into my sole, eliciting agony and ecstasy before she began to tape. "I know you both work hard, but sometimes I wonder if she underestimates you. You're just the strongest kiddo there is, and she should take full advantage of that. There are only so many opportunities in this life, and you shouldn't miss one. Not one. Including the Classic." She dragged a length of tape off its roll and tore it between her teeth. "'It's about exposure' my big, broad behind. If judges are going to see you, they should see you at your best. Otherwise you may as well stay home. That's what I think. You know what? Maybe I should just call Jennifer real quick. Smooth things over. You can finish up here, can't you, honey?" She didn't wait for me to answer before she used my knee as leverage and located the portable house phone. "Hi, Jennifer. It's Mrs. Wheeler calling. I'm so very sorry to be disturbing you, but I just wanted to touch base and maybe run that Gienger past ya one more time. Give me a call back whenever you get the chance. I'll just be here going through my coupons. Call anytime."

As I CHOKED egg whites and a clementine past my blubbering, I repeated Lucy's text in my mind. *Nobody will care about your face when they see your Gienger.* What I looked like wasn't as important as what I did. And I could do what most couldn't.

My mother rapped her knuckles against the kitchen table beside my plate. "Don't dillydally there, Sera. You were at a disadvantage before, not being a blond-haired, blue-eyed pixie. Now we really have work to do."

My father lowered his coffee mug from his mouth. "Charlene."

"I'm not saying she isn't pretty. She is my daughter. Of course I think she's pretty. I'm just saying she doesn't have the typical look the judges are after." She gripped my chin and swung it side to side, examining my face. "And I'm not thrilled about this."

Upstairs I stepped into my warm-up suit. I wouldn't dress in the performance leo—the cost of which had gotten us into this mess—until we arrived in Chicago. At least one thing should be unsullied that day.

Before addressing my face, my mother tackled my hair. She wet it in the bathroom sink before the water warmed, stuck me on a stool in my bedroom, and went to work, comb in hand, clips in mouth. As she parted and pieced my hair into different sections, she tugged enough to incite a headache, but pain was part of the process. Pain was required for success.

"Don't you worry. We are going to fix this. We are going to work this out," she said as she twisted and braided routes along my scalp. Her hand dipped down to wipe a tear from my cheek and then returned to the top of my head, where she joined all the braids and twists into a ponytail and secured it with a satin amethyst ribbon.

My mother began practicing complex updos on my dolls after my first competition, when I wore a simple bun and all the other girls arrived as if for the senior prom. We wouldn't be upstaged again.

After my hair was stiffened with half a bottle of spray, it was time to mask the rash. We migrated back into the bathroom, where there was better lighting thanks to vanity bulbs over the mirror. "Like a dressing room," my mother might have said if she were in a better mood, but that morning she was all business. While I perched on the hunter-green toilet, she unrolled her makeup case on the mosaic vinyl flooring.

When she looked up, it was as if she were seeing the damage for the first time.

"It could be worse," she said, which meant this was the absolute worst-case scenario. My breath was pleated by sobs.

"No more tears now. It'll smudge. I told your father you

had no business doing anything outside the gym. Especially not yard work, of all things. You aren't a landscaper, for crying out loud. Gymnastics is your job."

My father, who had crowded with my brother in the doorway, cleared his throat and said, "There's no harm in teaching her to do her share of the chores."

My mother scoffed. "No harm? Look at her face."

"He didn't know there'd be poison ivy," I said.

She selected a tube of liquid foundation and began dabbing it on the welts. "You don't have to defend him."

My father ignored her. "Sera really shouldn't participate in this state."

"It isn't in this state. We have to go to Illinois. That's why I can't go to Timmy's party. Remember?" Joe said.

"I meant in this condition. She should stay home."

My mother retracted her chin to get a better look, and then, deciding it wasn't enough, continued layering on foundation. "If she doesn't compete, she can't make the junior national team."

"So she'll try for it next year."

I pinched the seams of my polyester pants. I'd already dedicated six years to gymnastics, forfeiting the traditional joys of childhood and adolescence: birthday parties, sleepovers, beach days, school friends, town fairs, neighborhood kickball, sledding down Cherry Hill, jumping in the quarry, chasing the ice-cream truck—everything. I was a twelve-year-old who had resigned herself to living in pain. Now, thanks to all that sacrifice, I had the opportunity to qualify for the junior national team, and my father wanted me to wait another year? If he didn't understand why this was so important, he didn't understand me, his daughter, at all. But I didn't have to protest. My dream had an advocate in the room.

My mother rotated to provide my father full view of her disbelief. "Wait an entire year to compete internationally and train with the junior national team at the Balogh Ranch, all because you wanted to teach the value of hard work to the girl who clocks in twenty-five hours a week of training after school?" She turned back to me and rolled her eyes. "Really, Bob. The things you say sometimes."

He rolled his eyes in synchrony with her. "The Baloghs, the Baloghs. I'm sick of hearing about the dang Baloghs."

My mother capped the foundation and scanned her collection. "Get used to it. They're gymnastics royalty."

"All hail the kings. My point is that poison ivy resin is sticky. Nearly impossible to completely wash off. If Sera competes, she might transfer the oil to the equipment and spread it to the other girls. That wouldn't be fair, now would it?"

My mother plucked up a palette of metallic glitter eye shadow. "Don't talk to me about 'fair.' Sera worked too hard for too long to give this up. We both have. So I'm sorry, but I don't give a flying squirrel about the other girls. Tough tomatoes to them. That's what I say." While she normally used a brush, this time she coated her fingertip, despite the warning my father had just issued. Perhaps she thought direct skin-to-skin application would go on thicker, and bold color might attract attention up and away from the redness on my neck, jaw, and cheek. What she wasn't thinking about, or apparently didn't care about, was contracting the rash herself. She stroked my eyelid with surprising tenderness.

"But we did learn a valuable lesson today, didn't we?" she said. "Sera should never do *anything* outside the gym." When she finished, she sat back on her heels and clicked the eye shadow case shut. "Now we're loaded for bear."

CHAPTER 3

Charlene Wheeler

I was twenty-eight and on the verge of going stale when we found gymnastics. Then everything changed, and just in time too; I was about to lose my mind, I swear it.

I was easy on the eyes back then, and that's a blessing, I know, but it doesn't get a married girl out of the house. It doesn't give her something to *do*. After I dropped the kids at kindergarten, I did the wash, paid the bills, dusted, and took the sweeper around the house (my kitchen was always a mess, but give a girl a break; I was saved by grace, not by works). Then I faced the ten-thousand-dollar question: What the heck do I do now?

Oh, I found silly ways to occupy myself. I watched Oprah and snuck a peek at Jerry now and again, though it'd take a couple spritzers to get me to admit such a thing in mixed company. I strapped a bag of frozen peas to my belly with

my robe belt because I read about fat freezing in a magazine but couldn't afford the technology. I cooked, and when
I couldn't imagine putting together another hotdish, I had
food delivered and transferred it to a Pyrex container so it
would look to Bob like I'd made it. Melissa, a woman from
down the street—she might be a couple sandwiches short
of a picnic, but she's sweet enough—welcomed me to the
neighborhood with one of those concrete yard geese, and I
said, "Oh, what a fun idea," even though I thought it might
have been the stupidest thing I'd ever seen. But when I got
tired of rearranging the knickknacks in my china cabinet,
I thought, what the heck, and made Gilda—that's what I
called her, Gilda the Goose—little outfits and dressed her
for all sorts of occasions: Thanksgiving Pilgrim, Christmas
elf, her Sunday best, and a yellow slicker for when it rained.
Looking back on it now makes me want to stick my head
in the oven.

Then one day I picked the kids up from the YMCA—Joe
from peewee basketball and Sera from gymnastics—and
Miss Nancy, Sera's teacher, asked if she could speak to me.

I'd scrubbed the toilets that afternoon and looked like
death warmed over, plus there were groceries in the car, including a tub of ice cream, so I didn't exactly want to shoot
the breeze.

"You betcha," I said, and hoped my eyes would do their
magic of communicating the opposite.

Miss Nancy was a round and dense woman, the kind

who might have been part of a softball league, if you know what I mean. And her breasts were as ample as anything. Never mind a chest, she carried around a commercial freezer.

"Sera is doing well. Flourishing, really," she said.

I thought, I should hope so, because as soon as that girl learned to tumble, she didn't want to do anything else. She cartwheeled across our front yard until the sun went down.

Miss Nancy continued, "What I mean is, she's talented."

"That's nice of you to say," I said. Joe was beginning to fidget, and I was imagining my ice cream turning to milk; it never refroze right after it liquefied. It always just tasted like ice. I'd have to throw it away, and we didn't have enough in the grocery budget to buy another since I'd already blown a few extra bucks on Noxzema cleansing cream and a tube of toasted almond lipstick.

"I'm not saying it to be kind," Miss Nancy answered, with more snap than I appreciated, to tell you the truth. "I'm saying it because you might want to do something about it."

"Sorry, there. It's been a long day and my brain is fried. I don't think I'm following you."

"I'm just a YMCA instructor. But there's a gym an hour from here. Elite Gymnastics in Indianapolis. I know it's a bit far, but the coach is very good."

Saying "heck no" would have been bad-mannered, so I said, "Thanks for thinking of us, but I'm not sure I can fit that trip into my schedule."

"It's up to you, but Sera has natural ability. And she's six now. Many girls her age have already started training. You might want to consider it before it's too late."

"Too late for what exactly?"

"For becoming an elite gymnast. Competitions. Junior Olympics. The Xcel Program. Who knows?"

Well that just made me sit right back on my heels.

Joe dipped his nose into his collar and stretched it, even though I had told him a million times that was a good way to ruin a shirt, hand-me-down or not. Through the fabric, he asked, "Can we go now?" I gripped the top of his head and forced it straight.

"My Sera?" I asked.

Miss Nancy could tell she'd gotten my attention and tossed her hands up. "Hey, I'm no expert, but Sera picks up gymnastics movements like they're the next things she's supposed to be doing. She could have a future in it. But not here. This is for fun, nothing more. Talk to Jennifer."

"How about that," I said.

When once I'd been in a hurry, now I was hanging around, hoping to hear more words like "elite" and "Olympics." But Miss Nancy had made her case; she was finished. So I leaned over and kissed the top of Sera's head. This girl—my daughter—could turn out to be something special. Go figure.

"We sure have something to discuss with Daddy, don't we? Good thing I made chicken biscuit bake. His favorite."

Bob wasn't thrilled, I'll say that. But you don't get eight years into a marriage without learning what to say or how to hold yourself to get just what you want.

Pretty soon, instead of my life being a dull swampland of sitting water, I was a spring so fresh you could bottle me.

I drove Sera to Indy two and then three and then four times a week. I met seasoned gym moms who gave me tips on which parents to avoid and which meets to attend and how to keep white leotards from graying. I tailored warm-up pants. I brought brownies to every one of the gym's bake sales, sometimes even making them myself rather than plucking them off the clearance rack at Kroger's. I arranged travel to big competitions. I treated rips and styled the perfect bun that wouldn't interfere with a back extension roll on floor (hint: it requires one hundred bobby pins and a quarter bottle of hair spray). I bought performance leos that made even Sera's rippling abs and cut limbs look feminine. I discovered you could become quite fond of the other girls, but when it came to the moment of truth, you prayed those little prisses slipped on the beam so that your daughter would beat them. I mastered the gymnastics scoring system and tracked Sera's numbers so I knew just what she had to earn on her last event to place. When Sera performed like a darn rock star, I told her she did just fine so her head wouldn't inflate, and I congratulated the other mothers and their daughters whether they medaled or not to teach Sera that being great was only a few letters away from being gracious. I captured competitions on my phone and touched up the photos my-self. I made meals that Sera could eat on long drives, checked in about her homework and all the items in her gym bag, always, constantly, every day remembering to ask, "Do you have your grips or are they in your locker?" Too many days cooped up in her cubby gave them that jockstrap stink that was just about impossible to get out.

Familiarizing myself with the realm of gymnastics was like learning a different language, a different culture. Soon I wasn't just the person who gasped when a girl fell. I was the person who winced knowingly at the more subtle mistakes, like when a girl missed her vertical on a bars pirouette, or who noticed when a wrist guard came undone during a floor routine. I understood the benefits and ramifications of lifting the difficulty ceiling in the new scoring system. It was like *I* was the one acquiring new skills. And maybe I was. Maybe that was exactly the point. I was alive. And not just that. It was like I'd been sleeping since the twins were born and now I was finally awake.

And Sera—well, I hate to boast but this is just the g-d truth: she was a star. She may not have had the fair com-plexion of her Scandinavian-heritage peers, but she was so darn strong, and she had oodles of natural talent and a work ethic to boot. She was so good, she twinkled even without the glitter, but I rubbed on heaps of shimmer just the same because, what the heck, my daughter wasn't going to be the only Plain Jane east of the Great Plains.

She leapt from one Junior Olympic level to the next, and before I knew it, it was Easter Sunday and Miss Gilda the Goose was still wearing her Uncle Sam costume. There was so much to do, I didn't have time for concrete waterfowl anymore—thank the good Lutheran Lord. So I dragged Gilda's patriotic tail feather to the curb and hoped the garbage truck would haul her off before Melissa from down the road could see what I really thought of her gift.

I mean, really. A concrete goose. Good grief.

CHAPTER 4

The Chicago skyline was set onto the horizon like the Lego pieces Joe used to leave all over the living room floor. In just a few hours, I'd be inside one of those tiny buildings, moving through my routines with thousands of eyes watching me, maybe even 2008 Olympic all-around champion Nastia Liukin, who glided across a beam like water poured from a pitcher, or rising star and highest all-around scorer at the American Cup in New York, Gabrielle Douglas. The thought of it agitated my intestines.

My mother was gnawing on her fingernails in the front seat. She practically pulsed with nerves. "This will be quite a day. I don't mean to pressure you by saying that. Well, maybe just a little. Because pressure isn't always a bad thing. Pressure is what pushes people to be great. Maybe I could have used a little more of it." When she looked back to me, her expression was manic, like something in her brain had come unhinged. "You're gonna get us to international competition next year. I just know it. I'm already saving for Japan."

"Japan? Like ninjas and samurai swords? Will I get to go too?" Joe asked.

My mother swiveled toward his bucket seat, her expression frozen in animation. "What do you say, Joe? Do you need a snack? I've got corn chips or Ho Hos."

His eyebrows cranked together, but then they released. "Ho Hos, I guess."

As she rummaged through her bag, she said, "*Konnichiwa.* Konnichi-freakin-wa."

GYMNASTS MILLED AROUND the edge of the UIC Pavilion, warming up, stretching, and considering last-minute advice from coaches. Others were on the apparatuses on the platform above for precompetition practice. Media crews set up equipment; their cameras wore bulky lenses like telescopes, both designed to see stars up close. Newscasters conducted sound tests. The arena echoed with chatter and the soft thuds of landing feet. A banner read "Secret U.S. Classic" and the neon lights on the scoreboard beamed the same message. This was it. The road to the Olympics began here, and though I'd be testing the route on training wheels, I was on the road just the same.

A flood was rising in my torso; it churned, foamed, and spat. I tried to trick myself and the whirlpool inside me. *It doesn't matter if I do well. It's just for exposure.* But then I saw my mother's confidence, her excitement. *You're gonna get us to international competition next year.* And the waters roiled.

Physically, I was halfway through a hundred jumping jacks. Mentally, I was in the midst of my beam routine, about to launch into a roundoff double back dismount. After I hit the hypothetical landing, I looked into the stands where my family sat. My father and Joe were playing cards on a piece of cardboard box. My mother was taking in the scenery, as if she were on a safari and the gymnasts, coaches, and judges were exotic animals she'd been waiting her whole life to see. When she realized I was watching, she whacked the shoulders of her husband and son and they all waved.

Vanda Balogh and the other judges filed in and sat at their tables. The whey protein shake I'd sipped in the car lurched in my stomach.

"Sera!" Lucy hurried toward me with her arms flattened against her sides, walking as quickly as she could without looking unprofessional to the judges. Her ponytail was curled in perfect ringlets that bounced, and she'd caked her face with cover-up to mask her freckles. "It isn't as bad as you made it sound."

My chin dropped to hide the rash. "I'm Shrek in a leo."

"You can hardly see it. The judges will have no clue." Her lips glistened with the pink frost gloss she always wore for competitions. It smelled like cake icing. When we wanted dessert, we huffed it like glue sniffers. "Does it itch like crazy?"

"I want to scratch my skin off."

"I'll buy you a cookie if you don't."

When it was time, all the junior gymnasts assembled in a room off the pavilion. Some girls were giddy, beaming and bouncing, asking one another where they were from, if this was their first Classic, and how many times they'd watched the Beijing Olympics. Others were somber. I fell into that category. I pictured the poison ivy sinking beneath my skin and roping around my organs. My heart convulsed against its snare. I wondered if I might die.

"Want to play the tickle game?" Lucy asked. My consciousness had floated to the crown of my head, and my brain was so woolly, her voice sounded far away. "Close your eyes and tell me when I get to your elbow crease." Her fingertips tickled my wrist.

Having something concrete to focus on crystallized the fuzz in my brain. I waited until her touch felt high enough. "There."

"Not even close."

"Hey, girls." Edward Levett wore a short-sleeved collared polo and a lanyard with his credentials hanging around his neck. He smiled like we were old pals. "Remember me?"

Of course we remembered him. He was famous. What was surprising, and immensely flattering, was that he remembered us.

"Hi, Eddie," Lucy and I chorused.

"Big day. How are we feeling?"

How do you express that you're excited to demonstrate

all that you've dedicated your short life to, nervous you'll blow it in front of your heroes and the judges who will one day decide if you can attain your dream, and also terribly, terribly itchy?

Eddie inhabited this world; he understood. He was like one of those allies that existed in myths to help the hero along his (but in this case, her) journey.

He said, "I saw you perform at the ranch. You deserve to be here." He bent forward and examined my face over his glasses. "Got yourself a little case of poison ivy?"

I covered my cheek with my hand.

"It isn't noticeable at all. I only caught it because I'm a doctor. But I'd hate for you to be distracted. I can give you an antihistamine to reduce the itching. Would that help?"

"Really?" I asked, disbelieving my luck. "Thank you."

"That's why I'm here. To help you girls."

WE MARCHED AROUND the pavilion and then arranged on the floor mat for the national anthem. I placed my hand over my heart and felt it flutter like a trapped sparrow. Lucy was on one side of me, and a stranger from Ohio was on the other. We all wanted the same thing, but despite our talent, despite how hard we worked, it was very possible, likely, even, that none of us would get it. Lucy rocked her hip so it knocked into mine. Would she be happy for me if I made the team and she didn't? Would I be happy for her? I rocked my hip back.

When they called my name, I was sure I'd throw up. I wondered if they'd broadcast that on their live stream, if I'd be part of competition bloopers. Vanda would remember me all right—the girl who puked.

Jennifer placed her hands on my shoulders. I concentrated on her eyes, Aegean blue with flecks of gold. I made her face the only thing I could see, her voice the only thing I could hear. She was composed but serious. She called this—an expression stripped of fear, frustration, or sadness—a gym face. It was the stoicism she expected in training, and I imagined it was what she wore to her own college competitions a decade earlier.

"Good, solid form. Show them you know the moves. Simple as that."

The bottom half of my body was numb; I was surprised I was able to ascend the stairs to the podium. Was I going too slow? Could the people in the stands see me trembling? Or worse, my poison ivy? Did I look nervous *and* hideous?

I reached into the chalk pedestal and broke off a piece to rub between my palms and on the bottoms of my feet, and then I stood at the start of the runway. My shoulders lifted and fell with a giant shuddering breath. I flapped my arms up and held them above my head to salute the judges.

The vault looked small, on the other side of all that blue. An ocean away. *Good, solid form. Simple as that.* There sure were a lot of people there, but their attention would be divided. Gymnasts were performing on the other apparatuses.

And they were probably better than I was. No one would be watching me but my mother, and she'd seen me do this a hundred times. The only people who hadn't seen this were my father and brother. I would show them what I'd learned. I'd show them their sacrifices were for something real.

I sprinted.

My feet pounded the mat and my arms pumped at my sides. The vault seemed to charge toward me like we were in battle, the medieval kind where knights on horses galloped toward one another, swords extended. But I wouldn't fight. I was too agile for that. Too cunning. When my feet hit the right spot, I catapulted into a roundoff. My heels planted onto the springboard and I propelled into a back handspring. I angled my body at the leather, hit my challenger from above, and stole his strength; it was enough power for an additional rotation. I outwitted my enemy and finished with style.

My feet sunk into the mat and my knees bent to absorb the impact. I froze in that chair position for a moment, stunned, perhaps, that I'd stuck the landing in that setting. A near perfect Yurchenko layout. And they'd all seen it.

My face burst into a grin my cheeks felt sore containing. I saluted the judges again and stepped off the mat. I searched for my family in the stands, which were getting more crowded the closer we got to the senior segment. Joe clapped his hands over his head and whooped. My father applauded in slow but thunderous whacks. And my mother slapped her hands with more unfettered furor than she'd rehearsed for the cameras.

Jennifer met me at the uneven bars, handed me my grips, and assumed her position beneath the bars. "Hold that handstand."

I dipped my hands into the chalk tray and coated them before wriggling into the leather wrist guards. I felt electric, a live wire pulsing with adrenaline. This high couldn't be replicated outside an arena.

I'd gotten the attention of the audience with that vault. Their eyes were on me. They wanted a spectacle. I wouldn't disappoint them, and I wouldn't disappoint my mother, who believed in me, who wanted the world—or, at least, Japan.

Nobody will care about your face when they see your Gienger.

I hopped up on the bar and swung through my routine—glide kip, backward giant with straddled legs, stalder swing with half turn. I felt strong, capable—maybe even invincible. Now was my opportunity. I wouldn't have another chance to make the junior national team until next year; it was time to fly.

I rushed the handstand. Jennifer would be annoyed; it was the one thing she wanted out of this routine and I'd lose a partial point. But she'd forgive me when she saw what was coming.

I oscillated down with force and thrust up with all the strength my mother knew I had. Then I was in the air. And I got the height. I was higher maybe than I'd ever been, soaring and spinning, a marvel, an asset, someone meant for the national team, someone Vanda wished was old enough to represent the United States of America in London that summer. When my body had enough climbing, I began to drop back down.

The bar was back in front of me; my hands reached for it. But my arms had shortened during my meteoric rise, or the bar had inched away. It was too far. Fear lit in me like a firecracker. I reached harder, my fingers outstretched to their limit. But they missed. I couldn't grab it; my fingertips grazed the wood coating. I kept falling. The floor rushed up and I crashed into it, belly flopping on solid ground. The impact juddered through my body and snatched my breath.

The arena gasped. All the chatter dissolved and people were still.

To fall on a simple Gienger when I still had the triple back dismount in my pocket was a travesty. I felt the hot sting of tears in my throat and eyes. I squeezed them shut. The only thing that could make this moment more humiliating was if I cried.

Gym face. Gym face.

Jennifer touched the shoulder that ached from impact. "You okay?"

My eyelids pinched shut. If I opened them, I'd see Jennifer's face. It would be concerned, not bitter, though I'd defied her, though she'd been right all along. I'd see the piteous expressions of the judges, or more likely, their judgment; that was their job, after all. I'd see fellow gymnasts who'd interpret my catastrophe as their good fortune. And I'd see thousands of people in the stands watching me pick myself up off the floor.

I had only thirty seconds to get back on the bars; I couldn't earn difficulty score credit for elements I didn't perform.

"You're courageous. Everybody knows that now. Finish it," Jennifer said.

I wanted to ask if I could just go home, but I knew the answer, and hearing my desire out loud would reinforce how desperately I wanted the impossible.

I let Jennifer help me up to a spattering of applause that sounded a lot like pity. Excess chalk whitened my heels and toes. My feet looked cadaverous as they approached the bars again. Dead woman walking.

I never felt more alive than when performing gymnastics, but at that moment, my heart convulsed in my chest; I was sure I was experiencing the rare preteen myocardial infarction. At least then there'd be an excuse for my mishap. The commentators would say, "She fell on the Gienger, but she *was* having a heart attack."

But though I was experiencing heartache, it wasn't the medical variety.

Gymnastics wasn't like other sports. You didn't get another two pitches or a free throw without penalty for the previous misses. Though I could get up and complete the routine, my error could never be erased. The difference between winning and losing was a fraction of a point. A hesitation. A wobble. My mistake had been disastrous.

I hopped back on the bar, but the shadow of what came before coated each movement like tarnish.

Beam was next. I didn't know how I'd manage it; I was still balancing on the edge of my composure.

During a pivot turn, I remembered flying higher on the bars than I could handle, and I cut the rotation short. During my switch ring leap, in which I tossed my head back, losing sight of what was below me, I relived the rushed handstand and landed so off-balance I had to grab the beam—the deduction equivalent of another fall. During my prize move, the one I always stuck—the roundoff double back dismount—I stumbled backward and landed on my ass.

And the crowd cheered.

I scrambled to my feet, frantic, mortified, only to find that they weren't reacting to me. I was no longer worthy of their attention.

Across the arena, on the floor, a gymnast was springing through her next tumbling run: a roundoff, one-and-a-half-twist walkout, roundoff, back handspring, double pike. She bounded so joyfully and with so much height, she could have been made of rubber. It was a privilege to watch, the kind of performance that made you feel you were witnessing something rare and sacred, that you were in the presence of once-in-a-lifetime greatness. She served as a reminder of what I was not.

My floor routine wasn't a disaster, but it was messy—I stepped out of bounds, wavered to maintain balance, my legs came apart in my double pike—certainly unimpressive in the wake of Simone Biles.

When it was Lucy's turn, Jennifer bent so they were forehead-to-forehead and whispered last-minute instruction. It didn't matter what she was saying. I was sure behind all her guidance was the message *Whatever you do, don't be like Sera*. As I passed them, Lucy smiled at me in a way that expressed kindness and condolence. She knew how poorly I'd done. She knew too much. Heat flushed my cheeks. I climbed the stands to join the only people in the arena who might not comprehend the extent of my humiliation.

The men of my family weren't gymnastics experts, but they knew enough that my father laid a comforting hand on my back and my brother handed me his half-eaten package of Sour Patch Kids.

"At least your vault didn't suck," Joe said.

I tried to catch my mother's eye, but after offering me a tight smile, she kept her stare locked on the remaining routines. The candy wrapper crinkled as I retrieved a gummy; my tongue pressed it against the roof of my mouth and held it there, letting the sour sugar punish.

Joe continued, "That girl before you on the floor was crazy good."

Tears slipped down my cheeks. My father looped his arm around me and pulled me into his side. "You were good too," he said. "Just getting here is good."

"But not great," I said.

My father craned his neck to consider my face. His eyes were wet. "I think you're great."

LATER, WHEN THE seniors marched in, a thrill sparked inside me, but it was dampened by my own disgrace. There was Nastia Liukin, the image on my wall come to life, wearing a pink leo and her hair in her signature blond messy bun—an Olympic-medal-winning Barbie doll. There was McKayla Maroney, famous for her Yurchenko two and a half on vault. There was Gabby Douglas, who trained with Liang Chow, the same coach as Shawn Johnson. There was Aly Raisman, who jammed more elements into one tumbling run than I thought possible, making room for a one-and-a-half twist through to double Arabian to layout front. All the greatest talents in the nation, there to audition for Vanda. Just like me, only better.

And I probably gave them poison ivy.

As I watched gloomily, a man clambered up the stands toward us. He was tall and dense in the way men were when their muscle converted into something malleable but still robust, and his skin had been toughened by what appeared to be a thrashing sun. Hair circled the base of his head like a crown made too large, but that he wore with pride. Further north, his bald scalp made his skull seem fragile, like it was one careless bump away from cracking open; it was the only fragile thing about him.

He was breathless when he reached us. "Hey, kiddo," he

said, and his paw thumped my upper back with spontaneous familiarity. "Sorry about today. You must be pretty bummed." His hand remained between my shoulder blades until my father inched nearer to me. Then it shot in front of him and he clasped my father's hand. "Lou Gently. I run Champion Gym in Cincinnati."

"Nice to meet you," my father said unconvincingly.

"I'll cut right to the chase, since I imagine that sorority sister you call a coach might join you any second. I saw your girl out there. It wasn't her best showing, am I right?"

His words hit their targets directly. I gaped into the industrial lights and hoped they would evaporate the moisture in my eyes.

My father hugged my shoulder and pulled me into his side. "She did just fine."

"She could be better with the right teacher."

My father said, "I think we're happy with—"

"What are you suggesting?" my mother asked, bending over Joe.

Lou folded his leathery arms over his chest. They were covered with black hairs, like so many spiders crushed against his skin. "Coach Jill is a pretty young thing, I'll give you that. But she's soft, and that touchy-feely everybody-gets-a-trophy approach isn't doing your kid any favors." He unfolded his arms and offered his palms up to the ceiling. "She isn't my daughter, but here's what I'd do. I'd train her myself. I was a world champion gymnast back in the day.

Look me up. Gently. Spelled like 'gently,' but with a hard *g*. My gym is right around the corner from you."

"I wouldn't call Cincinnati right around the corner. It's two hours away," my father said with a humorless laugh.

Lou's face lifted with a Cheshire cat smile. "It's worth the drive, believe me. It's state of the art, designed for elite gymnasts. We've got the safety belts and harnesses you need to learn high-level skills responsibly, a pit bar, all the bells and whistles. Not to mention, a qualified coach." He pounded his chest, apelike. My father moved to speak, but Lou plowed over him. "And if you feel uncomfortable with a man, I get that. I have two daughters myself. I'm a family man, so there's nothing to worry about there." He rubbed his hands together as if warming them beside a fire and then slipped them into the pockets of his Nike warm-up pants. "Listen, no need to make any decisions now. I just wanted to introduce myself and make the offer. If you aren't interested, it's no skin off my back. I just felt an obligation to be honest with you. Jill is a sweet young lady. But if you want the best for your darling girl here, you have to be selfish and smart. Not sentimental."

"It's Jennifer," my father said, although he seemed to know the correction was futile. As Lou walked away, my father released his hold on me. "That man is not from around here."

"Bob," my mother said, understanding that was my father's version of an insult.

"What's a man doing coaching girls' gymnastics, anyway? He couldn't find any boys to coach?"

"Trust your instincts," a woman two rows up said. She wore denim cutoff shorts and a distressed trucker hat that read "Gymnastics Mom." With her accent, her words sounded parabolic, like a kayak rolling over a swell. "I've got two competitive gymnast daughters. After a while, you get to know the people. I heard Lou Gently worked one of his athletes so mean she broke her leg on purpose just to get out of training with him. I know people take this sport seriously, but these are still kids, you know? It's got to be fun. And he sucks the fun right out of it." She lifted a can of Diet Coke and used it to gesture at my father. "If you ask me, he's a dirtbag."

I still wore only my leotard; sweat chilled on my skin and I began to shiver.

Joe poked my shoulder. I was sure he was about to reiterate Lou's criticism or point out another gymnast who was better than me. I swung to face him, ready to bite back. Instead of lancing with a snide remark, he held out my warm-up jacket. I slipped my arms through the sleeves as tears slid down my cheeks and eroded a clean river through my foundation.

AFTER THE COMPETITION, we splurged for dinner at Applebee's. A group of men across the restaurant were drinking, laughing loud and openmouthed, and slapping one another on the back. They celebrated while we mourned. I'd received the lowest score of all the juniors that day. Strike that, I'd *earned* the lowest score.

"That was quite an experience," my father said with depressing buoyancy. "You'll always be able to say you competed at the Classics, and that's pretty special. We're proud of you."

I didn't even bother correcting my father that it was called the Classic, not the Classics, plural. There wasn't any point. We'd never be back.

The collar of my expensive plum leo was visible beneath my warm-up hoodie. I pulled the zipper up to hide it. Then I tested how hard I could punch my thighs from only an inch away.

While Joe set out to devour his bacon cheeseburger and I picked at my undressed salad, my mother plucked a fry from my father's plate and held it between her thumb and index finger.

"I think we need to move to Texas and beg the Baloghs to take Sera on full-time," she said.

My father choked on his whiskey sour and clanked his glass against the table. He drew his hand across his chin to wipe spilled droplets. "Are you out of your mind?"

My mother's hair had flattened and her makeup had worn. But her features were set into the cliff of her expression. "Sera, please explain to your father how Dominique Moceanu got to the Olympics."

I stared into my plate. It would be the highest honor to be trained by the Baloghs, but I wasn't sure I wanted to trade Jennifer and Lucy for someone cold and intimidating in a place I found as exciting as it was stressful. Besides, after my routines that day, what made my mother think Vanda would take me? I wasn't cute or congenial or talented. I wouldn't be worth her time.

"She trained with the Baloghs," I said.

"And where did her entire family move from to be close to the ranch?"

"Florida."

I'd answered correctly and was off the hook. She pointed the limp French fry at my father. "That's exactly right."

My father's expression was agape, as if he still couldn't tell if my mother was joking. "Charlene," he said, as an entreaty.

"And Gabby Douglas? The one who trains with Chow? I heard she moved to Iowa from Virginia without her family. She lives with strangers. I know you don't want that for Sera."

He said, "Didn't that girl—Gabby—didn't she just place, what, thirteenth, fourteenth?"

"But she had the highest all-around score at the American Cup. And you saw her height on those uneven bars. Nobody can do them like her. Mark my words—they'll want her in London."

He clutched a napkin and worried it between his fingers. "I don't care about her or any other gymnast. I only care about Sera. Our family."

While he unraveled, she remained tightly wound. "That's what this is all about. It's a hard choice, I grant you that. But life isn't an ambrosia salad. It's full of tough choices and we don't want to look back and think 'woulda, shoulda, coulda,' do we? The next Olympics are in four short years."

Her earnestness settled on him and stiffened his posture. "The Olympics? Charlene, really." He stole a glance at me and then shifted toward her, boxing me out. "This has been an exciting ride, but come on. Nobody makes the Olympics."

"Five families do. There's no reason it shouldn't be us."

I was the ball in their tennis match. *Thwack, thwack, thwack.* I bore down for the next impact.

My father pivoted further and spoke from the side of his mouth. "Isn't today a reason?"

The more he huddled into the corner, the more she unwrapped her body, like a blossom opening. "One off day and we give up on her? Jesus had forty days and nights in the wilderness, but he didn't let the devil beat him."

My father sat back against the booth, lifted his whiskey to his lips, and smiled apologetically at me over its rim. He swallowed big and winced his next exhale. After a few more breaths, his shoulders relaxed. I could almost see him slowing his own heart rate.

He said, "So we don't give up. That doesn't mean we should move the family to Texas on a wing and a prayer."

We wouldn't quit gymnastics, and we wouldn't move to Texas. My glute muscles released.

"Fine. But we have to do something. You saw her scores. It's time we pull her out of school so she can train more, like all the other gymnasts at her level."

Although Joe's Coke was two-thirds full, he held the straw near the surface to make it slurp and looked at me over his glass. He seemed to think this was a bad thing, a punishment. But my education and fellow classmates meant little to me. Gymnastics, competitions, the Olympics—that was all I cared about; why shouldn't I make it my full-time job? I wanted to stop disappointing my mother. I wanted to be great at something. Special. And I wasn't—yet.

"I can't believe most twelve-year-old gymnasts train forty hours a week," my father said, but when he carried the whiskey to his mouth again and administered it like medicine, his objections almost visibly dissolved. "Fine."

My mother popped the fry in her mouth. As she chewed, I caught an uptick at the corners of her mouth and realized all at once that she had never wanted to move to Texas. She offered it as an extreme so they could compromise on something he wouldn't have settled for had she used it as her starting point. She'd conned him. Being a Midwestern woman, an identity in which language is a dance, she'd already had a foundation for such maneuvering, so I didn't know if she'd been conniving all along, or if, while I worked on aerials and arabesques, this was the skill she'd been honing.

Perhaps this was part of the reason I was attracted to gymnastics, where people were scored to the tenth of a point for content, difficulty, execution, and artistry. When you made errors, you received deductions. You knew when the people around you were good, when they were bad, and by how much. You didn't have to interpret tone, timbre, and the space between words. You knew where you stood, and you knew how you could be better, if being better was what you wanted.

In real life, there were no points to tally. There were no ranks. There were only guesses. Make enough guesses and you were bound to be wrong some of the time. Your mother, who you thought loved your father, could trick him. Your father, who you thought was smart, could fall for it.

And a doctor, who you thought was good, could be the most dangerous person in your life.

CHAPTER 5

I didn't miss school, the boys who ignored me, or the girls who didn't invite me in on their jokes. They might not have guessed it by my sharp nose and mousy hair, but I was destined for something they could never touch.

Every morning I ate egg whites and wheat toast; popped three Advil; checked my gym bag for wrist guards, tape, body adhesive, a callus shaver, hair spray, elastics, clips, Icy Hot patches, sandpaper to file down the edges of my grips, resistance bands, and a frozen water bottle; dressed in my practice tank and warm-ups; drove an hour to Indianapolis; trained for four hours; broke for a lunch of boiled chicken; trained for two hours more; and drove an hour home. There I iced my wrists, wrapped broken toes and raw palms, drained the bubbles of blisters, massaged sore muscles; sprayed Icy Hot on my knees and slipped sleeves over them; swallowed three Advil; lay in bed, hurting all over; and psyched myself into doing it again the next day. I skimmed school materials in the car and during meals. But academics were secondary. I answered to a higher calling.

Some nights I wanted to quit. The pain was too much. The frustration of slow improvements—or no improvement at all—was discouraging. I'd hear my father say, *Nobody makes the Olympics*. If I couldn't make it that far, what would have been the point in all this hurt? In bleeding my family's finances? In making Charlene an all-out gym mom?

But by morning my dream would be refreshed. Nobody made the Olympics, except for the ones who did. Like the Fierce Five. Lucy and I gripped hands before the gym's television while Russia chased the Americans through to the last London event. My mother and I propped pillows against her headboard and sat hip to hip as Jordyn Wieber was edged from the all-around by the two-per-country rule; as Aly Raisman lost bronze after a tiebreak; and as McKayla Maroney missed gold on the most challenging and typically consistent Amanar vault when she landed on her backside, prompting her to arrange her lips like a curtain pulled aside during her medal ceremony, an expression that would go viral, and which Lucy and I would mimic when skills didn't go our way.

My father would be so surprised and my mother so happy when Lucy and I were on the podium in Rio.

I was a full-time gymnast. I wouldn't mess up another opportunity. I'd make the national team that year, and then I'd train with the Baloghs outside the camps, just like Lucy, who'd made the junior national team. I'd travel to compete as a representative of our country, just like Lucy.

I'd be great, just like Lucy.

December 2012

We used to fear him. He was the bloodthirsty dragon that guarded Rudi's cave. We imagined his muscles rippling as he pawed the grass. Spit flecking his loose muzzle as he growled and snarled. His chain snapping. Incisors sinking into our necks.

It had been six months since I'd been to the Balogh Ranch for the last camp, and I still feared the brindled pit mix tied up outside the Balogh cabin. But Lucy had returned several times in between to train with the rest of the junior national team. As we approached the savage on four legs, Lucy bent forward with her palms on her knees and cooed, "Hey, Roscoe. Did you miss me? Who's a good boy?"

At the sound of her voice, his stub of a tail wagged along with the lower half of his body.

It wasn't just the dog. Ranch coaches nodded to Lucy. She'd trained alongside the senior national team, even members of the Fierce Five, who'd gone to the London Olympics. So when we spotted Gabby Douglas, the first African American woman to win the all-around, my heart squeezed at the celebrity sighting. She greeted Lucy by name.

Vanda Balogh didn't just recognize Lucy, she was familiar with her skills, and she cared enough to push her. While I was home in Indiana, Vanda had begun grooming my friend.

Lucy was training the standing Arabian on the beam, a salto with a backward entry into a half twist so early it becomes a forward salto. She had graduated from landing on stacked mats to training on a floorboard with only a thin cushion for landing. But she was stumbling on the finish.

"You are rotating too late. You have to finish the twist by the time the salto is coming back down," Jennifer said. She wore the new warm-up Lucy and I had given her for Christmas, and her blond hair was tied in a messy bun at the top of her head, like Nastia Liukin.

"This skill was made for a girl like you. So light. Not much to manage in the air. Like a bird." Vanda's glasses were black and cat-eyed, and the edges of her frown looked like they were sewn into her jaw.

Lucy nodded, but instead of climbing back to her feet, she hugged her gangly knees and sighed.

"You can't be tired," Vanda said.

Lucy flexed one leg. "Something is funny with my knee."

"If it's so funny, why aren't I laughing?" Vanda asked.

Lucy massaged it and winced. "It hurts."

"It hurts because you aren't landing properly. Get better and it won't hurt so much."

I was working on the full twisting double layout on floor. I wanted to yell, *Turn around. Look at me. See how I land properly.*

Jennifer considered Vanda and then squatted beside Lucy. She tested her knee between her thumb and index finger. When Lucy cringed, Jennifer said, "Maybe you should see Eddie."

"Everybody here has something that hurts, but they don't whine. Tape it up and keep training. We don't stop unless we're bleeding," Vanda said.

Jennifer spoke directly to Lucy. "A knee injury could be serious. You've already trained for three hours. It's time for a break. Why don't you see Eddie? If he says nothing is wrong, we'll pick up where we left off."

Torn between Vanda and Jennifer, Lucy seemed brittle. Just as Vanda had described her—like a bird. A skinny pale freckled bird.

"Okay," she said.

As Lucy limped toward the door, I shot her a thumbs-up as a question and she mirrored it weakly.

Vanda exhaled her disapproval and began to walk away, but when she saw me, she paused. My spine elongated. As she scanned me from head to toe, I felt so naked I covered myself with my arms.

She said, "If you're just going to stand there and watch, you belong on the sidelines. Not on my mat, taking up space."

THAT NIGHT, WE played MASH (Mansion Apartment Shack House)—gymnastics edition—a game to determine the

Olympic year in which we'd compete, the medal we'd win, and on which event.

Lucy's legs were straddled with an ice pack balanced on one knee, which Eddie had diagnosed as swollen but nothing to worry about. He'd also manipulated her body to realign and prevent the injury from reoccurring.

I arranged myself in my friend's open lap so she could comb my wet hair. She continued brushing long after there couldn't have been any knots left. In a life riddled by discomfort, this was how we showed love.

Just as I calculated her MASH results—predicting Lucy would compete in the 2020 Olympics, winning silver on beam—a male voice called from the hallway, "Knock, knock," and the door opened.

Eddie usually wore a short-sleeved collared shirt marked with a Nike or Under Armour logo and khakis. But that night, he was in his civilian clothes: a Michigan State University T-shirt and sweats. He stepped into the room and closed the door behind him. "May I come in?"

I was aware of the intimacy he caught me sharing with Lucy and shifted to rest against the wall.

"I thought Lucy might need a refresher for that knee," the doctor said, holding an ice pack. His other hand was hidden behind his back and he revealed it with a flourish, like a circus clown presenting a bouquet of plastic flowers. "I happen to know Hershey's Kisses are your favorite. The Baloghs have a strict no-candy rule for team members, but you could use a little soul medicine. I won't tell if you don't."

"Thanks, Eddie."

Lucy's grin absorbed her eyes and usually endeared her to me. Now it stirred bitterness like dead leaves in the wind.

"And how are you, Ms. . . ." As Eddie trailed off, he cringed.

Maybe my mother was right about me not having the classic look that appeals to judges, to all people. I'd have to charm him so he'd never forget me again. I fixed my expression into congeniality.

"Sera," I said.

"Of course. Sera. I was going to say that." He smiled, but when he turned to Lucy, his expression warmed into something softer and sweeter, like melted chocolate. "Ms. Lucy. How's it feeling?"

"Better," Lucy said.

"I told you it'd be just fine. I'm going to keep you in peak training condition." He swapped out her old pack for his new one, positioning it just right. "You'll come see me before you leave, won't you?"

"I will."

He thumbed her nose. "Good. And add me to your Christmas card list, if your family does that type of thing. I like to hang cards from my favorite patients."

When the door closed behind him, Lucy said, "He's going to treat me off-season. No charge or anything, because he knows my parents don't have a ton of money. Isn't that so nice?" When I didn't respond, she reached for the paper and pen in my hands. "Time to do your MASH."

Resenting Lucy was like resenting Minnie Mouse. It felt unnatural, wrong, and undeserved. It wasn't Lucy's fault that I didn't make the team. It wasn't her fault that famous gymnasts said hello to her, that Vanda Balogh was invested in her future and not mine, and that a renowned doctor was interested only in her health. Still, I felt like her success was at the cost of mine, and knowing something is irrational doesn't make it feel any less true. I didn't want Lucy to be nice to me while I was begrudging her for something she couldn't control, so I slid off her bed without looking at her, punishing her special attention by withdrawing mine.

"It's a stupid game," I said. "Let's just go to bed."

CHAPTER 6

May 2013

Lance Armstrong confessed to doping. President Obama was inaugurated for his second term. Bombs exploded at the Boston Marathon. McKayla Maroney retweeted me. Eddie examined Lucy in his basement. And we trained and we trained and we trained.

Five months after the last Balogh camp, there was a hot spot just below my knee.

Sure, my entire body twanged. It always did. I had stone bruises in my heels. Cuts between my toes. Tenderness in my wrists and ankles. Muscle pains I patched with an ice-and-fire combination of menthol and lidocaine. But this was different. If I were a dog, I would have been licking it, shielding it from the world; I would have growled if another dog approached. It was sensitive and swollen and had been for weeks. I'd doubled my Advil intake, burned through a roll of athletic tape a day, clenched my teeth during training, and snuck frozen packs to bed at night.

I had only a month left to perfect my routines before the next Classic. This was no time for bellyaching. This was the time for gym face.

But then it became a problem I couldn't gym-face away.

When I was training the Arabian double front dismount off the beam, landing for the first time on the mat rather than in the foam pit, my upper shin was seared by an invisible iron. My leg collapsed and I cried out.

Jennifer's hands guided my shoulders so that I was lying back on the mat, and her fingers traced the outer edge of my hurt. "How long has it been like this?"

Lucy's and Jennifer's faces hovered over me like two pale moons, and beyond them I saw stars. "Only since Tuesday," I lied.

"You should have told me then."

"I'm sorry."

Lucy tucked a strand of hair behind my ear. "We're always hurting somewhere. How are we supposed to know which injuries are serious?"

Jennifer sighed. "I was afraid of this when I agreed to train you forty hours a week. You can only keep that up for so long before your body burns out. But your mom insisted."

Could my thirteen-year-old body have already burned out?

Lucy clasped my hand. "Maybe it's just a little puffy, like

mine was at the ranch. I was also training an Arabian. Maybe you just need to ice it."

An X-ray confirmed what Jennifer and my orthopedic specialist already suspected: Osgood-Schlatter disease, an inflammation of the growth plate at the top of the tibia caused by overuse.

I stared at the X-ray, still stuck to its light box. It looked like the ultrasounds I'd seen in the movies, but instead of a baby inside a womb, the objects of our concern were fragments trailing off my shinbone like the shattered tail of a meteor.

The treatment consisted of ibuprofen, stretching exercises, and rest.

"Rest for how long?" my mother asked. She stood uncomfortably, as if she didn't want us to know somebody was pricking the bottom of her feet with a tack.

"Until the pain is gone," the doctor said. When my mother raised her eyebrows, prompting a finer point, he sighed. "Six weeks. Maybe eight."

She laughed. "Sorry there, but it's competition season."

"You mentioned that."

"There's got to be another way."

"I'm afraid not."

"Athletes train through injuries all the time. It's part of the process. She certainly isn't the first gymnast to have Osgood-Schlatter."

The doctor nudged his glasses further up his nose, as if to see my mother more clearly. "Rigorous activity might result in a fracture through the growth plate. Then she would re-quire surgery, and many months to heal."

Forbidding me from practicing gymnastics was like tell-ing me I couldn't speak English. It was the only language I knew. I looked up at Jennifer and knew my voice would tremble even before I opened my mouth.

"But the national team," I said.

"There's always next year," she said, speaking tenderly, as if she knew each word pressed into a bruise.

My well of motivation wasn't bottomless. In fact, with all these setbacks, it was drying up. It might be arid before I ever made the junior national team, never mind the senior, or even more improbable, the Olympic. I squeezed my eyelids against my tears, but it wasn't enough of a dam to keep them from leaking hot and fast down the sides of my temples.

MY MOTHER STARED blankly at the road and didn't, perhaps couldn't, say anything to console me, so I wrapped my arms around my knees and hugged myself.

"When Lucy's knee hurt after her Arabian, Eddie had her ice it the rest of the day and she was fine. But I have to be out for months. It's so unfair."

"Who iced her?"

"Eddie. Dr. Levett."

My words were like oil to her rusty joints. As they ab-sorbed, she reanimated. "Sera, that's a great idea. The quack we saw today wouldn't know a kip from a flicflac. But Eddie?

He knows gymnasts. He'll be able to tell us if you really need to rest this thing or if that orthopedic downer back there is just protecting his own hide from malpractice. Where does he practice when he isn't at the ranch?"

"Michigan, I think."

"That's not too far. Maybe a four- or five-hour drive? Easy peasy."

I released my shins. My breath still rattled, but the sobs were tapering. "You think he'd see me?"

"You're a future Olympian. Why wouldn't he? Besides, doesn't he know you from the ranch?"

I thought of when he visited my dorm to see Lucy and didn't remember my name. "Sorta."

Renewed hope filled my mother like she was one of the inflatable air dancers in front of my father's car dealership, and she held the steering wheel to keep herself grounded. "You're a personal friend. Of course he'd see you." Then she glanced over at me and her nose wrinkled. "Sweetie, there are tissues in the glove compartment. Wipe those tears before your face sticks like that."

She tapped the radio on and hummed to Carly Rae Jepsen's "Call Me Maybe" while I watched suburbia pass by outside the window. It was a cool spring, so the dogwood trees were late to bloom. But there they were now, their flowers opening like thousands of white and pink fists unclenching.

"You know what?" my mother said as she veered the minivan to the side of the road. "Let's just get this appointment settled so we can move on with our lives."

We were only a few miles from home, but she sifted through her purse, pulled out her phone, and muttered, "Levett, Levett," as she searched the internet for his office number. While the phone rang, she said, "It's better this way. Before we forget," and then held up her finger to silence my nonresponse when the other line picked up. "Hi there. I'm the mother of a Balogh Ranch gymnast and, if it's not too much trouble, then, I'd like to make an appointment with Eddie. . . ." she said, and paused for a response. "First-time patient but not new to the scene by any means. She's met Eddie several times." My mother winked at me and nodded. But as she listened to the person on the other end, her head stilled. "There must be something sooner. . . . I'm sure he is a busy man, but we're approaching competition season. Heck, the Classic is next month. . . . I don't mean to be rude, but Eddie knows my daughter. . . . Do me a favor and tell him it's Sera Wheeler, from the ranch. . . . I think you're going to feel very silly when he hears you're giving us such a hard time. . . . I understand he has a lot of patients, but . . . No, she's not on the national team, but she will be soon and, like I said, she's attended camps at the ranch many times. Eddie knows her." She faced forward and rested her head back against the seat. "I see. Yes. Well, thanks anyway." Without looking at me, she cleared her throat, shifted the car back in drive, and eased onto the road. "That receptionist thinks she's all high and mighty because she holds the keys to the castle," my mother said, bending forward to peer over the steering wheel, as if her vision was suddenly impaired. "We'll think of something, Sera. Don't you worry."

We wouldn't.

THAT NIGHT, I lay on my bed with my computer on my lap and a bag of ice melting on my knee, watching Jordyn Wieber's floor routine from the 2012 Olympics, when she competed with a stress fracture in her right leg. If I didn't let this heal, that could happen to me, a bone cracking at the worst possible time. She scored only a 14.5, finishing seventh, but seventh in the world wasn't so bad with a fractured leg.

Gymnastics necessitated control in all things. A balance beam was only four inches wide. You had to jump, flip, twist, straddle, pike, planche, handstand, and return safely to that narrow leather. If your angles fell a degree out of alignment, you might not be able to readjust your body with the beam. The consequence of failure was your shins, knees, hips, thighs, crotch, or head smashing against the covered wood or burning against its surface. We learned to demonstrate absolute command over our bodies or we paid the price.

There was no way to avoid discomfort when pushing to greatness, but serious injuries were a taste of powerlessness. An instance when the body that you'd kept so disciplined betrayed you.

My phone buzzed and I knew it was Lucy before I looked. We texted each other before we went to sleep, usually ending with "Good night, smoochie," a parody of Jennifer's endearment with her husband.

What'd the ortho say, smoochie? Do you have mutant healing powers? FIG might think that was cheating, but I won't tell.

I responded with the poop emoji and added, That doc was dumb. I have to see someone who knows what he's talking about.

Then I had a thought—a thought my mother might have called my second great idea of the day. I typed, Will you ask Eddie if he'll see me? His appointments are booked but he might make an exception for his favorite patient. JK. But kinda serious too.

The response dots oscillated. I stared at the screen, awaiting an "Of course. He's so nice, I'm sure he'll make room for you." The dots disappeared. Her end was blank for several excruciating moments. I was about to type "Pretty please?" but then her text bubble appeared.

I'm really sorry, but I can't.

A black thought flickered to life in the lizard part of my brain. I was Lucy's friend, but I was also her competition. She was withholding Eddie to keep me down now so she wouldn't have to oppose me later.

I knew the idea was sinister, and completely unlike Lucy. I turned from its smoke, but I didn't extinguish it; I let it burn.

CHAPTER 7

July 2013

Lucy held a split handstand on the concrete floor of my basement. She'd applied so much hair spray, her locks were darkened from red to brunette and appeared wholly unaware that they were hanging in the wrong direction.

We'd descended into the damp underground because she wanted to show me a change to her beam routine. Now that we were down there, me in a lawn chair covered lightly in spiderwebs and Lucy alternately upside down and stretching on a beach towel, we remained.

Lucy had earned silver on beam at the Classic the previous week. I'd watched the event from my bed with a box of tissues on my lap while I pinched the soft underside of my biceps until it purpled.

My dad had paused in my doorway. His frown tugged

down the edges of his mustache. "What do you say we go out for ice cream? Get your mind off it?"

His face reflected my own heartbrokenness. I snatched another tissue from the box and crumpled it in my fist. "I can't. Especially when I'm not working out."

"Not even a kiddie size?"

Then my mother was behind him. The tip of her nose was nipped red and liner splotched like watercolor under her eyes. "It's tough tomatoes, that's for sure, but you'll be training again next month." Then she gestured to the hand weights in the corner of my room. "No sense letting your upper body atrophy too."

In the basement, Lucy didn't mention her new medal. Because she pitied me, I was sure. She thought I was beneath her. We both did. And that fact wedged distance between us. Perhaps I could have vanquished that distance by pulling my friend close, reassuring her, congratulating her, and asking for a firsthand account of the competition. But I didn't.

From her handstand, Lucy said, "I'm thinking about piercing my nose. What do you think?" Her elongated throat strangled her voice.

Gravity towed Lucy's shirt up to her ribs, revealing a taut belly. She was a fourteen-year-old with a six-pack. All gymnasts were ripped. Well, except me. Although I'd been adhering to my food regimen, I was sure my belly had softened, and I wrapped my arms in front of my stomach.

"Vanda won't like that."

Her legs lowered to the floor one by one in swift but controlled movements. She had complete authority over her body. She swung into a sitting pike position and folded her upper body onto her knees.

"I wish you could go to camp next week. I don't want to room with anybody else," she said. "You'll be back for winter camp, though, right?"

"Yeah. Definitely."

"Thank God," she said, and then ventured, "Maybe Eddie can examine you then?"

My words were barbed. "I won't be hurt then."

She lifted her face so that her nose hovered over her legs. From there she bounced gently to stretch. "He examines me whether I'm hurt or not."

"To keep you aligned. And because of your stomach issues."

"I guess." She drew the soles of her feet together until her heels pressed against her inner thighs and her knees cocked, and then she dropped the weight of her torso onto her lap. "Do you think it's weird he always checks—" Her wrists flicked as a substitute for words. "My doctor in Indiana never checks down there when I see her about IBS."

She looked so graceful on the concrete floor—thin, strong, elastic—a perfect picture of a gymnast. She was one of the best in the country and would soon be an international competitor. There I was, rickety, collecting dust, standing still while everyone moved on without me. Maybe it was all those bonus visits with the best gymnastics doctor in the country that had preserved her body, prevented her from getting Osgood-Schlatter disease or anything else. Maybe if I had been one of Eddie's prized girls, if he'd brought me chocolate and provided treatments and tips on form, I'd be on the national team too.

"I think Edward Levett knows exactly what he's doing. But if you think it's so weird, you should stop seeing him," I said. My words were sharp enough to break skin.

At that, her expression blanked into gym face and her stare fell from mine. She gripped her feet and fluttered her knees like butterfly wings.

"Lucy didn't want to stay for dinner?" Joe asked around a mouthful of green bean hotdish, which he washed down with three gulps of red Kool-Aid.

Lucy and I had evaded each other like estranged spouses until she finally suggested she leave. I didn't disagree, and so she'd called her mother, who'd been visiting a friend nearby, to come pick her up.

"Is everything all right?" I heard her mother ask through the phone.

Lucy's deadpan stare skated to me, found no traction, and slid away. She answered flatly, "It's fine."

I answered Joe by saying, "She had to go."

Although I'd stopped eating family meals long ago, we

still pretended I participated by spooning me a portion that was inevitably wrapped for my father's lunch the following day. I poked the serving on my plate. Steaming cream of mushroom soup oozed from beneath shredded canned greens while the fried onions sprinkled on top moistened. How many calories were in each bite? Thirty? Fifty-five? How many cartwheels would be required to burn off an entire meal—cartwheels I couldn't do? How many pounds would I gain if I actually ate this plateful, and where would they land—my thighs, upper arms, stomach?

"Why aren't you eating, Sera? Not feeling well?" my father asked, referring to my untouched side dish of hard-boiled egg whites and raw string beans. A rubber-ducky-patterned tie hung loose on his chest and a bit of cream clung to the follicles of his mustache, bobbing with his question.

My mother smiled prettily. "Sera doesn't have to eat if she isn't hungry. Let her be." Although she was defending me, it felt like criticism, like she thought I didn't deserve dinner.

I dug my fork into a heap of hotdish. I was impressed by its weight. I suddenly knew exactly how it would plop into my stomach and seep into my sedentary ass. I shot her a glare that made her flinch.

"Maybe I *am* hungry," I said, and shoved the entire mass into my mouth.

"Good girl," my father said. "Eat up."

My mother watched me, shocked and maybe a little disgusted, while I cleaned my plate. But she didn't say a word.

Later, I stared up at my bedroom ceiling. Lucy and I had never fought before. She was the person who mocked a reprimanding coach, who celebrated my accomplishments, who didn't require setups to stories because she already knew the details. She was where I went to vent. Where would I go now that she was the subject? Who would text me good night?

Our interaction sat in my memory as upright and uncomfortable as the meal sat in my belly. I rolled it over, examined it from all angles, held it under different lights. She was being selfish, wasn't she? Preening on the floor like a prize rooster while my wings were clipped, griping about how she was too loved by our franchise. She was the one who should be lamenting our moment in the basement, not me. And then there was that strange business about Eddie that my mind refused to digest.

The green bean hotdish squatted at the top of my stomach, and then it lurched. I stumbled to the bathroom just as it heaved its way out, burning my throat and singeing the hairs in my nose. And though my mouth stung, though the ugly taste would linger well beyond a toothbrushing, my stomach was gratifyingly empty.

When I was back in bed, my mother ascended the stairs and paused in the hallway outside my door. I thought she'd come to apologize. Maybe she'd heard me vomit and wanted to make sure I was okay. Instead, she stepped into the bathroom and peered over the toilet. Then she glanced across the hall into my room, but I shut my eyes and pretended to be asleep. She flushed the toilet again and went to bed.

So I reached for love from the only person I trusted to provide it.

I'm sorry I was mean and jealous. I'm proud of your silver. Can you forgive me, smoochie? I typed, tacking on silver-medal, heart, applause, and kiss-face emojis.

Her dots bounced to life. I was just picking up the phone to text you. We are soul mates, smooch-smooch. I wish we'd medaled together. But we will. I just know it.

CHAPTER 8

Charlene Wheeler

I felt different the moment my babies were conceived. Fuller, and a little sick. Bob lay in bed beside me in the spent way he always did, and I felt restless and a little ashamed the way I always did. But this time there was something else too. I snuck out of bed and tiptoed into the bathroom, where I squatted over the toilet and peed on a stick. It came up negative, of course, but I knew just the same.

My doctor didn't believe that I could vouch for the exact date. Doubt hid behind his smile, as big and fat as I was about to become. He looked at me like I was a foolish woman and said, "Isn't that something?" But it *was* something. I'd felt the seed plant in my womb and it wasn't just one baby, but two; maybe that was why the impression had been so strong.

I had a similarly undeniable feeling when Sera stepped

out at the Sears Centre Arena for the 2014 Secret U.S. Classic. Was it nerves? You betcha. But it was also the exhilaration of having the future laid out before us—that thrill when the Buick was packed, the oven was off, the house doors were locked, everyone had piled into the car, and we pulled onto the expressway, not knowing what adventure awaited, just that it would be new and shiny and the next time we saw the boring walls of our house, we'd be a little different.

And I was right. Sera placed silver on bars, bronze on beam, and fourth overall. It was more than enough to make the junior national team. Thank the good Lutheran Lord because I don't think she could have missed it a third time and gone on for a fourth. A heart can only endure so many disappointments before it surrenders. If it were me, I would have flopped down on my bed and taken up scrapbooking a long time ago. I'm not too proud to admit my flaws, and I've always had a low threshold for negative feedback. But not my Sera. She didn't mourn every setback with the flair I would have. She was quiet for a few days, kept to herself. And when she emerged, her head was down, but her eyes looked forward. Being great at something requires talent, sure, but sometimes I wonder if most of all it means giving up later than most people.

I don't know where she came from, because she didn't get her determination from Bob either, I can tell you that much. It was like my uterus had all the qualities built in, pre-furnished, and she and Joe split them down the middle. Joe got charm and street smarts. Sera got ambition and strength. Or maybe my womb had all my own limitations, and God placed his all-knowing, all-mighty ingredients in the mix. The Creator made us a lean, mean, fighting machine, and I thank Him for it.

I wasn't blessed with my daughter's resolve, but I prayed I'd find my share. It wasn't easy for me as a mother to watch my daughter in harm's way, and as a woman of Christ I knew better than any other that there were plenty of devils roaming free. They took the form of stingy judges, precompetition flus, and who knew what else. But if the Virgin Mary could watch her son on the cross, I could manage this.

One such devil knocked Sera off-balance when she was eight years old. She fell from the beam and fractured her wrist. I swear I heard the snap echo in the gym. I felt it in my own bone. Ever since then, I have anticipated her next slip and watched her practice with an open mouth. Fear has lived on my tongue like a sacrament refusing to dissolve. My heart has performed all the jumps with her. When my girl suffered, I suffered. And when she soared, I soared.

After the Classic, I was so proud I wanted to roll down my window at every stop-and-go light to ask the driver beside us if he had heard about Sera Wheeler. It was all I could do to get through small talk at church the next Sunday without bursting, "She did it, and she did it so well."

Her friend Lucy did super too. She's always been a sweetie, supporting and strategizing with Sera, and complimenting me too, taking notice of new shoes or earrings or what have you. It's been precious watching them climb the ranks as they matured from girls to young ladies. There's nothing quite like a childhood gal pal. I didn't tell Sera that such friendships rarely last. Some of life's letdowns you just have to find out for yourself, but I'm sure the tenacity gymnastics has instilled in Sera would make that eventuality a breeze to weather.

After the Classic, I wanted to see where my girl stacked among other athletes, so I went to the "July 2014 United States sports" Wiki page. There was the Major League Baseball All-Star Game, nine tennis championships, five car-racing events, golf, and the NBA Summer League. Fine, those were deserving of a spot, but then there was a kid's choice ceremony and the CrossFit Games, of all things. Without an Olympic year to remind everybody of our importance, gymnastics wasn't in sight. The 2014 Secret U.S. Classic was just that—a secret the average person hadn't been let in on. It wasn't universal enough. If Sera wanted to be a household name, she'd have to go bigger.

And she would. I was sure of that too. That's why I took out another mortgage on the house. The loan might have been in my name, but it was betting on hers.

CHAPTER 9

September 2014

Over the course of the next year, Sochi hosted the Winter Olympics; Eddie was put on leave at Michigan State University following a Title IX complaint and police report, but his suspension wasn't advertised and he treated patients elsewhere, including at the ranch and in his home; my tibial tubercle healed, I returned to rigorous training, won Vanda's attention at the next Classic, and was placed on the junior national team; Lucy's and my goofy gymnastics photos were reposted by the USA Gymnastics Instagram account; and Eddie was cleared for treating MSU patients once again.

At the monthly national team training at the Balogh Ranch, Jennifer fed me pointers beside the high beam while Vanda stared down its barrel at me. It was like she could see into my soul and didn't like what she found.

"Keep your entire body over the beam on this series,"

Jennifer said. "Strong legs from the beginning. Tight core. Lead with the head."

Vanda squinted. She was a human calculator with only a subtraction key, ticking off every deduction: a flexed foot here, a bent arm there. From her constipated expression, I wasn't sure I had any points left.

As I paused at the head of the beam, I bobbled and jerked to regain balance. Vanda's mouth tautened. Another 0.3 deduction. *Crap*.

I spun on the pads of my feet, bent forward, swung my arms, and launched into a back handspring, hoping to erase Vanda's memory of my falter. I was airborne and upside down, and then my hands caught leather and pushed me back up again. As my feet landed one by one, I thrust my head again into a second back handspring. I had to fit another skill into only seven remaining feet, so I channeled my force into vertical rather than horizontal movement. With the third and final takeoff, this time into a layout stepout, I ensured my arms were a firm frame for my body to operate inside. Vanda had already told me I was lucky I had acrobatic abilities, because I had zero artistry. No flow. No rhythm. No flair for performance. Like a Russian robot, she said. Until I developed style, I wanted to remind Vanda of the reason I deserved to be there. This needed to be the best layout stepout she'd ever seen.

I was arcing beautifully above the beam. An inverted dolphin out of water. But as the crown of my head crested the curve, I searched for Vanda's approval, finding only a blur of tan skin and red nylon sweats, and my wandering gaze misaligned the course of my landing.

My right foot compassed my body and returned to the beam, catching only the edge of the wood. It slipped, and the inside of my leg burned down the side as the beam rushed up and axed my crotch with all the power of my gathered velocity.

Fireworks exploded inside my pelvic bone. It was thunder and lightning. It was molten lava that sent sparks into my fingers and toes. The pain blinded me.

My shoulder crashed onto the floor mat. I curled into a ball and wailed.

"Breathe, breathe," Jennifer said. Her fingers were cool on my bare arms, but their comfort just slid off the sphere of my pain. My pelvis was still detonating. I grasped it and wept.

I'd never split the beam before; it felt like I'd been hammered in half. I was sure I'd fractured my pelvis. I couldn't afford another recovery only a year after my last injury.

"I need Eddie," I moaned.

"No," Lucy said, beside me. She tugged my wrist until I relinquished my hold and pressed an ice pack into my hand. "You just crotched the beam. I've done it before. It hurts like heck, right? I know. But you're okay. Here, squeeze my hand as hard as you can." She slipped her hand into mine.

It was rough with calluses. A tough, hard-worked hand. I squeezed through the throbbing and opened my eyes. Her cheeks were flushed from training and her eyes were so very kind. They glinted from the overhead lights. "There, better already, right?"

Vanda appeared as a shadow over Lucy. Her expression was unchanged by my accident. She nodded to the beam. "Again, before the fear sets in."

AFTER SIX HOURS of training, hunger consumed you. That night, we ate our self-provided meals with other juniors in our common room. That was one stark difference between TOPs camp and team training at the ranch: during team training every month, the ranch didn't provide meals. You brought your food or you didn't eat.

Bruises were already seeping down my inner thighs, so I numbed my lap with a bag of ice.

"I remember when I did that. It sucked so bad." Kelsey, a blonde from Arkansas, pointed a carrot stick at my injury and then snapped the tip between her teeth. "I didn't get back on the beam for months. Then I was so afraid it'd happen again, I cartwheeled with my butt out like a grandma."

My skin stung from the cold, but I ignored it. Skin wasn't as important as muscle and bone. The ice crunched as I rearranged the bag into the curve of my pelvis.

"Don't you think I should have seen Eddie? Just in case it's serious?" I asked the room.

Ada, a dark-haired girl with bushy eyebrows, snickered from the corner. "That would have made the Crotch Doc's day."

"I know," Kelsey said, hitching her shoulders as if to tuck her head between them. "He massages there for everything. He even sticks his finger—"

"He does that to me all the time," Cindy, a Californian, interrupted. "It's weird, but it's the treatment. It's normal."

"You think it's normal he gets a hard-on touching you like this?" Ada set the plain yogurt she was eating on the floor, her eyes flicked closed, and her fingers worked the air in front of her.

Giggles spattered around the room; they all seemed to be in on the joke. I smiled even though I didn't get it and looked to Lucy, but she was occupied with her salad. Her mouth was set.

Just then, someone cleared her throat in the doorway, and a hush settled over the room. "Dinner is over. Time for room checks," Vanda said.

We tossed what was left of our food in the trash and filed down the hall to our dorms. I brushed my shoulder against Lucy's. "Hey, smoochie. You okay?"

She gnawed her lip and considered me like she was taking stock—of me, our friendship, her experiences, everything she knew to be true and all that she didn't. She was like an appraiser measuring goods, unsure if it would all add up. But what was in front of her was all she had. It would have to be enough.

She tugged me by the wrist and shut our dorm room door behind us. Although we were the only people in the room, she stood close enough that I could see the rough edges of her freckles. My ice pack dangled from my fingers and chilled the outside of my thigh.

"What Ada said in there . . ." she whispered, squeezed her eyes closed, and shook her head, as if her vision was too distracting. When the rattling of her questions didn't settle into answers, she opened her eyes and said, "I don't know. She has a point. His treatment is weird."

We remained almost nose to nose. Her urgency bound us together like coconspirators, the two of us against everyone else.

"But it's Eddie. Helping us is, like, his mission in life," I said. But Lucy wasn't moved by my reassurances. "Have you asked your mom about it?"

"No way. You know how she is. She'd freak."

I nodded somberly, disguising my pleasure that I was her person. It was my job to make her feel better, as I always did when she was insecure about a new skill or an upcoming competition. I knew this responsibility by heart; aside from gymnast, it was my most prized role. "But your mom was with you during your appointments in Michigan, right?"

"Yeah."

"And he still did the treatment then, right?"

"Yeah."

"So it must be fine."

"I guess." Lucy stepped back. Some of the tension escaped in the expanded space, and the whirring in her head seemed to slow. "It kind of hurts, though."

"Everything we do hurts. Just look at me." I contorted my features and clasped the ice pack against my groin. To my relief, Lucy giggled. "It's just one more painful thing we have to go through. Whenever it stings, just grit your teeth and picture us on the cover of *Sports Illustrated*. You and me, the bests in the world."

THE NEXT MORNING, the juniors scattered around the gym to warm up. We jumped rope, swung arms, circled shoulders and hips, curled feet, rolled heads and wrists, jogged in place, squatted, and skipped, all while descending into the mind space necessary for hours of training bodies that were still tired from the previous day. We repressed unsettling dreams. We forgot that spotty cell reception prevented us from calling our parents, who we missed, because we were children and it had been days since we'd last heard their voices. We ignored hunger pangs after paltry breakfasts. We covered our bodies in tape. We manipulated tight muscles. We wrapped joints. We drained blisters. We swallowed pain relievers. We stopped giggling and got serious. Because when the metal doors clanged opened and the Baloghs walked in, we couldn't still be getting our acts together. That would be an insult to their time and talents. We had to be ready, so we got ready.

Maybe it was because of this single-mindedness that I didn't notice something serious was happening.

Natural light poured in with the open door, and then it was shut out so only the wan yellow fluorescents illuminated Vanda and Rudi.

Normally, without even a good morning, Rudi would clap his thick hands together, signaling that we should begin sprinting around the gym. He'd continue to drill us through a warm-up so rigorous the room would begin to spin. So I got into position. I was poised on the pads of my feet, ready to launch into a full-out run at his command, pulsing groin and all.

But Rudi didn't thump his hands and bark urges to run faster, harder, like we meant it. He stood against the wall, his fingers knitted before him, like a bar bouncer with a bushy white handlebar mustache.

Vanda's announcement was delivered not quite loud enough to carry across the sprawling space. We had to strain to hear her, and we did. We held our breath to listen.

"Last night we found contraband in Ada's room. She was sent home this morning. Ada wasn't national team material. Very sad. I hope the same isn't true of you."

I looked to Kelsey, Ada's roommate. They were so different. One with dark coloring and one with light. One a brassy Northerner, one a demure Southerner. But that far from home, your bunkmate was your closest friend. Kelsey's chin wrinkled. The other gymnasts glanced at one another but didn't say anything. I wondered if they were thinking what I was thinking: that there was now one less person to vie with over precious few spots.

Ada was just an acquaintance. My family was doing without Christmas presents, vacations, red meat, and new clothes to give me this chance. Their sacrifices would be meaningless if some other girl got the glory. So it didn't matter how funny or hardworking Ada was. She was my competition, and this was survival of the fittest. It was an ugly feeling, and one I wasn't proud of, but it was mine.

I waited for Lucy's gaze so we could exchange the loaded, covert look of partners, but she was in a split stretch, doubled over so flat it was as if an invisible coach were sitting on her back.

Ada had disrespected a USA Gymnastics official. She'd raised her voice above ours to be heard as an individual when we were supposed to be a uniform team. But I sensed the shadow of something else too. Something wicked. It was a transparent amorphous thing that hovered and then floated through me, lingering for a moment in my gut, casting dark threads down my extremities, before it moved on, drifting into the distance. Ada's expulsion wasn't just about contraband—forbidden candy or even cigarettes. It wasn't just about disrespect and individuality. It was about something larger. Something I couldn't comprehend, even if I tried.

But I couldn't try. Like homesickness, like the pain in my pelvis, I had to subdue those thoughts. Save them for another day. Because in the Balogh gym, there wasn't room for thinking or feeling. There was only room for training.

After Vanda finished, Rudi stepped forward and smacked his hands together, and the remaining gymnasts sprung into obedient motion.

CHAPTER 10

I thought I'd banished Lucy's anxiety about Eddie. Such arrogance was one particular to a girl who hadn't lived long enough to appreciate how little she really understood. I thought an almost-fifteen-year-old could solve a problem whose complexity was beyond the bounds of her experience. I thought I was enough. Wisdom, I suppose, is learning your own limitations.

My presumption was naive, but I meant well; I wanted to be Lucy's answer. I wanted to be the only person she ever needed, as she was for me. I'd later come to realize, if you don't see somebody's hurt, that doesn't mean it isn't there—it might just mean she isn't showing it to you.

WE HELD OUR bodies together with foam and tape.

Back in Indiana, Lucy and I met at Elite Gymnastics half

an hour before training to prepare each other's joints, muscles, ligaments, and skin for the demands of the day. Jennifer had issued us our own keys, so we sat along one wall, lit only by the bulb directly overhead. The rest of the facility was shrouded in darkness, and emptiness echoed against the high ceiling. It was equal parts spooky and peaceful, like an abandoned church, which was fitting, as the gym was where we worshipped. It was our cathedral.

Though we tended to each other wearing only sports bras and spandex briefs, this was pure business and platonic affection. It was a nurse changing dressings. Sisters applying sunscreen. It was for the preservation of self and of the person closest to us.

Lucy's index and middle fingers climbed my back until she found a point where my muscles cried out.

"There," I said. Her finger marked the spot until her other hand placed a medicated patch.

First there was the rush of coolness. I reveled in it for as long as I could, because I knew what was coming. Soon that relief was burned away as heat singed pain signals and paralyzed what would otherwise be sent to my brain.

We trimmed kinesiology tape according to the shape and needs of its placement, peeled off the adhesive backing, and applied the neon stripes precisely, even lovingly, to each other's backs, shoulders, hips, knees, thighs, shins, and ankles. By the time we were done, we'd be so colorfully banded we could direct traffic.

I held Lucy's foot in my lap. It was like a moonstone, pale and hard, and her toenails were brightened by chipped blue polish. I fixed one edge of the tape two inches above her ankle, rolled it over the joint, tugged the elastic to reach over the side of her heel, and pressed it against her sole.

"Are you gonna throw skills on the trampoline or swing bars first?" I asked.

Her stare rested above my head, like she was trying to see something in the dark behind me. "Not sure."

I assumed she was visualizing a floor skill she'd been honing: the Cojocar. So I said, "I brought a scrunchie for you to loop around your shins so they won't come apart in the front two and a half."

Her voice sounded as if it were rising up from a well. "Thanks."

I finished with her feet and, in practiced unspoken choreography, we pushed to standing, and she presented her back to me.

I knew this expanse better than she knew it herself. There was the solar system of freckles across her upper trapeziuses. There were the wings of her shoulder blades. There were the embankments of muscle running along her spine. There was the birthmark on her left buttock, like a small tea stain on linen.

"My mom posted the video of me doing a full-in pike on Facebook and hashtagged it with 'grateful,' 'thankful,' 'blessed.' She was all pissy because she only got thirty-two likes. She doesn't realize the gymternet is all about Insta," I said.

Lucy said, "Can you double the KT Tape on my low back? Eddie told me if my spine doesn't realign soon, I'll need to up my appointments. And, you know, it's such a long drive."

"I miss Eddie. How is he?" I asked cutely, the way teenagers often do when affecting a closer connection than actually exists.

Lucy's wings beat together once and then stopped, as if abandoning the notion of flight. "Fine, I guess."

Now it was undeniable. She wasn't just bothered by a skill that had been eluding her; something else was off.

Lucy had fallen so behind in her at-home schoolwork that she'd been held back a year. She claimed she didn't care, but maybe she did. Or maybe her parents were fighting again. Or maybe she was in the midst of a bad bout of irritable bowel syndrome.

I didn't like being on the outside of her interior life, but I also didn't want to draw attention to the fact that she hadn't invited me in. So instead of asking what was wrong, I sought to win her back.

"I tried this new odor spray in my gym bag," I said. "But it has this, like, chemical evergreen scent, so now it smells like a grandpa's armpit."

Lucy sniffed as a weak nod to a laugh.

We finished with the vibrant flexible adhesive and moved on to prewrap foam and white sports tape. We wound it round our ankles for extra support, and then our feet so our toes wouldn't split with the impact of acrobatics. We looped it in and out of our fingers and circled it around our wrists. It was like we were trying to mummify our youth. We went through a mile of tape a month. Maybe the true testament of an Olympic gymnast was if she'd used enough tape to circumnavigate the country she was representing.

While Lucy encased my hands, I tried to grab hold of her detachment. "See my palms? I was too lazy to get my callus scraper from the car last night, so I just used a cheese grater. Life hack."

"And your mom probably didn't even care. Anything for gymnastics, right?" Her words came from intimate knowledge, but an aloofness had cooled and set them aside.

When our bodies were bound and reinforced by unnatural materials, we stepped into our practice leos.

Lucy was right there beside me, but I still felt apart, like whitewater tubers drifting down a river, on our own separate islands dragged by the same current. I couldn't stand it. I rummaged through my gym bag and retrieved a cylinder just larger than a bottle of foundation.

"Before we warm up, can you do me a favor?" I stood and swiveled, bending over to display my rear. Then I held the stick out behind me. "My leo is loose around the seams. Be a smoochie and rub on some butt glue."

Lucy took one look at me in this pose and her tautness slackened. We used adhesive only for competitions, so she must have known I was petitioning for her favor. Her mouth softened and spread, exposing chunky teeth that still retained their childlike ridges. Her cheeks lifted and crinkled her eyes.

"You are such a dork," she said, and extended her hand. "Give it here, smoochie. I'll gum up your slippery bum."

CHAPTER 11

July 2015

Over the next eight months, dozens of women accused Bill Cosby—America's Dad—of sexual assault; Aly Raisman performed gymnastics nude for *ESPN The Magazine*'s *Body Issue*; Walter Scott was shot dead by police; and after another competition season, Lucy and I made the senior national team, which we celebrated by biting into opposite sides of a chocolate chip cookie, snapping a photo, and then throwing the rest of the cookie away.

Vanda paraded us before the TOPs campers like we were show dogs. We were well trained, desperate to please our handler, to get a pat on the head, maybe even a treat (we were so hungry). We waved and beamed at the young gymnasts, who wore expressions of awe and adoration we recognized. We were their idols, especially Gabby and Aly, who were already Olympians. The remaining thirteen were potentials. The children studied our faces. They memorized the shape our names took in their mouths.

We lined up before the bleachers of wide-eyed aspirers and Vanda pulled us forward one by one. She arranged her arm around our shoulders like we were important to her. Then we demonstrated our strongest events.

In that moment and moments like it, I believed she loved us. Her commendations felt like sunrays. Her warmth proved kindness existed in the harsh world of discipline, that she pushed us for our own good. All the yelling and mocking—*you're lazy, useless, fat*—was worth it. The cortisone shots into my feet and knees were worth it. The hunger was worth it.

When I was introduced, Vanda hugged me, turned to the crowd, and said, "Meet Sera Wheeler, a new member of the senior national team. You'll be seeing a lot of her. Don't be surprised if she's in Glasgow at this year's Worlds."

The World Championships. Vanda thought I'd be one of the seven she'd send to the freaking World Championships. My head felt like it was pumped with so much helium, my crown lifted and, inside my brain, a little egg of ego cracked, hatched, shook open its wings, and flew out the top.

I worked my ass off on the uneven bars, my showcase event. The campers oohed and aahed, but it was Vanda I looked to when I stuck my landing.

I thought she loved us. But now I know better. We were just things. And you can't love a thing. Not really.

THE NEXT DAY, Lucy and I found Rudi and Vanda in our dorm with our bags upended on our beds. There was my phone charger, plantar wart cream, a pumice stone, makeup, underwear, and the note my dad always slipped into my luggage. My private, personal belongings were tossed about as if they were trash.

I thought of the room search the previous year. The contraband found in Ada's dorm. The announcement that she'd been sent home. Worlds. Glasgow. Everything could be lost, at Vanda's discretion.

When Eddie visited Lucy the previous night, he'd gifted her another package of Hershey's Kisses and, for the first time, brought something for me too: a twelve-pack of Bubblicious. I was delighted to be remembered, and chewed a piece to demonstrate my gratitude, even though the saccharine juice tasted like Pepto-Bismol. Now, with the Baloghs sniffing around, searching for reasons to give up on us, I could have used the real digestive relief.

Vanda lifted the bag of chocolate and shook it in Lucy's direction. "This is why you stumble on your beam dismount. Too much extra weight."

Rudi snatched the Bubblicious and tossed it in a basket on the floor that contained other items, presumably from room raids that preceded ours: animal crackers, Cheetos, Twizzlers, M&M's. Were they also tokens of Eddie's affection?

Rudi's features danced when he spoke. "Sugar is no good for you. Vegetables, fruit, protein. That's what makes an Olympian. Go ask Aly. She'll tell you. This? This makes a fat pig. Are you fat pigs?" he asked, and then he oinked.

"You eat too much, you'll get too tall. Too wide. You'll outgrow gymnastics. Nobody wants to see a Thanksgiving turkey squawking on the floor. They want girls. Tiny girls. Not oafs."

Vanda was right. A growth spurt would be a death sentence. Breasts and hips interrupted the clean lines that made gymnasts little missiles. Puberty messed with aerodynamics. Petite balanced better. Smaller girls flew higher and could perform the challenging skills that were becoming more and more necessary.

I'd be sixteen in a few months, and every time I used the bathroom, I prayed I wouldn't find a splotch of blood on my underwear. Menstruating would mean I'd let myself go. I hadn't operated with enough self-control. I'd let my body beat me. I didn't care about the warnings of my physician, who cautioned that not having a period meant my body wasn't producing the appropriate amount of estrogen, the lack of which would contribute to bone weakness. That was a problem for later. For now, victory was my top concern.

"Eat only what you need to feed your current size," Vanda said. "And if you eat more, fix your mistake."

I knew exactly what she meant. I'd learned just where to jam my fingers to empty my stomach when my discipline slipped. Other gymnasts favored laxatives—enema, suppositories, you name it. Diuretics used to be relied upon for shedding water weight to look slimmer for competitions, but they were prohibited by the World Anti-Doping Agency in 1988 because they could also be employed as a masking agent to hide steroid or stimulant use. Luckily, shitting your brains out was still permitted. Lucy called laxatives a roll of the doody dice. I preferred the control of purging, knowing where and when I'd unload my occasional slipup.

But at the ranch, purging wasn't necessary. I was burning over 2,000 calories a day.

We trained long hours, warming up under Rudi's direction. He screamed: *If you want to be a slug, go home. This place is for winners. Not fat and happy losers.* Then we moved on to individual training with our personal and ranch coaches. Vanda and Rudi circled the room and studied us. *Again, better, faster, higher.* And if we didn't improve the second or third time, they clapped until the room slowed and gathered the other coaches and gymnasts around to watch. *Now,* they said, with all eyes on us. *Do it.*

At the end of every day, the Baloghs posted a sheet that ranked our performances. Vanda was particularly hard on Lucy; although she wasn't the weakest, she was inevitably listed last. Eddie assured Lucy that Vanda pushed her only because she believed in her. But it didn't look like faith, and I imagine it didn't feel like it either.

"What is this face you have?" Vanda asked after Lucy's floor routine. She bared her teeth and her eyebrows shot up her forehead. "That smile. Are you going to bite someone? Is that why you show your teeth like this?" Her facial muscles relaxed as she restored her own hostile expression. "Nobody wants an ugly Olympian. Do it again. But this time, pretty face."

Throughout the imitation, Lucy stared back as if she were deaf and blind to Vanda's criticism. Every negative comment Vanda threw in my direction was like an ax aimed at a stump. It took all the fortitude I had not to crack open, to maintain a proper gym face even though her blade gouged me. Lucy didn't seem to be affected, but I figured that was just another part of our training she'd perfected.

After one of Lucy's bar routines, Vanda crossed her arms over her chest and asked, "Why are you landing on the left side?"

Lucy picked a foot off the ground and rolled it. "My right ankle hurts."

Vanda scoffed. "Everybody here has a hurt ankle. You don't see them favoring a side. Do you need to see the doctor?"

Jennifer laid a hand on Lucy's upper back and bent to whisper. Lucy listened and nodded. Her shoulders rose and fell with a full breath, and then she reached and jumped onto the bars.

Now, in our dorm, Vanda lugged the basket of illicit items off to the next room, but her husband lingered. Rudi Balogh was most famous for the moment at the 1996 Olympics when he scooped up the injured Kerri Strug and carried her to the podium to receive her gold medal, Team USA's first. It was a tender display. But insiders knew that when Kerri's foot snapped after her first vault, it was Rudi who urged her to go on and complete the second round.

Rudi unwrapped the silver foil from around a Hershey's Kiss, looked from Lucy to me, and popped the chocolate into his mouth.

ONE HUNDRED PERCENT of elite gymnasts get hurt. The impact of acrobatics is a toll on bones, muscles, ligaments, and joints. Only a superhero could be immune to its damage. So, as a national team member, being treated by Eddie was inevitable.

Vanda was watching me train my beam dismount. We had only a few more meetings in Texas before she selected the team for Worlds. Her attention was precious, both for her expertise and favor.

"Press the landing. Press," she said as I spun through the air.

I drove my feet into the mat like stakes through the earth.

A flare shot up my right calf and exploded in my knee. I buckled. But I was a soldier who wanted to prove worthy of battle, and Vanda was my commanding officer. I couldn't let her see weakness. What if she left me behind? I climbed onto my good leg and minimized my limp as I headed back to the beam, prepared to go through my routine again.

Vanda wasn't fooled by my performance, but she didn't object either. She eyed me, perhaps daring me to surrender. Jennifer wasn't so bold.

"Sera, what hurts?"

"I'm fine."

"You could make it ten times worse," she said. I paused and considered her warning. My good leg held the weight of my body as I lifted my bad leg from the ground like a hound with a spur in its paw. Jennifer continued, "You know if your body isn't right. Is it right?"

Vanda's expression was carved from sandstone. She wanted me to be impervious. I wanted that too. But my knee was throbbing; what if it was on the verge of a ligament tear, or if this was susceptibility leftover from Osgood-Schlatter disease, and my tibia fractured on the next dismount? We had an expert on the grounds. Perhaps he could prevent further damage.

"It isn't right," I whispered.

Eddie treated girls in a room off the back of the gym. I hobbled the perimeter, meeting the eyes of those who pitied me, but who might also hope that this injury would remove me from the race.

The door was ajar, and I caught the doctor's profile through the narrow opening. The glow from his laptop lit his face with an eerie green hue. I almost saw the reflection of his screen in his glasses, but then he noticed me in his peripheral vision and slapped the computer closed.

He spent one week a month at the ranch, when the national team was training, and his small office showcased his impressive work. The walls were like a portfolio, decorated with autographed photos of Olympians, handwritten thank-you notes, and certificates of achievement.

"Oh no, Ms. Sera. What happened to you?"

My knee smoldered. I was overcome with pain, but also with the frustration that I was hurt when I needed to practice, and embarrassment that it had happened in front of Vanda. But Eddie was an expert. I was lucky to have him.

He encircled my waist and braced my weak side as I hopped onto his table. "Let me just have a look here."

He squatted and eyed my knees, regarding one and then the other, level with my groin. I tugged at the seam of my leotard and realized I probably only drew more attention to the area and cursed my self-consciousness, but he was too focused to notice. His fingers pressed the tender area around my already swelling knee. To distract myself from the sting, I focused on the cleft in his chin.

"In a perfect world, I'd tell you to rest that knee. But time is a hot commodity while you're here. So how about we wrap it up and we can keep this as our little secret. What do you say?"

I exhaled through pursed lips. "That'd be great."

He slipped my foot into a knee compression sleeve. "While I have you, I'm just going to do a quick scan to make sure this wasn't caused by a misalignment. We wouldn't want things to continue popping out of place, would we? So if you could just lie down, I'll get started, and send you back out there in a jiff."

As I lowered back onto my elbows, the thuds and claps of the gym soundtrack outside the office were interrupted by a shriek, and then the other noise quieted. Eddie and I both froze and listened for the activity to resume, for all to be well. But then we heard someone shout, "Get Eddie."

Eddie patted my good knee. "Duty calls."

Back in the gym, a crowd huddled around the vault mats. Eddie made his way to the center. Lucy was the only one whose attention wasn't focused on the scene. She hurried toward me.

"I was weight training and didn't see you get hurt. By the time I heard, you were already with Eddie." She pulled my arm around her neck and hugged my ribs to support me while I walked. We were both perspiring, but our bodies were always damp; we were used to sharing sweat. "How'd it go?"

"He's letting me train. That's all that matters."

"But did he"—she looked at me meaningfully—"examine you?"

"Yeah," I said. But I sensed that my understanding had

come dislocated, a ball needing to be popped back into its socket. "Wait, what do you mean?"

"Never mind." Her attention fell in front of her, but she pulled me close. "I'm glad you're okay."

IN ORDER TO address a growing list of problems—high arches, irritable bowel syndrome, hip misalignment—Eddie worked on Lucy midday in his gym office and nightly in our dorm room. Those calls had become so routine, I'd come to know him as a fisherman knows a lighthouse: a steadfast presence, a symbol of safety, a friend at the ranch who encouraged us and snuck in items that the other adults prohibited. He brought a water bottle from the London Olympics, an autographed photo of Kerri Strug, a USAG sweatshirt, and always, *always,* Hershey's Kisses.

When he arrived, Lucy was ready in a sports bra and a baggy pair of shorts. She lay facedown on her bed while I analyzed the footage of my routines that Jennifer had recorded on my phone. But it was difficult to concentrate with Eddie chattering away, asking about our summer plans, which coaches we liked best, or who we thought would win the primaries. Lucy was slow to respond, perhaps because the adjustments were uncomfortable, so conversation fell to me, unless questions were addressed to her directly.

"Does this hurt?" he asked. "If it hurts, I'll stop."

"No," she said. Her face was turned to me and the clay

of her features had been fired in a kiln, made as hard as ceramic. "It doesn't hurt."

Gymnasts weren't supposed to feel pain.

WE HAD FIVE minutes before morning training and Lucy wasn't in our bedroom. All the other girls hastened toward the gym, religious disciples answering the call to prayer. But not Lucy. She wasn't waiting outside, and I knew she wouldn't have gone ahead without me. I hurried to check the bathroom.

The door was propped open and Lucy was beyond it, gripping the edge of the sink and glaring at her reflection in the mirror. There was something about her pose that made me stop and watch without announcing myself. She sucked air in through her teeth. Her chest swelled with each respiration. Then she released the grip of her right hand, inhaled again, and slapped herself across the face, hard and fast. I flinched. She whimpered and struck herself again.

"Lucy," I said.

Her hands dropped to her sides and she rotated to face me fully. Her eyes glistened. "I'm going to say I fell in the shower. I want to go home."

She hadn't closed the door. She knew I'd come looking for her. Maybe she wanted to be found. Maybe she wanted me to ask what this was really about.

"It's only one more day."

Her hands worked into fists by her hips. Her mouth thinned and released, thinned and released. Maybe she was waiting for a question. She couldn't give the answer if I didn't ask the question.

I stepped forward cautiously, as if approaching a cornered animal. "Come on," I said, and gently towed her by the wrist. "It's only one more day."

By the time we entered the gym, the other girls were running laps around the perimeter. Jennifer jogged toward us, her face fixed with worry. "I was just about to come looking for you. Where have you been?"

"You are late," Vanda said. A line dug between her eyebrows, but her mouth puckered in a way that suggested she enjoyed this. "That is a disrespect to your fellow gymnasts and to me. If you don't care enough to be on time, you don't care enough to train at all. Go on then. Go home," she said, jutting her chin toward the door.

I worried Lucy would take her up on the offer. I clenched my butt cheeks and dug my fingernails into my palm.

"I'm sorry," I said, standing as tall as my height could manage. "Please let us train today."

"I fell in the shower," Lucy said lamely.

Vanda turned to face Lucy and Lucy alone. "If you're going to be lazy, that's your choice. But don't bring your friend down with you. She's a good girl, and a good gymnast. She's going to Glasgow, unlike some people."

In any other circumstance, I would have swelled with the compliment. But Lucy's spine bowed, and I remembered the clap of her hand against her cheek.

I looked beyond Vanda to the gym equipment. It wasn't state of the art, like one might expect for a renowned facility where the best gymnasts in the country traveled to train. It was ripped and run-down and dusted with chalk. In need of a good scrubbing, repair, or maybe replacement altogether. I looked back to Vanda, who appeared suddenly foul herself.

I said, "Lucy isn't lazy. She works as hard as the rest of us. She fell in the shower. But she's here. What does that tell you?"

Vanda turned toward me. With her next swallow, liquid paste seemed to travel through her body and cement. She wasn't a tall woman, but in that moment she was a craggy mountain, something I would never have the strength, endurance, or courage to climb. Her eyes narrowed into blades and her voice gathered into a blunt mallet. She hurled each word with precision.

"It tells me she's as clumsy outside the gym as she is in it. And she's always making excuses. Falling in the shower? Poor baby. That is no excuse. I don't care about fevers or sprains. I don't care about little aches and pains. Unless you are bleeding, you train or you go home. Your issue, though," she said, and nodded toward me, "is new, and not good at all. I am not happy to see it. Very disappointing."

Ada had been expelled for piping up, so I expected further

discipline: to be kicked out of the gym, or at the very least be made to run extra laps. But Vanda just stepped aside. My heart pounded as we bypassed her toward the equipment.

Later, Vanda spotted my flight series on the beam: three layout stepouts in a row. On my final landing, Vanda caught me by the upper thigh, although I'd landed steady. A sharp pain stung my left butt cheek. She'd pinched me, deliberately or not, I couldn't be sure. The nip blossomed into a petal by the time I returned to Indiana. I was home, but her presence remained.

CHAPTER 12

Charlene Wheeler

The night Vanda was going to announce the lineup for Worlds, Sera sat at the kitchen table with her knees pulled into her chest, a tuck held in suspension. Even with her width widened by thighs and calves, she still looked slight, prone to snapping. But I'd seen her crash so hard the slap of her body against the mats stung my ears—and she didn't snap. Most of the time she hardly even cried.

(She got her small size from me. I was always an itty-bitty thing until I had children; I've had to go on and off Weight Watchers ever since. I keep telling her she should enjoy it while it lasts. If there's one thing I've learned, it's that nothing lasts, good or bad.)

Sera reached her arms around her legs to rest her fingers on her laptop keys while I tapped the screen.

"Exit the window and open it again," I said.

Vanda had all but promised a spot to Sera, but it was going to be something special to see her name spelled out on the USA Gymnastics website as an official international competitor. Everyone around the globe was going to be hearing about my daughter. It wouldn't be her last hoorah—not with the Olympics around the corner—but it'd be her grand debut. This moment was ten years in the making, and I couldn't wait another minute.

There was also prize money to be had at Worlds, and I'd just opened a new credit card Bob didn't know about. I can't say how much debt I'd accumulated, so I'll just say this: if Sera had never picked up gymnastics, I could be driving around town in a brand-new sports car.

Sera said, "I don't have to close the window. I already hit refresh." Then she twisted to look at me. Agitation made me feel like bursting out of my skin, so I'd started doing squats behind her. "Will you just sit down?" she said. "Jeez."

"At least I'm burning calories. You should think about applying your energy to something constructive. If you keep bunching your eyebrows like that, those wrinkles are going to set. Believe me."

At sixteen, she was already more accomplished than most adults, but it took only one good eye roll to strip away all that expertise and make her look like just another teenage girl.

"It'd serve you right if you got stuck that way. Now turn your little hiney around. Vanda might have made the announcement while you were sitting there making faces."

The screen cleared and reassembled into something new, like tea leaves reading our future.

Sera's feet dropped to the floor and she leaned forward. The light of the computer made her skin look sick.

"I'm not there," she said, her voice as flat as her hair, abs, and chest.

"Oh, for heaven's sake." I hunched over to search the page myself.

"No, really. I'm not there." She pushed off the table's edge and sat against the back of her chair, crossing her arms over her stomach.

I was sure we were just so eager to get through the list of names that we'd skimmed right over hers. So I read and reread. The problem was, I just kept skipping it, no matter how slowly I looked.

"Well, this just can't be right," I said, although grief was rising up fast and dense from my toes.

"It's right. I wasn't picked."

Sera's face became a drywall panel her true feelings could hide behind. She'd mastered the Midwestern woman's custom early: how we appear polite when our eyes are really saying, "Up yours, pal"; how we wave to our neighbor at the store and reply, "My day is fine. Thanks for asking," whether we won the lottery that morning or buried our pooch. Maybe that's why girls of the Plains are predisposed to gymnastics—they've been bred to manage great success and great disappointment with poise, or at least to appear to manage them.

But just as I was remarking on her resilience, a crack ran through Sera's Sheetrock. (What a fitting name that is—it may have some of the properties of stone, but it's as thin as a sheet.) The fissure was immediately followed by a pulse, the force of which was too much for her to bear, and cracks branched in every direction. She dropped her face into her hands and her tiny shoulders shuddered.

They say to be a mother is to watch your heart walk around outside your body. If that's true, then to be the mother of a gymnast means letting your heart not just walk, but vault, swing, leap, and flip. In this case, it was to watch my heart be promised the Worlds, only to have it yanked away. This was perhaps the furthest Sera had ever dropped, including releases from the high bars.

Her hurt was excruciating. It made me murderous.

"I'm just going to call Vanda real quick," I said.

Sera went as rigid as a pike. "Don't."

"There's been a little bit of a misunderstanding, but it's nothing a phone call won't clear right up."

"It's not a misunderstanding. I wasn't picked."

"But she kept saying you would be, and if you really aren't, that isn't right. She should explain herself."

"She doesn't have to explain anything. She's Vanda."

"I—"

"Just don't call her." Sera pitched her words at me like hammers and nails flung simultaneously.

Any other time, I would have propped my hands on my

hips and said, "I don't care for the way you're talking to me, young lady." But before I considered it, Sera melted enough for me to see the true shape of her pain, and it looked like a small girl, rejected and so very sad.

Heartache is just that: a sting in your chest.

Sera whispered, "Mom, can you promise that you won't call her?"

I nodded, but I didn't say a word. At least then it wasn't a lie to God's ears.

Of course I was going to call. Vanda was the one who got us in this rotten mess. And if Sera didn't like it, well, tough tomatoes for her. She might have been the talent, but I was the mother, and that still counted for something.

I pretended to go out for antifungal cream for Sera's foot and left her in the emotionally constipated company of her father and brother. The two of them sat on opposite ends of the couch, sneaking sideways glances at Sera, as if she had a disease they didn't want to catch, while one of the those late-night talk show hosts—an expensive suit who thought he was funnier than he was—pranced on the television, desperate for approval.

Two blocks from the house, I pulled to the side of the road and threw on my hazards. A light mist turned the glow of streetlights into a row of halos. I took that as a sign from the good Lutheran Lord.

I probably shouldn't say this in today's day and age when everybody gets so uppity about everything, but even Vanda's hello made her sound like that she-villain from the cartoon about a flying squirrel and his big moose friend.

"I'm sorry to bother you," I said, and allowed her the chance to fill my pause with assurances that I was no bother, but I was met only with expectant silence, making it seem I was very much a bother indeed. I wanted to say, "You know what, Vanda, let that be a lesson to you about raising a mother's expectations." Instead I said, "It's just that we are confused, Sera and me. According to the list, it looks like she isn't going to Worlds."

"So you are not confused then."

"Well, we are pretty disappointed over here, as you can imagine. We were under the assumption that she was a shoo-in."

"She once was going to Worlds. Now she isn't."

"And what changed, if you don't mind me asking?"

"Sera isn't as consistent as I once thought."

"Is it the triple full? I thought she had that down?"

She paused, and my Midwestern intuition told me that space was filled with meaning all its own. "I need girls who are dependable."

"You can count on her. Take my word for it." But even as I said it, I realized my words meant nothing to her. *I* meant nothing; I was just another parent of a child who wasn't making it. I really thought Sera was different. Special. One of the exceptions. I thought I was different too.

"This decision is final. If she wants a better result for the

Olympics, Sera has eight months to prove she is someone to rely on."

"You're a busy woman, so I better let you go. Bye-bye, now." My thumb jabbed the screen to end the call, and then I pressed the top edge of the phone against my forehead so hard it left a mark.

Six mothers would snap pictures of their daughters wearing warm-ups in airports, on their way to Scotland; marching around an arena; saluting the judges, vaulting, swinging, leaping, tumbling; standing on a podium, wearing a medal, wrapped in their country's colors. Six mothers would share those photos on social media for all their contacts—neighbors, distant relatives, their parents, high school friends they hadn't talked to in decades—to see, but most importantly, to envy.

But not me.

"It could be worse. It could be worse," I said out loud, but there was no one around to convince but me.

THE HOUSE WAS all buttoned up for the night by the time I got back, which was just as well. I thought I'd be returning a hero, kicking down the garage door, trumpeting good news like a darn one-woman marching band. *We are going to Glasgow! I told you it was all just a big mistake!* Instead I tiptoed along the upstairs hallway, praying everybody I loved was dreaming a reality sweeter than the one we got.

"Mom?"

A sliver of light sliced through Sera's door. I pushed it open. She almost looked infirm, like she was lying in a hospital bed.

"Yeah?"

Her nostrils were aggravated and her sniff was congested. She asked, "Are you okay?"

"Oh, sweetie." I sighed, and in that sigh I said, *I am heartbroken*. Because my daughter had lost everything and yet she was worried about me. Because I'd lost everything too. I slipped into her room and eased the door behind me. "What are you doing awake? We've still got to get up early for practice tomorrow."

"I just got off the phone with Lucy."

Of course. Lucy hadn't been selected either. "How's she taking it?"

Sera pinched her nose. "It's weird. She doesn't even seem that disappointed."

"She's probably in shock."

"I don't know. She's been weird in general lately."

My daughter was a lot of things—determined, athletic, tough—but she wasn't one for heart-to-hearts. Not with me, anyway. But I felt a pull from her then, so I sat on the edge of her bed. "Oh yeah?"

She tugged on a loose quilt string. "It's like . . . I don't know . . . like she isn't happy anymore."

I thought, well, duh—she's a teenager. That was hard in and of itself before the added burden of being an elite athlete.

When I was that age and my father moved us from northern Wisconsin to Indiana, plopping me down in a school where I didn't know anybody, I was so sullen and lonesome, I latched onto the first person who complimented me, saying I could be Brooke Shields's sister. That happened to be Bob, and the rest is history.

"Girls this age can be funny," I said. "And she's heading into an Olympic year. Not everybody can handle that pressure, you know."

Sera nodded, staring into her lap the way she did when she was waiting for judges to post scores she knew wouldn't be flattering.

"If I tell you something, do you promise not to freak out?"

I thought of scenes in *Grey's Anatomy*, when the doctors shock a heart back into life. That's what was happening in my chest, thinking Sera had something terrible to confess. She'd shocked a heart that had been hurt but was otherwise doing just fine.

"Sure."

"Lucy has said some weird things. About Eddie. She mentioned it a while ago, and she made another comment on the phone just now."

I had met Dr. Edward Levett in person at the Nastia Liukin Cup in Texas. He approached me and Bob but reached to shake my hand first, which was a point in his favor. "Your daughter has what it takes. And I don't say that to every-

one." He leaned in closer. "I only say that to four or five families a cycle."

I fell in love with him then, dorky glasses and all.

"What could she possibly say about Eddie?" I asked.

Her shoulders bobbed like the cubes in her ice baths. "She
thinks his treatments are creepy or something."

"Creepy?"

"Yeah. Because he touches"—she looked wide eyed to the
place covered by her blankets—"down there."

My eyes followed. When I understood, my cheeks burned.
We treated sex the same way we treated anger and sadness:
by ignoring it completely. If our hand was forced, we came
at it sideways, using euphemism. But now we were looking
at it directly.

"Oh for heaven's sake."

When I moved to Indiana and didn't know anybody
from Adam, I met some teenage girls who were pretty
prima donnas that aimed beauty and meanness at parents,
teachers, boys, and, often, me. They'd already established
their allies by the time I arrived. They didn't need another
friend; I was more valuable as the subject of their ridicule.
Hey, Wisconsin, does your badger bite? The rumors they spread
were as wild as they were vulgar: *Charlene is from so far north,
her vagina is a glacier, her nipples make cheese, she's mounted a
Mountie.* They didn't understand the consequences of their
words.

Lucy was leagues sweeter than those strumpets, but even the nicest girls are guilty of gossip every now and then.

I told Sera, "It sounds like your friend might be going through a crisis. Hormones, the stress of competition, not getting picked for Worlds, the embarrassment of having everybody on God's green earth studying her young body. Heck, there are strangers making comments about her thighs on YouTube. That's a lot to take, and this whole Eddie nonsense is a by-product of that. The best thing you can do is not indulge her story. It might feel thrilling to play make-believe, but if that's what she wants, she should join drama club. These stories won't feel so fun when it bites her in the rear. So, as her friend, you've got to focus, for both your sakes." Sera's eyebrows drew together, and I pressed my pointer finger in between them to remind her to relax those lines. "Let's just keep our heads down and get through the next month. When we're at the Olympics, missing Worlds will be just another chapter in the bio package that will make your triumph all the more satisfying." I squeezed her foot and prompted, "Right?"

Sera sniffled and ran her sleeve across her face. "Right," she said, and when she looked up at me, she smiled, and I thought maybe I'd managed to scrape some disappointment from her, like frost from a windshield. Maybe I'd been of use.

As I turned for the door, I noted all the gymnastics posters taped to her walls and felt sure that one day her image would be among those encircling a little girl with big dreams.

"Hey, Mom?"

"Yeah?"

"Thanks for not calling Vanda. I know that took a lot of restraint, and I appreciate it."

I was in the doorway now. At the end of the hall, my bedroom was already dark. Sera's was the only light on in the house.

"Okay, sweetie," I said. "Night, night."

CHAPTER 13

December 2015

In October, six American gymnasts and one alternate flew to Scotland. They medaled in every event, and I wasn't one of them because I'd stood up for Lucy and insulted Vanda publicly. Vanda held the power—she *was* the power—and I'd all but spat in her face. I couldn't believe my irresponsibility, my carelessness. I lost so much in one breath.

We were entering an Olympic year. *The* Olympic year. It was likely my only chance before I was too old and worn to continue training at this pace. I had to win back Vanda's favor. Fast.

Our first morning at the ranch, I rushed Lucy out of the dorm so we'd be the first girls at the gym.

"What's the point? The Baloghs roll in after we're all there anyway," Lucy said, still pinning down stray hairs.

By the time the other gymnasts filed in, I was already in a center split stretch, visualizing my double twisting Yurchenko on vault. In it, I was a corkscrew thrown into the air, whirling and twirling with complete control. And when the gym doors banged open to reveal the Baloghs, my brain snapped off and I was instantly back on the mat, springing to my feet.

But before I set off into the daily warm-up run, another person appeared behind the Baloghs: Donna Jenssen, the medical director of USA Gymnastics. Just beyond middle-aged, Donna had limp colorless hair cropped around her ears and loose jowls that half swallowed her chin. She was a familiar face on campus, sometimes working as a trainer alongside Eddie.

She raised her voice to address us. "I'm afraid I am the bearer of bad news. After almost thirty years of service to USA Gymnastics, Eddie has decided to retire. He wished he could be here to tell you personally. You mean so much to him, and I know he means a lot to you. He was a wonderful doctor and will be sorely missed. I'll be on campus if you have any concerns this week. Don't hesitate to stop by and see me."

Eddie was leaving without warning, only months before the Olympics? The news severed a tether in my brain, and my equilibrium pitched.

The other gymnasts were also unsteadied. Murmurs

rushed around the facility. Eddie wasn't just kind. He had a record of restoring and preserving gymnasts' bodies. If we had an accident, could we trust Donna with the vehicle we were pushing to its limit, especially at such a crucial time? No, we wanted Eddie. *I* wanted Eddie.

Rudi clasped Donna's shoulder to thank her, or to guide her backward, out of the spotlight, which he assumed. Then he clapped his hands and we fell in line.

Lucy ran beside me, which was unusual. We normally used this time to finish sinking into our gym personas of fierce, focused athletes. She wore the pink practice leo Vanda had told her didn't serve her skin tone. I watched her in my peripheral vision.

"We have to tell them," she whispered.

"Tell them what?"

Her profile was resolute, almost statuesque. "About Eddie."

I thought about my mother's counsel: this was a cry for attention, a desire for drama or diversion. I had to treat Lucy the same way I'd treat an old, nagging injury—by ignoring her. My feet kept pounding.

Her chin angled toward me. "Sera."

"What?"

She looked ahead. "Most sports doctors don't visit rooms at night," she said, and her gaze flicked south. "Most sports doctors don't touch their patients down there."

The sound of eighteen pairs of feet sticking and unsticking reverberated around my head while I skimmed through everything I'd come to know about doctors. Hospital billboards. Brochures. Television shows. I touched every positive association I had to confirm they were still secure in their place. I tapped all the assurances for Eddie in particular. The image of him reaching for Kerri Strug after she tore two ligaments at the Olympics. The gifts and letters from former patients that decorated his office. The coaches promising, *You can trust Eddie. He's the best.* The other athletes gushing, *Thank God for Eddie. He saved my life.* There they all were, just where I'd left them.

And then there was my mother's concern about Lucy. My friend was struggling through something. She certainly appeared to be struggling when she withdrew into herself on the floor of my basement, when she trained with a vacancy in her eyes, and when she'd slapped her face in the ranch bathroom. This Eddie story was a symptom, not the source.

Lucy said, "I'm telling Vanda."

I tripped.

Team members couldn't make their individual voices heard. We'd seen what happened to deviations. They were discarded—like Ada, like me before Worlds—to preserve order. Lucy's Olympic dream, our dream, would be shattered in a single utterance.

My voice was insistent without attracting attention. "You can't."

"Why not?"

What could I say? *Because it isn't true? Because your lie will needlessly ruin everything?*

I said, "At least wait until after the Olympics."

"That's like a year away."

"Ten months."

"Why can't I just tell her now?"

My eyes flashed to Vanda talking with Donna. Even though they were the same height and held similarly high-ranking positions in the organization, Donna appeared dwarfed by Vanda. Perhaps she was afraid of her too.

"You don't want to make her mad."

"Eddie isn't part of USA Gymnastics anymore. I'm not bad-mouthing our organization. I'm just bad-mouthing some guy."

"Since he isn't part of USA Gymnastics, you don't have to work with him anymore, and reporting him can wait."

"He's still a doctor somewhere." Lucy pulled her bottom lip between her teeth, perhaps considering her future the same way I had. She came to an entirely different conclusion. "Vanda won't hold it against me. She's a bitch, but she isn't a monster."

We were rounding the corner. I hurried to deliver my final plea. "So don't wait until after the Olympics, just until after the team is announced. That's only seven months. Besides, he said he was helping you. Pelvic manipulation. Myofascial release. Don't you think it could have been medical? Shouldn't you know for sure before you say anything?" I grasped that same old thread as everything unraveled in my hands.

Vanda looked up just in time to see my lips finish moving. She raised her palm, directing us to stop. We did, and I burrowed my toes into the mat.

Vanda crossed her arms over her chest. "What is so important that instead of warming up you girls chat like chickens?"

I turned to my friend and all at once I knew she would do it, that she'd toss it all away.

"Lucy," I said, breathless.

She was breathless too, but not supplicating, as I was. She was emboldened. She held herself with the graceful but powerful lines of a gymnast.

"Dr. Levett touched me in an inappropriate way for years."

Donna's eyebrows shot up her forehead and she went rigid. But Vanda's expression was unaffected. It rested on Lucy so long, I thought maybe she was considering her seriously. But then her stoicism broke and she snorted.

"That's ridiculous."

Lucy faced me, her best friend, fully. Her body language was open. Unprotected. Even after others had broken her trust, she still had faith in me.

"Tell her, Sera."

But he didn't do anything wrong. She was just confused, struggling with how uncomfortable it was to have thousands ogle her, the upset of missing Worlds, and looking down the barrel of the Olympics. She wanted to release some of that pressure by focusing attention on somebody else. But Eddie? He touched that area for medical reasons. Lucy would get him in trouble after he was so nice to us for so many years. It wasn't fair. I didn't have time to think this through. I wanted to cry. To disappear. My face burned.

"I don't know. He worked on her," I said.

Jennifer was suddenly beside us, her hand on Lucy's shoulder. "Lucy, why do you think it was inappropriate?"

Lucy turned toward our coach, but her eyes were locked with mine. She regarded me skeptically, like there was a small part of her that suddenly didn't recognize me, but the rest of her was reminding that part: *She's your friend. Your best friend. Remember?*

"He touched my chest, and my backside. And he stuck his fingers up my . . . me. He stuck his fingers up me."

Jennifer's mouth dropped open, and she looked from Lucy to me. I couldn't tell if our coach was shocked by Lucy's description or because her athlete was complaining about a legitimate technique. But Lucy seemed validated. Her wavering voice solidified.

"You saw him, Sera. Tell them. Tell them about his treatments."

Everything blurred. Lucy and I had talked about this; we'd agreed that Eddie was just doing what he had to do. He was a good doctor. The best. His treatments worked—the results spoke for themselves. He was kind and generous when no one else was. I hadn't felt his touch. I didn't know where his fingers went or if that made a difference. I didn't want to complain about a former USA Gymnastics official from inside the void of all this not knowing. I didn't want to say anything at all.

Gymnasts were trained to be silent. Nadia Comăneci had blood poisoning by the time she told anyone she'd sliced her hand. We performed through pain. We were hungry, but we didn't eat. We sucked it up. We didn't complain. We didn't listen to our bodies or our instincts. That's why we had coaches. The adults were the experts. They knew better than we did. The movements were too dangerous to risk ignoring the advice of experts. They told us we could trust the doctor, so we did. Simple as that. We trusted him. We smiled for the judges.

But Lucy was a year older than me, that much closer to the age of womanly knowing. She was the one who lived through Eddie's exams while I lay supine on the adjacent bed watching gymnastics routines on my phone. If Lucy said his touch was wrong, maybe I should believe her. I should stand with my friend.

The other gymnasts were still running the perimeter, but their paces had slowed. They watched. We got along well enough, comparing injuries in the common room, swapping

PowerBars when our own flavors grew tiresome. But when it came down to it, if Lucy and I didn't make the Olympic team, two of them could take our places.

Vanda studied me with narrowed eyes. She could shut me out of the Olympics the way she'd shut me out of Worlds, all because of a delusion. Hadn't I sacrificed enough? Now Lucy's eyes rounded. Her jaw jutted. She was begging. But she was troubled and self-sabotaging. To deny her would be to help her.

My exterior hardened and the soft part of me who treasured Lucy and our friendship shrank and hid behind the gym persona that was necessary to survive in our sport. I took a deep breath the way I did before each routine.

I could ask Lucy's forgiveness. I couldn't ask Vanda's.

"I didn't see anything. I don't know what you're talking about."

Lucy's next inhale was a small gasp. Her lips parted and her arms rose and wrapped around her belly, as if to catch her insides before they spilled. It was like my betrayal had disemboweled her.

"You should be ashamed of yourself, Lucy. Dr. Levett helped you, and now you slander his name," Vanda said. "Good gymnasts don't spread such lies."

Jennifer's forehead touched Lucy's, the way she did to issue last-minute reminders before we competed. "Did he really touch you like that? Because that would be wrong. So very wrong. What you said—is it true?"

I didn't know what was true anymore. I'm not sure Lucy did either.

Her tiny nostrils flared as she struggled to stay on top of her upset. She looked into Jennifer's eyes and her chin quivered. Then she looked past our coach and her stare bored into me. I fidgeted under her attention and watched as she slowly receded into herself, where it was safe. She blinked until her breathing slowed. Then she turned back to Jennifer and shook her head.

"No," she said. "It isn't true."

CHAPTER 14

January 2016

Lucy didn't show up for practice after the New Year, and when I asked our coach where she was, Jennifer answered, "She fell down the stairs and sprained her wrist. Didn't she tell you?"

No, she hadn't. She wasn't answering my texts.

I don't know what you're talking about, I'd said.

But I'd said it for Lucy, who was struggling through a crisis that made her paranoid or fantastical or melodramatic or I didn't know what. It might have looked to her like self-interest, and maybe that was part of it, but I had her dream at heart too. Still, nausea roiled through my stomach when I remembered her expression, stunned and dumb, like that of a gutted widemouth bass.

I felt the urge to pay penance, the equivalent of what my mother called the Cuckoo Catholic rosary.

YouTube recognized my name after only seven letters. I'd have to compensate for that pleasure too.

I navigated to the video of my floor routine at the 2015 American Cup. I didn't have to watch the performance; I knew each beat. I'd long ago gone frame for frame to identify and memorize each deduction: the slight hop to maintain balance, the arm swing, falling out of tempo with the music, an overrotation. These errors were seared onto the folds of my brain. I scrolled past the video and entered the dark, dank world of the gymternet.

Only thirteen comments. That was a blow in and of itself. Most were positive, from fangirls who sandwiched extra *o*'s inside the word "wow." But I was there for the trolls. I wanted to press their talons against my carotid artery.

Watching anyone but Simone is a giant waste of your time.

Wheeler is doing her best here but she's so stiff. Look at her hands during the dance moves. They're like hooks.

Her hands! I can't unsee her hands!

Now we know how a reanimated cadaver would perform.

I can't even watch her acrobatics. I'm too busy staring at her butt jiggle. Not muscles like Simone. It's a miracle she lands anything.

I systematically clicked through ten videos, immersing headfirst, eyes open. And it stung. But it didn't absolve me of my guilt, which poisoned my blood like an infection. For that, I had to see my friend.

I TALKED JENNIFER into a half day of training and took a bus to Kokomo. If I hurried, I'd beat my mother back to Elite Gymnastics and wouldn't have to explain a thing.

Lucy lived in a charmless brick apartment building. She once told me the amount her parents spent on gymnastics each month was equal to their rent. If she wasn't so passionate about the sport, they could move to a three-bedroom, or even buy a house.

Her mom buzzed me into the building and answered the door wearing a black velour sweat suit whose fabric was threadbare beneath her armpits and too tight around her rear.

"Lucy won't come out of her room. But feel free to go to her," she said. As I walked by, she squeezed my forearm and pulled me toward her. "I don't know what's with Lucy lately. Has she said anything to you?"

Good gymnasts don't spread lies.

"No."

Lucy sat on her bed eating buttered popcorn by the fistful while *Grey's Anatomy* played on a small television on her dresser. Her wrist wasn't in a brace or sling, and there weren't any ice packs in sight. Although she didn't look in my direction when I entered her doorway, she knew I was there.

"I think I'm done with gymnastics," she said.

It was like hearing she was done being a woman, done being part of her family, so intrinsically was gymnastics woven into our identities.

"But we're so close."

Lucy wore an oversize Jonas Brothers T-shirt and plaid pajama pants. Her cat, Wilbur, a Maine coon the size of a bobcat, with long fur and tiger eyes, rubbed his body along her shins and gently bunted her knee. She scratched behind his ear and spoke as if she were confiding in the gentle giant.

"I just think I'm done, you know? You give and you give, and they just expect more. It's never enough with Olympic sports. You do a double axel and they want a triple. You ski eighty miles per hour and they want ninety. At some point, you're risking your life for a stranger's entertainment, and I'm done with that."

"What would you do instead? Swipe through Tinder at Starbucks with a bunch of other girls wearing matching yoga pants?" The idea of either of us being so provincial when we'd brushed against the exceptional was a preposterous waste. "Go to prom?"

She pawed absently at the surface of the popcorn. "You're only a teenager once, right?"

"You can be normal the rest of your life. You can only do *this* once."

"Well, I've done it. I've had enough."

I'd been in Lucy's room innumerous times. It'd been the

backdrop to almost daily FaceTime calls and WhatsApp sleepovers. But now I viewed it again through the lens of her new revelation.

Decals of a silhouette moving through a back walkover stuck to the wall atop her bedframe. Issues of *Inside Gymnastics* magazine were stacked so high she used them as a nightstand. Coat hooks had amassed medals. A collage of our silly photos was displayed on her bookcase. Practice leos were lined up, ready for action, in her open closet. Almost everything in that room was flavored with gymnastics. She still loved the sport; she must. We'd dedicated ten years to it. That was longer than many marriages lasted. Such devotion might dull over time or evaporate like water off the surface of a lake, but you weren't just released from a love like that. It tunneled into you. Or, more likely, it originated from your center.

She was the other half of our two-person secret society. I was desperate to lure her back, to save her from herself. To save us. But I didn't know how.

"If you quit, what was it all for?" I asked.

She tossed a kernel in her mouth and crunched down. She smiled at me, but there was something gruesome about it, like the expression had been carved into her face.

"Nothing. It was for nothing."

I wanted to remind her of when things were simple, when we ate what we wanted and we weren't in pain and we flounced around the gym, filled with unsullied joy because it was fun and we were free and we loved it. I wanted to talk about our victory dance. When was the last time either of us had been that silly? Didn't she miss it? Didn't she miss me in the month she'd shut me out? Because I'd missed her. I felt like I'd gone through the holidays without one of my appendages. I wanted to say, "You're acting like I betrayed you when you're the one who made this whole thing up. But I forgive you. This life we chose could drive anyone mad, and you went a little crazy, but that doesn't mean you give it up." I'd prevented her from taking her story too far. She didn't have to quit. Our dream of standing together on the podium, two best friends from Indiana up there for all the world to see, had been protected. I wanted to convince her that by the time she realized what a mistake she was making, it'd be too late; she wouldn't be able to come back to this moment and do it differently. Most of all I wanted to say that I was sorry I couldn't fix her hurt this time.

But I didn't say anything.

She watched me, perhaps hoping I'd surprise her. Then her mouth tightened as she gave up on me for good.

I felt like my insides were pieces of fruit left on the counter so long they'd grown soft and brown and their cloying, sweet smell was attracting flies. I didn't know if this was grief or guilt or what, but I wanted to scoop it out as soon as possible, but also keep it forever, because without it I'd be empty.

Lucy pointed to her dresser. "Want some Hershey's Kisses?

I got a bag for Christmas, but I can't eat them anymore. They make me sick."

And beside the bag was her rubber bracelet, the other half of my mantra, hollowed without her bones and blood.

OVER DINNER, I considered all that I was losing—no gripping Lucy's hand on the front page of *Sports Illustrated*; no sharing a room in Rio; no Olympic best friends; heck, we might not be friends at all—and longed for my family to console me, but I didn't know how to ask for such tending. So I just stated the facts.

"Lucy might quit," I said, and was caught off guard by my own coolness.

My mother's fork clanged against the edge of her plate. "Did she have her period?"

"I don't think so."

She patted her lips with her napkin and it came away with a kiss. "Then what would possess her to do such a thing six months out from the Olympics, for cripes' sake?"

While my family ate ground beef tacos, I bobbed my spoon in a cup of fat-free Greek yogurt. "Things are weird between her and Vanda."

My mother's chest nearly dipped into her sour cream as she leaned forward. Gymnastics dirt was her soap opera. "But Lucy knows better than to mouth off to Vanda."

"She didn't mouth off, exactly. She said something about Eddie."

My mother rolled her eyes. "Not this again."

Her incredulity gave me further permission to dismiss Lucy's claim. "I know. Eddie was just being nice and she took it the wrong way. And now she's making it this whole big deal and ruining everything."

My dad, usually bored by gymnastics talk, now asked, "What'd he do that was so nice?"

"Little things. He asked how we were doing and if Vanda was pushing us too hard. You know, small talk. And he brought us candy at night so the Baloghs wouldn't catch us pigging out."

"What do you mean at night? In your room?" he asked.

"Where else would we be? In the woods?" I said, but the size of the joke didn't match the hole I was trying to push it through, and it came out misshapen.

My father's elbows dug into the table and his hands worked together. "You're telling me he came into your room?"

"Yeah."

"Was Jennifer there too?"

"No," I said, lengthening the word into a question.

"So an adult male was in a room with female teenagers, unattended?"

My mother laughed nervously. "What is this, Bob? An interrogation?"

He lowered his voice. "Did he touch either of you?"

"Bob," my mother said shrilly.

"He was our doctor," I said. "He touched us like a doctor."

My mother's lips compressed, but she forced them into a smile. "See, Bob. Like a doctor. Your mind, sometimes. I swear."

He studied me, perhaps waiting for me to admit all that I knew about Eddie and some things I didn't. Then he pushed himself back from the table.

"I don't like this. I don't like it at all. It's inappropriate. Lucy's right."

I made a last-ditch effort to win back the vote my father didn't realize he was casting. "It wasn't inappropriate," I said. "They were just pelvic manipulations."

His eyes bulged. "*Pelvic* manipulations?"

"Yeah. She has pelvic floor dysfunction. It's common with gymnasts. Muscles and tendons shorten from the impact of our landings, so he elongates them."

My mother said, "Makes sense to me."

"You're telling me he conducted these types of manipulations in your room at night?"

I was trapped between my father and my own fault. I had to barrel through him. "Lucy admitted what she said wasn't true."

His features bunched and he shook his head. "You said yourself he was in your room and he explained the so-called pelvic manipulations. So what about it wasn't true?"

I felt the chill of my guilt as cool as cinder blocks against my back. "That the manipulations weren't appropriate."

"It can be confusing for a teenage girl to be treated in an intimate area, especially by a male doctor. She probably just misinterpreted. As a man, you wouldn't be able to understand." My mother's voice was playful, teasing, and she flicked her wrist to dismiss my father's perspective. Then she faced my brother. "So, Joe, how is your winter workout schedule going for football? You look like you're bulking right up."

Joe hadn't expected to be the subject of conversation. He hastened to finish chewing, but before he could swallow, my father asked me, "So what is being done about this doctor? Other than Lucy suddenly quitting gymnastics right before the Olympics, that is."

"Nothing. Because who knows if he really was inappropriate? Like I said, Lucy admitted she was making it up. Or, not making it up. Exaggerating. Misunderstanding. Whatever. And he doesn't even work for USA Gymnastics anymore."

"That's convenient, isn't it?" my father asked. He steepled his fingers. "Seems to me that something should be done."

"Bob," my mother said, as if reprimanding a child. "We're talking about Joe now. Don't you think our son deserves our attention more than a doctor we met only once?"

They faced off in a silent duel, but my father had no chance of winning against the fastest glare in the Midwest. It didn't take long for him to regrasp his fork and stab his frustration onto a clump of meat.

Outside, the evening had already sunk into complete darkness and the air was cold and wet. Though the last snow was still heavy enough to bow branches, the forecast was anticipating much more to drop.

THAT NIGHT, AS I combed through the medicine cabinet for Benadryl to put me to sleep, I heard a rustling in a different part of the house, followed by a muffled but charged voice. I would have figured my parents were arguing, but my mother was in her bedroom, letting a homemade sour cream face mask set. I tiptoed down the stairs. The door to the garage wasn't fully closed, and through the crack I watched my father pace beside the wall of gardening tools, his cell phone pressed to his face.

"I don't give a damn that he's a respected physician, and I sure as heck wouldn't consider it a privilege for my daughter to receive this kind of private specialized treatment. He's got no business examining girls in their rooms. I wouldn't want the president of the United States alone with my daughter at that time of night. . . . You're USA Gymnastics and he was your team doctor, so yeah, I do think you're responsible. . . . Well it doesn't sound like you're taking my claim seriously. It sounds like you're blowing smoke. . . . Tell me this: Have you gotten other complaints? . . . It's a yes-or-no question. . . . Well, maybe the police would be interested to hear my story. . . . Yes, I am threatening you. I thought that was obvious. . . . You think I care so much about my daughter's future in gymnastics that you can bully me? . . . It could very well have been above-board. But he shouldn't be doing it at after hours. They may be athletes, but they're still girls. . . . All I'm asking is that you look into this. . . . So I've done my part. Right? I've done my part. I can sleep tonight. Now it's on you."

He scowled at the phone and then his thumb punched the screen to end the call. His breathing was ragged, but it calmed after several exhales. When his hand lowered, it seemed his rage had passed, and my own muscles unclenched.

I couldn't help but think how much easier my father's life would have been if he didn't have me and my gymnastics constantly coming between him and his wife, him and his wallet, him and his son, him and his principles—if he didn't have a daughter whose demanding lifestyle turned him into the furious and unfamiliar stranger currently standing in our garage.

But with the passing moments, he was returning to himself, and that was a sweet relief.

Then he jerked his arm back and hurled the phone against the drywall. It bounced and clattered to the cement, splintering into pieces and making enough noise to conceal my gasp.

CHAPTER 15

Between the Classic competition and the Olympic team selection, twenty-five of the best gymnasts in the country, gymnasts who, like me, devoted their lives and their families' lives to the pursuit of this singular artistry, sacrificing time, money, their bodies, and all other interests—friends, hobbies, education—all with the shared dream of one day representing her country at the Olympics, were whittled down to five team members and three alternates, leaving seventeen equally or very nearly qualified athletes devastated, and three severely disappointed.

For most, this was their one shot. By their second Olympic cycle, it was likely their bodies would be too tired, too worn, too mature. Too old. This was it.

I was ready. I trained forty hours a week. I treated my

body like a machine, feeding it fuel rather than food, consuming just enough that my muscles operated at their highest capacity without being weighed down by extra fat. I wrapped whining joints and draped myself in heating pads. I popped Advil. Blisters rose on my hands and tore. My feet bled. My back muscles spasmed. I worked through pain and the regular desire to quit. Between workouts I dressed in layers to keep my muscles warm, and after workouts I blasted Eminem and lowered myself, excruciating inch by excruciating inch, into a tub of ice water, screaming at full volume until I was submerged. Then I started hyperventilating. Rapid breathing was the only means of surviving the cold. I focused on that. Breathing was everything.

I also used that breathing exercise when I reread the text messages I sent to Lucy that went unanswered. Thinking about Lucy became a ritual, a sort of meditative masochism I practiced in spare moments driving to the gym, stretching, treating sore body parts, or lying awake at night. It was a hair-tugging or scab-picking whose sting contained its own dark pleasure. It was an act of living—of feeling—and an act of punishment. And so I'd dwell on the discontent. I remembered the moment I denounced my only friend and saw Lucy recede into herself. That split second before she withdrew was the last time I'd ever see her fully. Then she was lost—at least to me. Our friendship was lost.

I panted breaths to outpace my heart.

I RANKED SO well at competitions leading up to the Trials, my family didn't make summer plans. We were bound for Rio. Joe made Carnival samba dancers his laptop wallpaper. My mother had bathing suits waiting in online shopping carts, ready to press the purchase button, and she rented Portuguese Rosetta Stone CDs from the library. *"Boa noite,"* she said from beneath her headphones as she dusted the living room. *"Boa noite."*

My father had already put in for his vacation at work. "I just want to learn to say one thing," he said. "'That's my daughter.' I'm going to say it to everybody in that arena. By the time we leave, I'll be an expert at it."

I tried to temper my excitement, but it was futile. I couldn't help but imagine what it would be like to hear the entire world chant my name.

It would change all of our lives. Aside from the fame I could taste on my tongue, sponsorships and the Olympic athlete tour that followed the Games would pay enough so my dad could stop working weekends. It could send my mom on a European vacation. It could cover Joe's college tuition. It would settle the credit card and mortgage debt established on my behalf. I knew I might never be able to repay my family for putting me at the center of their lives for over ten years, for throwing every spare cent they had toward my pursuits, but this would be a start.

So I would live our dream without Lucy.

THE 2016 OLYMPIC Trials were held in a sold-out San Jose arena. I was one of fourteen athletes wearing performance leotards in red, white, and blue, as if we wanted to trick the board into thinking we were already representing our country. *See how I look in the shades of our beloved flag? I am your American girl.*

My family wore shirts printed with my name, which the gym had sold to raise funds for the trip, mostly to younger gymnasts who wanted to be in my position one day. I autographed their purchases like I was already someone special. And for a minute, I felt like I was.

When other athletes fell, my reflex was to share my panicked sympathy and shameful relief with Lucy, but of course she wasn't there. She was back in Indiana, watching the competition or not. I thought about texting her, asking her, but I resisted—I couldn't be distracted by her silence, or worse, harpooned by a response. So I treated her absence the same way I treated the four toes that purpled after I fell off the beam the previous week, one losing a nail: I sprayed the injury with anesthetic.

Over the course of the three-day event, I survived on protein shakes, Gatorade, and adrenaline. Even though I wasn't eating much, I felt like my body couldn't contain its excess energy. My leg jostled as I watched the performances; Jennifer laid her hand on my knee as a silent reminder that said: *You are being watched. Even this, on the sidelines, is part of your audition.*

When my name echoed over the sound system, I shut out the sounds of the crowd. Everything slowed, and the overhead lights distorted. I breathed in through my nose and out my mouth and let my body do what so few bodies were trained to do.

I danced and split. I scaled, leapt, circled, and swung. I unfurled an Arabian double, a double somersault dismount, a double twisting Yurchenko, and a double twisting double tuck on bars.

Yes, I took an extra step on a tumbling pass. I faltered on the beam. I bounced on my vault landing. My performance wasn't flawless. No one's ever was. But on this I will never waver—it was damned good.

The crowd agreed. Their cheers were an enthusiastic punctuation to the satisfaction that was already rushing up from my heels when I stuck each landing. I hadn't just averted disaster. I'd performed well. I'd demonstrated what I was capable of doing. The floodgates of my emotions opened, and relief and pride surged through my veins at such a strong force, if I jumped into the air, I thought I might rocket into the California sky.

Jennifer met me at the platform edge, squeezed me tight, and kissed the top of my hair. She'd never kissed me before. When we separated, there were tears in her eyes. This wasn't just about me; she'd worked hard too.

"That was so good," she said. "So good."

My father whacked the shoulders of those around him

and pointed in my direction. I could almost hear his tagline: *Essa é minha filha*. My mother clung to Joe and jumped up and down. I imagined the applause sounded to her ears like bossa nova music.

I scanned the roaring arena to absorb the sights and sounds of that moment. I never wanted to forget what it was like to look up and see my face on a Jumbotron, grinning back at me. I never wanted to forget what it sounded like to hear a mob chant the two syllables that defined me: *Se-ra, Se-ra*. I never wanted to forget what it was like to believe my dreams were coming true.

Ranks were announced without great fanfare, because that day wasn't about rank alone. It was about who made the Olympics, and that was decided by a committee, based on what they determined to be the needs of the team. My name fell in slot number five. According to that day's scores, I was fifth best in the country. If the team was decided solely on points, I'd be on it.

The only sure thing was Simone Biles, the three-time World Champion who'd ranked number one at the Trials. The winner of the Trials got guaranteed a spot. The rest were elected, which was why it had been so important to gain the esteem of Vanda.

Officials corralled the gymnasts and their coaches downstairs to wait while the selection committee deliberated. The room was an appropriate holding cell: The walls were cinder block. Time ticked by under a dropped ceiling. Jennifer sat on a metal folding chair. I paced behind her. I felt like my belly was full of frogs—squat, potbellied, and slick with mucous coating. I felt plagued.

Above us, the crowd chanted: "U-S-A, U-S-A." Down the hall, Vanda Balogh sat with two other members of the selection committee. They compared ranks from the Trials and the championships held earlier that spring. They discussed our strengths and weaknesses. Surely Vanda contemplated her personal favorites, which disciples had been loyal and which hadn't. They had eighteen minutes to decide.

In the arena, a singer performed patriotic hits to help the audience pass the time, and occasionally a belted note of "Proud to Be an American" or "America the Beautiful" drifted into our room. Most us of didn't speak. We couldn't even look at one another. But a few gathered in a corner and giggled like a gaggle of geese whose necks I wished to wring.

Was Lucy thinking of me? Was she rooting for my success or for my failure?

Jennifer turned in her chair and smiled. But there was a rigidity to her mouth, like sympathy.

The door opened and the selection committee members filed in along with Steve Penny, president and CEO of USA Gymnastics.

My heart trilled like dragonfly wings.

I didn't make it, I didn't make it, I told myself, trying to construct a quick wall of words to ward off disappointment. But those words felt false. The wall was a prop. It was no match for the confidence I had in the price I'd paid.

Vanda wore her warm-ups, as if she were prepping her muscles, her mind, for a performance. And, in a way, she was. She'd announced that this would be the last year she'd be the national team coordinator for USA Gymnastics. She'd still run the camps at the ranch where the national team trained, but as far as having so much influence on the organization, she saw this as her last hurrah. She carried a clipboard and looked around the room like she owned it and liked what she saw. The other committee members wore pencil-skirt suits, and after they offered me courteous acknowledgment, they rested their stares elsewhere.

My left hand pinched the skin between my thumb and index finger, trying to draw it out like taffy.

"If we could send you all to Rio, we would," Vanda began. "But since that is impossible, here is the 2016 Olympic team. Simone Biles . . ."

Every time she opened her mouth, I anticipated hearing: Sera Wheeler. And each time, the sounds passing her lips— Aly Raisman, Laurie Hernandez, Gabby Douglas—were so different. It was like hearing gibberish when you expected your native tongue. I was jarred until I realized she wasn't speaking anymore.

She'd announced all the names and none of them were mine.

Eight girls were hugging, congratulating one another, and

crying. Someone was distributing official Team USA warm-ups so the gymnasts would be in uniform when they were introduced upstairs. There'd be smoke, pump-up music, and flashing lights. Rally cries from the crowd. All while I was downstairs.

Jennifer's fingers grazed my shoulder. "You're still a member of the national team. There's always Worlds next year."

I backed up until I felt the chill of concrete against my skin. I needed to feel something real and immediate to anchor me, and I didn't want it to be human.

"I know this is disappointing, but you should be proud. You did so well."

Wind roared in my ears. My body wanted to shut down. I might have passed out if I'd let myself. I heaved in gulps of air to stay awake.

This was my only chance. My family's only chance. I'd abandoned Lucy, in part, for this. I was Judas Iscariot—only, he'd been paid his silver.

Then I was slapping myself. Beating my face, shoulders, and torso with open hands. I was used to pain and I wanted to hurt. When slapping wasn't enough, I shrieked and slammed my shoulder against the wall.

"Sera!" Jennifer yelled. She grabbed my biceps, but I tossed her off. "Stop it. Just stop it." A male coach's thick arms straitjacketed me until I surrendered. Jennifer's eyes were wide. I was a wild animal; I scared her.

Later that night, some commentators would call overlooking me an upset. That was the understatement of a lifetime. Others would rationalize my strength was bars, and the team already had Gabby. (*Who placed seventh!* I wanted to scream at the replays of the event footage, and sometimes did.) Still others would say I stumbled on the beam, proving I wasn't consistent—I was too young, not seasoned enough to be reliable.

Nobody but Vanda and I knew exactly how reliable I had been.

But there was that hateful look Vanda had fixed on me after my public defense of Lucy. Maybe my subsequent loyalty had not been enough, and Vanda was taking advantage of her final moment of power as team coordinator to drive the stake through my career, ensuring I didn't go to Rio— that I wouldn't hear samba drums, see the hills of Pão de Açúcar, feel the sand of Copacabana between my toes. But most importantly, that I'd never carry an Olympic medal around my neck.

All my work, my years of dreaming—it had been for fool's gold.

CHAPTER 16

Charlene Wheeler

My parents were nice people from good northern Wisconsin stock—still are—but they never expected much from me, and I guess I'm the sort of person that lives up to expectations.

The agricultural machinery factory where my father worked went under in the early nineties, the summer before my senior year in high school, and when he announced we'd be moving for a few years to Indiana, where my uncle had secured him a job, I nearly choked on my bratwurst.

"But I was going to the Minneapolis College of Art and Design," I said. I hadn't really known that's what I wanted until the option was pulled out from under me, but now it seemed so clear, and so very tragic.

My father snorted, and when my mother looked to him,

her mouth was disapproving, but the rest of her expression shared the joke.

"To do what exactly, dear?" she asked. Her eyes were magnified behind glasses whose pearlescent frames claimed the majority of her face.

"I don't know yet."

My mother nodded, as if that settled it. "What do you think of the potato salad today, Norm?" my mother asked my father. "I added a little paprika. Thought I'd try something new."

"I've never even seen you pick up a crayon," my father said as he reached for the bottle of ranch dressing and squeezed a glob onto his potato salad.

I said, "They have things besides drawing. Furniture design. Filmmaking."

"Filmmaking," he repeated, as though somebody had tickled his ribs in the midst of the word.

"That's an interesting idea," my mother said. "But you know we can't be doling out money for your education when we have two older boys who didn't even go to college. They're doing just fine and so will you."

My father shoveled in a mouthful. "You're pretty and you're sweet, Charlene. You'll make someone a better wife than they could have dreamed of. And that's enough. No need to get fancy."

They didn't see me, only what they wanted me to be. A small-town girl, happy to one day be a small-town wife.

When my daughter landed her first tumbling pass at a Junior Olympics competition, I sobbed right into my soda, because in that moment I was sure she'd be different. I understood when none of the names announced at the Trials belonged to my daughter that this was just wishful thinking.

In twenty years, when Sera is at someone's backyard cookout, and her belly is paunchy from carrying babies, and her boobs—excuse my French—are hanging down to her collapsed belly button, nobody will give a hoot that she almost made the Olympics once, because almost doesn't count for anything. Her poster won't be taped to anybody's walls. Strangers won't recognize her name. She'll eat a hot dog and a slice of sugar cream pie in the company of housewives and math teachers and traffic cops. Normal people—just like her.

And me.

It would have been so sweet to call my parents up in Wisconsin—they moved back "to be with family" just after I got married, leaving me alone with Bob in Indiana—to announce that my daughter was an Olympian (and since my genes were swimming around in there, that made me half an Olympian, at least). I would have done a little happy dance in their stunned silence. I wouldn't even have had to say that they'd been wrong. They'd know it. We'd all know it.

That was my little daydream, but not anymore. Tough tomatoes for me, I guess.

I'd always been average, but at least I was beautiful. Once. I should have appreciated the last of my looks before they disappeared, because when I saw my reflection after the Trials, I didn't recognize the middle-aged woman looking back. How hadn't I noticed how quickly I was going to seed? Now that I wasn't the mother of an Olympian, I had all the time in the world for more drastic measures.

Eighty-one percent of moms feel more confident if they're happy with their hair—that's what I read in *Bloom Magazine,* Indiana's *Vogue*—so I started there. Kroger's had a deal on dye. And a good deal. A buy one, get one. Not one of those buy one, get one 50 percent off nonsense specials where they aren't giving me anything but the privilege of getting to purchase something twice. So I picked up two boxes of Radiant Red, described as a mix of cinnamon, fine wine, and auburn. I'd always had hair the color of wet potato skins, but I was looking for a change, and the model on the front looked like *Grey's Anatomy's* Kate Walsh. I could do worse than Kate Walsh.

I didn't leave it in a minute too long. I followed the instructions to the letter.

But I knew something was wrong when I rinsed my hair and the shower drain looked like I'd squeezed a hamburger too hard and shot ketchup out the back end. It should have been called Ronald McDonald Red, because that's who I looked like when I blew my hair dry. A fast-food clown.

I was too humiliated to let anyone see. Not even my family. So I got ahold of myself in the bathroom, honked my nose (now I looked and sounded like a clown), and wrapped the abomination on my head in a towel. Then I borrowed one of Joe's baseball caps and slinked out of the house. I drove to a Rite Aid two towns over, where I wouldn't run into anybody I knew, and purchased another box of hair dye at full price, this time a more sensible Neutral Brown. That's what it was called and that's what I was. Neutral: having no strongly marked or positive characteristics or features.

When I got home, I threw the free box from the BOGO in the trash. Buy one, garbage one.

With my hair salvaged, I turned my attention to the rest of me, sagging and fat everywhere but my thin lips. I used Scotch Tape to pull back my loose neck skin. I made my own lip plumper from a recipe shared on Facebook, mixing Vaseline with ground cayenne pepper—which I would have bet my last dollar I didn't have but was surprised to find collecting dust at the back of my kitchen cabinet.

Sometimes I found Communion wafers too spicy, so my mayonnaise palate sure as heck wasn't prepared for cayenne.

It started as a tingle, but before long it was all-out hellfire. Tears streamed down my cheeks while I waited for my phone timer to tick down from sixty seconds. I got to twenty before I stuck my mouth under the bathroom faucet.

Proverbs says, "Charm is deceitful, and beauty is vain, but a woman who fears the Lord is to be praised." Well, I'll tell you what—I may have been vain, but that experience put the fear of the Lord in me.

My lips smoldered even after the washing. And yeah, they

were fuller, because they were *swollen*. I may as well have asked a welterweight champ to punch me in the kisser. Jeez.

I was old and haggard and I guessed that was just the way I was going to stay. More than anything, though, I was tired. There was nowhere to go, nothing to do. Bob and the kids were doing fine without me. Sera was disappointed, of course, but trying to cheer her up would have been the depressed leading the depressed. At least she still had smooth skin, a flat tummy, and boobs that stood on their own. Not me. I was deteriorating by the minute. I might as well just get some sleep.

CHAPTER 17

August 2016

That summer, long-distance runner Abbey D'Agostino tripped over Nikki Hamblin, and then bent down, helped her back up, and encouraged her to finish the race; Michael Phelps swam his last Olympic lap; Usain Bolt sprinted his final race; Kate Ledecky set world records in two freestyle events; and Fu Yuanhui discussed menstrual pain on the international stage of pool tile. There were spectacles of sportsmanship and humanity. There was determination, and there was triumph. There was great disappointment.

But I didn't see any of it. We didn't even mention the Summer Olympics in my house.

Once I caught my father reading the sports section of the *Indianapolis Star* on a lawn chair in our backyard, but when I stepped onto the patio, he fumbled onto his knees and laid the pages onto a flowerbed.

"The only thing the news is good for these days," he said. "Smothering weeds."

My mother framed my old performance leos, stored them out of sight in the basement, and watched footage of my competitions, beginning from the days I was cartwheeling in the front yard to a month before the Trials. She relived our shared journey that led to nowhere with a tissue box in her lap.

I passed her, went upstairs, stared at myself in the bathroom mirror, smiled a stilted smile, and slapped it off my face.

One night during the Games, Joe invited me out with some of his buddies. His friend Tim drove a twenty-year-old Chevy pickup around town with two other teenagers up front and six of us bumping around the bed. We unloaded in a dirt pull-off, brandished our cell phones for light, and trudged down a path through the woods until we reached a circle of stumps and boulders littered with broken glass and cigarette butts. Someone had dragged a cooler along and now distributed cans of Pabst Blue Ribbon, which hissed and clicked as they opened. I'd never exposed my temple of a body to a substance lacking nutritional purpose. But my body wasn't a working temple any longer. It could be desecrated.

The beer tasted like river water. But after a few, my muscles loosened. I no longer sat rigidly. I was able to forget that I'd never had a casual conversation with unrelated nongymnasts.

Matt Simmons, a linebacker for the high school football team, ambled over to where I was balanced on a rotted log, lowered next to me with as much grace as a barking elephant seal, and slung his arm around my shoulder.

"Sera, tell me, and be honest. Which of the Final Five is the most bangable?"

The temperature was relatively warm and I wore a fleece zip-up, but the moisture from the log was seeping through my jeans and chilling my skin. I rubbed my hands against the denim on my thighs and looked to the others for help exiting the conversation.

"Hey, Matt." Joe's chin lifted as he called from across the circle. "Tell everybody what Schiffer said in precalc today."

Matt's eyelids drooped like two slouching sweatshirt hoods. "In a minute, J. I'm gathering important intel."

"Dude." Joe smiled, but it was waxy. "Let it go."

"No way. I'm thirsty for a gymnast. Like, parched. And we have an inside source here. When else will I be with some-one who has met the Final Five?" His words slurred and then his head swung back to me. "I know it isn't Simone. She's got too much spotlight to give me the time of day. Is it Madison? She's quiet. Cute. But not too showy. I bet it's Madison."

Joe's jaw shifted and his voice fortified. "Matt, seriously."

Matt pulled his arm from me so he could direct his body toward Joe. "You know what I'm talking about. You've al-ways had a hard-on for Sera's friend, going on and on about her as soon as you get three beers deep. What was her name?

Lindsay? It's not my fault you bet on her and she burned out. I still want to fuck an Olympian."

Joe flung his full beer at his friend. It landed at our feet and golden liquid gushed onto the soil. "We aren't fucking talking about Lucy, and we sure as hell aren't talking about the Olympics."

Conversation halted. Nobody moved, unsure if this would boil over into a full-out fight. While they waited, an owl hooted in the branches above our heads. Leaves whispered in the wind. Someone's phone vibrated.

"Matt's right," I said, because the only way I wouldn't start to cry was if I took ownership of the moment. If I was crass and mean. If I continued to be a liar. "If you want to fuck an Olympian, it's Madison Kocian for sure." And when I said the word "fuck," I drove it into the dirt like a trowel.

The Olympics came and went. I stopped training. What was the point? Worlds was a year away, and it just didn't seem alluring without the possibility of the Olympics behind it.

Without gymnastics, I had so much extra time and no idea how to spend it. I caught up on all the television shows I'd missed over the years: *Breaking Bad, Parks and Recreation, Scandal, Orange Is the New Black*. I rode my bike to the Dairy Queen for ice cream—a sickening delicacy of cream and sugar I'd never dared eat before. I went to church. I watched Joe's football practices. I read. I picked up a shift at McDonald's, a forty-year sponsor of the Olympic Games. Crowds once sang my name and now I was in a kitchen spooning fries into cardboard pockets. When once I wore sequined leotards designed specifically for me, now I wore an oversize, corporate-issued, collared red shirt. There hadn't been such a fall from grace since the devil himself. When I got home, I couldn't wash the grease off my skin no matter how hard I scrubbed. But my nearly realized dreams had driven my family into almost irreconcilable debt, and I was determined to pay them back one $7.25-per-hour at a time.

Occasionally, a customer at the drive-thru window would pause in their cars. "Hey, aren't you Sera Wheeler? The gymnast who lives around here?" they'd ask. And I would pass them their bags of fast garbage, already darkening with oil.

"Nope."

My mother laid on the couch in her terry bathrobe and watched soaps on mute. My father returned from work and whistled Johnny Cash songs in the kitchen, a hand towel draped over his shoulder like a sauce-stained priest's stole.

"What am I doing singing Johnny Cash like I'm on my way to the bank?" he mused to himself. "I'm making meatloaf, might as well sing 'Paradise by the Dashboard Light.'"

I smoked weed with Matt Simmons. At first it stung my athlete's lungs and sent me into a hacking cough, which made him laugh. But I wasn't a quitter, and it didn't take long before I was inhaling like a pro. I finally understood why they called it a high. It was like I'd released from the uneven bars and never came back down. I just floated in the air, contentedly.

Up there, it didn't matter that I wasn't standing on a podium as part of an elite group. It didn't matter that I'd deserted my friend when she needed me most. Nothing mattered.

THERE WAS A stain on my underwear, like a penny had melted and dried. It took a moment for me to realize what had happened. I thought the blood would be vibrant, like that from a fresh cut. But it seemed my uterus had aged and flaked out paint chips. I was at work and had to stuff toilet paper in my underwear until my shift ended. I stopped at CVS for supplies on the way home. Pads, liners, tampons. Playtex, Kotex, O.B. The options were overwhelming, and I didn't want any of them. I walked right out of the store.

BY THE TIME I returned to school in September, Matt and I were dating. Not because I thought he was clever or kind or altogether very handsome. In fact, his sense of humor was unimaginative, and often bullying. His head was boxy and his body mass was the bulky kind you knew would melt into fat as soon as football practices ended. But he wanted me. I might not have been selected for the Olympic team, but at least I had someone texting me before bed again.

When we were alone, he asked me to show off, and the simplest movements—a front walkover, a back tuck, even a handstand held for an impossibly long time—made his jaw drop. It was refreshing to impress so easily. No deductions. No competition. No rejection. I was the star.

For the first time, I held all the power. I wasn't answering to judges or a selection committee. I wasn't bowing down to those who would decide my future. I commanded the moment with a graze of my index finger along his waist. And when he reached for me, I controlled his success or his disappointment.

But the novelty of that wore down like an old pair of dowel grips. I stopped feeling a thrill. His hot breath on my neck, his fingers groping the clasp of my bra. It grew dull. Just as jokes weren't funny anymore. Just as school lessons couldn't interest me. Even driving a car for the first time elicited little. I felt like the walking dead, roaming among the living, together but separate. And I didn't want to be lifeless, understimulated. I didn't want to be a sixteen-year-old zombie. And so, in Matt's bedroom, his parents milling around downstairs, I lifted the roadblocks. I let his hands travel up my shirt. Down my pants. I allowed my hands to be guided by his. I watched his features set into an expression of wonder and pleasure so strong it looked painful as he rode his wave of ecstasy to shore, and then lay there, exhausted but gratified. He seemed to feel so much. All while I felt nothing.

Whatever I had with Matt, it just wasn't the sound of my name booming from a loudspeaker. It wasn't sprinting toward a high-stakes tumbling pass. It wasn't releasing my hold on a high bar and spinning free.

CHAPTER 18

September 2016

I was in Matt's bedroom. It was a school night, and the sun had been down for hours, yet my parents hadn't urged me home. They didn't even know where I was. Only a month out from the Olympics, they still tread carefully, like I was standing in the center of a pond that hadn't completely frozen over and they were afraid with one wrong movement I'd fall through.

Matt's room smelled of unwashed socks and bong water. He was kissing my neck when the text lit up my phone, an article from the *Indianapolis Star,* sent by a cousin.

Former USA Gymnastics Doctor Accused of Abuse

The sounds of Matt's mouth filled my ear, wet and too loud. I read the headline and shirked away.

"Come on. My mom's going to get home soon. Read that later," he said, groping my breast.

I didn't care to explain to him, this person who didn't much matter to me, why exactly this news was more important than his hard-on, a version of which seemed to ripen every fifteen minutes. I walked to the other side of the room, out of his reach, and skimmed the piece. Two gymnasts, one an Olympic medalist, had accused Eddie of molesting them during treatments. My heart flipped as if I'd gone over a vault.

But those were palpitations, medical manipulations, and sports massage designed to release muscles and pressure. Eddie had explained, using anatomical terminology, until it made sense.

"Sera. You can't leave me like this," Matt said, leaning back to showcase the bulge beneath his basketball shorts.

I navigated to GymHub, a popular gymnastics forum. The article was its main thread, along with thousands of comments ranging from "Don't believe these liars. Eddie is a healer, and he needs our support now more than ever" to "I called this years ago." Responses stacked even as I watched. "I feel like puking," "So upsetting," and "This is why girls shouldn't be wearing leotards. What do they expect?"

Four more *Indianapolis Star* links lit up my phone, this time texted by classmates and another gymnast.

Ada had said Eddie got erections during treatments. Did I ever notice? Did Lucy? Is that how she knew what he was doing was wrong? I wanted to tell Matt to shut the fuck up, but I was afraid if I spoke, the contents of my stomach would spew all over his worn carpeting.

LIGHT FLICKERED INSIDE the living room of my house, which was strange; after I stopped training, my mother began going to bed early along with my father. She slept in late too.

Matt shifted his car into park and laid his hand on my upper thigh. The streetlight illuminated half of his face and cast the other half in shadow. He smiled at me like he wanted to communicate something: attraction, maybe. Or something more significant. But his expression came across as dopey at best and, at worst, made my skin crawl—his smirk surfaced an image of Eddie standing in our dorm doorway with a bag of Hershey's Kisses.

"Thanks for the ride," I said, and pushed the car door open without looking back.

My parents sat side by side on the couch while the television played a sitcom rerun on mute. My mother picked invisible specks off her pants. My father tugged one edge of his mustache.

"Sit down," he said. "We want to talk to you."

Either I was in trouble or somebody had died, and since neither of them were crying, I figured it was the former.

"We were watching a movie and I lost track of time," I said. Another lie. They came easily now.

"It's not that, although we should discuss the parameters for your social life, now that you have one," my father said, and then shifted in his seat, perhaps sorry to have implied that I previously didn't have a social life. "What we wanted to talk to you about, what we need to ask you is . . ." He trailed off and looked to my mother. She raised her eyebrows, as if to say, *You're almost there. You might as well say it.* Judging by her silence, I had to assume this confrontation was his idea. His gaze drifted up to me and he pressed his lips into a frown. Finally, he said, "Sera, did Dr. Levett ever examine you at the ranch?"

They'd seen the articles. Of course they had. My mother had Facebook friended every gym mom she'd ever met and followed many of the gymnasts themselves. She claimed this was for research, but I knew she was just a forty-year-old fangirl.

But the articles didn't matter. It wasn't anything we hadn't heard before. These were just two more confused girls. Their stories didn't change anything. We'd already decided what was true.

"He was the team doctor. He examined everybody. And if I'd hurt my hips or if my back was out of alignment, I would have been lucky to have Eddie treat me. He's an expert in myofascial release therapy. He even teaches it."

My father ran his fingers through the hair at his temples. When his hands dropped to his lap, his hair remained fluffed out, making him look crazy.

"I'm afraid to know how wrong you are," he said.

I dug my fingernails into my palms. "You don't know anything about gymnastics. You always hated it. You're just glad to have a reason now. But Eddie is innocent."

I stormed up the stairs before my anger could dissolve. At the top, I paused before a portrait of a nine-year-old holding an arabesque on the balance beam. One leg was raised behind so that her pointed toe was in line with her head and her arms were flung back. Her hair was pulled into a bun at her crown and sprayed liberally. Her makeup was dramatic, complete with thick black eyeliner and blue eye shadow. But most striking was her expression, fully charged with an open, toothy grin; all watts burning bright. Lucy had been standing beyond the camera, impersonating a fashion model on a runway to make her laugh.

The girl in the portrait was strong. The muscles in her limbs were defined. She was confident and passionate. She was a gymnast. And she knew all those things, even at nine years old. She knew who she was.

Who was I now, years later, without gymnastics, without a friend? I had to be more than a girl who didn't recognize abuse when it was happening in the room beside her. I had to be more than that.

I MADE THE announcement on Halloween.

My mom's mouth gaped as she dozed on the couch corner opposite me. She'd begun taking antidepressants, which she called Mommy's little helpers, when she had something important to do—Joe's football game, the church's pancake breakfast, or on mornings of her therapy sessions, so she could confirm truthfully that she was on her medication. She didn't take them consistently because they caused electric sensations in her brain. My father argued this happened *because* she didn't take the pills consistently, but she just waved him away, saying, "Did you get a medical degree when I wasn't looking, Bob? 'Cause that sure would help pay the bills if you did."

My dad sat in an armchair with a lowball glass of whiskey on the end table, reading a John Grisham paperback, ready to serve candy when the doorbell rang. Joe boiled a hot dog in the kitchen, not because he craved a hot dog, but because he was dressed in a hot dog costume and wanted to make a joke about cannibalism. It was the third year in a row that he'd worn the costume, and he made the same joke every year. That was the line he used at home, anyway. The line he used with his friends was that he had the biggest wiener in the room.

"Are you sure you don't want to come to Tina's?" he asked from the stove. "Matt is gonna be there, but so what? He's a big boy. He can handle it."

I'd dumped Matt the day after the *Indy Star* article was published. He wept. I felt like I was in the audience of a bad play.

On the television, Bette Midler stroked her spell book and the eyeball opened. It seemed oddly sexual to me now. "I don't have a costume."

"You could wear your red leotard and go as ketchup. It's been a while since we wore matching outfits."

"That'd be so cute," my mother said, without enthusiasm.

My father dropped his book in his lap. "So cute I might have to get out the camera."

"Don't bother," I said. I didn't want to dress up; I was sick of pretending to be something I wasn't. For months I'd been acting like a normal teenager, a kid who was interested in drinking in the woods, smoking weed, and having sex. But I wasn't that. When the costume came off at night, I stared up at the ceiling and knew one thing for certain: I was an Olympic gymnast, just without her Olympics.

"I'm going to train for 2020," I said.

My mother pushed herself up, wrapped her fingers around my foot, and held it tight. She looked as if she'd been waiting for me to say those words since July, and now that I had, she almost couldn't believe it.

"Are you sure?"

I nodded. "I have to."

The pot of water behind Joe started to boil and steam rose toward the ceiling in a dense column.

"Why?" he asked.

"I'm just not happy."

My father gripped his book. "You're still adjusting. We all are. It feels strange, but give it time. You'll find a new groove, a different way to be happy."

"I've tried."

His voice was stressed, like he was trying to be reasonable, but beneath that was a force he fought to keep restrained. "Not very hard."

"I don't want to do school clubs or youth group or any of the other activities you've suggested."

My father smiled as if there were a gunman at his back telling him to do so. "How do you know if you haven't tried?" He placed his book on the end table and cradled his whiskey without drinking it. "Maybe you should reach out to Lucy. What's she doing postgymnastics?"

Lucy had blocked me on social media, but I didn't want to admit that. I tucked my feet under my body to sit taller. "I'm not postgymnastics. That's what I'm saying."

"But the Olympics?"

"I can do it."

His eyebrows rose. "Can you?"

My mother flattened her hair with her hands and tucked it behind her ears. "She's still young. She'll be just twenty."

"And a half," Joe added.

I said, "There have been older gymnasts than that."

"Maybe in the seventies. Now the movements they expect you to do are designed for preteens," my father said.

"Since when do you know so much?" I asked.

"You're my daughter. I educated myself."

"Then you know the average age of the Final Five was nineteen."

"That was an exception."

"Maybe not. Maybe it's the beginning of something new."

"That's right. Be part of the change." My mom shifted over so she could pat my knee. "This is very brave."

The doorbell rang but none of us moved for it. I waited for my father to greet the trick-or-treaters the way he had all night. *Look at you. Are you a ladybug? That's my favorite bug!* His wrist moved in a circle so that the whiskey dipped around his glass like a Hula-Hoop in slow motion.

I spoke quietly. "If I give up now, I'll always wonder."

My mother took my hand into her lap. "We're not ready to quit."

"What if *we* are?" Joe asked from the kitchen. In his costume, he looked like a food vendor who'd had a disappointing day at the ball field. The hot water popped and spit on the stove behind him, the hot dog likely bursting from its casing.

It was as if my mother hadn't heard him. She clapped my hand with hers and said, "Let's get those kids some candy and call Jennifer with the good news!"

My gymnastics career was her mood elevator, her most effective drug.

She insisted I make the call on speaker so she could hear Jennifer's excitement firsthand, so we placed my iPhone at the center of the kitchen table. My father sat apart from us, on the stairs to the second floor, and Joe must have been halfway to Tina's house by then, his hot dog still floating in the pot on the stove like a sad vacationer alone in a deactivated Jacuzzi.

I dialed, and the word "Coach" appeared across my phone.

"Hello?" Jennifer answered.

My mother jumped in before I could speak. "I convinced her, Jen. We're back."

"I'm sorry?"

"Hi, Jennifer," I said. After the Trials, my coach had begged me to continue training, but I just didn't have the motivation. She'd texted me occasionally to check in and encourage me to return when I was ready, but otherwise we hadn't spoken. "I want to train for 2020."

I thought our call had been disconnected, but the phone timer still ticked. Maybe she was waiting for a question. I opened my mouth to ask one just as she responded.

"It's great that you want to train. There's so much for you to pursue. Worlds, college track—you know how I feel about NCAA gymnastics. But I have to be honest. I don't think 2020 is an option."

I sat back. "Why not?"

"You've trained hard for three years. That's a lot. Your body can't take another four."

"Why don't we try and see?" I expelled a single burst of air I hoped would pass as a laugh.

"It'd be irresponsible of me, as your coach, to let you try. There's too great a risk for injury. You saw how tough it was to make the team this time around. It's only going to be harder when you're older, not to mention they are cutting the team from five members to four. The chance isn't worth the toll on your body. There are lifelong consequences to consider."

My mother sat taller, stiffer. "Are you saying you don't want to be her coach?"

Jennifer's voice rushed forward. "Not at all. I love working with Sera. And I think she can do great things. Like I said, at Worlds and in the NCAA."

"But you won't train me for the Olympics?"

Again there was a pause, but this time it was shorter. She didn't need the time. "I'm sorry, but no."

I tucked my feet under myself and wrapped my arms around the front of my sweatshirt. "Even if I sign a waiver or something saying you aren't responsible for injuries or whatever?"

"I'm not worried about you suing me. I just don't think it's wise, and I wouldn't feel right putting you through it." Jennifer sounded soft, like she cared about me. I wished I could believe that she didn't.

"Well, that's an interesting perspective," my mother said, her words steely.

Emotion flurried up my throat and stuck to the sides like bits of cotton. I clenched handfuls of my sweatshirt in my fists. Jennifer was thirty-four. By 2020, she'd be thirty-eight. In that time, maybe she'd want to have a baby. Maybe *she* wasn't prepared to train for the Olympics.

"I think I'm going to do it anyway." I glanced up at my mom. Her eyes were wide and she nodded vigorously.

"I can't stop you."

"No, you can't," my mother said.

"Right. And hey"—Jennifer paused, as if she were reconsidering what she was about to say, but then decided to go ahead with it—"did you hear about Eddie?"

I concentrated on the wood grain of the table. I didn't want to see either of my parents, especially not my father. "Yeah."

"And have you spoken to Lucy?"

I hunched over a bit more. "No."

"Have you spoken to the police?"

"No," I said, hardening. "Why would I?"

"Well, to give your statement."

"What is there to say? He's a doctor who did a medical procedure."

The line was so quiet, for a moment it seemed like even my phone didn't want anything to do with me. Finally Jennifer's voice rose from it like steam from hot pavement.

"Right, well," she said, tapering off, and then she cut the end clean. "Good luck to you, Sera."

I ended the call just in time for hot tears to rush down my cheeks. Jennifer had been one of the few people in my gymnastics-immersed life. Another person in past tense. I wiped my face with my sleeve.

"Jennifer just offered a professional opinion," my father said. "Shouldn't we listen to it?" Sitting on the stairs, angled forward with his elbow on his knee and his palm cupping his jaw, my father formed a triangular truss with his body, a structure designed to bear weight, and yet he looked as if he couldn't support much at all.

My mother pushed herself up from her chair and brushed her palms together, as if dusting off dirt. "I want a second opinion."

THE OVERCAST SKY was brightening into a lavender morning, and I-74 cut through flat, cheerless fields scattered with snow patches, but my mother and I each had a stevia-sweetened iced coffee in the cup holder and Justin Timberlake's "Can't Stop the Feeling" was playing on Q102. My mother's fingertips drummed the wheel and her shoulders pumped forward one at a time. My feet were up on the dashboard. We looked straight ahead at the expressway, happy to have a destination again, to be back in tune with the universe and each other. Things seemed possible.

People said Lou Gently degraded his athletes. Like the Baloghs, he drilled gymnasts as if he were a boot camp sergeant and wouldn't let them break until they got their routines right, depriving them of food and rest. He brought them to tears, to their knees. But he also brought them to the Pan American Championships and to Worlds. He got results.

I had had a supportive coach, but that alone wasn't enough to get me to the next level. If abuse cultivated greatness, I was at least willing to hear him out.

Lou wanted us to be at Champion Gym in Cincinnati at eight o'clock that morning, before his other athletes started for the day. The gym was still dark when we arrived. I wondered if we had the date wrong and expected the door to be locked when we pulled the handle. But it opened, and light radiated from a small room at the back of the facility. We made our way through the equipment.

He didn't acknowledge us as we stepped into the doorway

of his office. His fingertips continued thrashing his keyboard. Even when my mother knocked the frame with her knuckles, he acted as if he was oblivious to our presence.

"Should we come back, or . . ." I asked.

Lou's eyes remained fixed on his desktop screen. "If you give up that easy, we're going to have a problem."

Before I could counter, he hit the enter key with a flourish and swiveled his desk chair to face us. Four years had passed since we'd met at the Classic. Lou had weathered that period like a ship, still robust but his facade had been worn by the elements. Even though it was November, he wore a short-sleeved collared shirt and gym shorts that barely contained the mass of his thighs. His knees splayed open.

"So you're ready to go for the Olympics."

We slid into the chairs opposite his desk and he rotated like a clock's second hand to follow us.

I suddenly worried that he'd mistaken me for someone else. "I went for the Olympics before."

His fingers had been knit at his crotch, but then his hands fell open to match his legs. "I can't help you if you really believe that."

"I got pretty close."

He smiled cruelly. "And how did that feel?"

My stare dropped to the edge of his desk. The wood veneer was peeling in some places. "Not great."

"So we agree. It can't be like it was before." I nodded curtly, and he clapped his thick hands back together. The sound was full. "Good. I don't want to waste my time, so let's get a few things straight up front. Gymnastics will be your top priority, over school, friends, family, and your own physical and emotional comfort. Are you prepared for that?"

That was easy; I didn't know anything different. "Yes."

"Don't just say yes. You don't know what I mean yet. I mean you'll be in pain. Every single day for years. I mean you'll push yourself to the limit. You'll hear and say and do things the you sitting across from me today wouldn't dream you'd hear and say and do. Nothing will be out of bounds. Do you understand what I'm saying to you?"

"Yes."

"If you do what I say, no questions asked, I'll get you to the Olympics."

Hope was a sweet thing, a fresh thing, like dewdrops. I tasted it once again and felt renewed. Strong and capable. I sat like a trophy, like a flag stripe made vertical. I struck the straight lines of a gymnast.

"I'll do whatever it takes."

"Okay." He leaned back in his chair and crossed his arms over his chest so high his elbows cocked. "I don't want to see you for eight months."

"What?"

"It's forty-five months until the Olympics. That's too long to sustain an Olympic workout regimen. Until the summer, I want you running, swimming, and doing light routines. I'm talking Junior Olympic routines, just to keep your hand in it.

We'll start training at thirty-seven months, take a month to ease into it, and then work hard and strong for exactly three years. Do you understand?"

"Yes."

His gaze traveled up and down my body. "How much do you weigh now?"

I crossed one leg over the other and thought of the filth I'd ingested as I tried to be someone I wasn't: ice cream, beer, and pot munchies. "Ninety-five pounds."

His eyebrow cocked. "How much?"

"One hundred and one point seven."

"When we begin in July, you'll weigh ninety-five pounds flat or I won't work with you. It'll be over before we've begun. It doesn't matter how you get there. Just get there. Got it?"

My gut seemed to expand in front of me, pregnant with all my indulgences—the stuff of human weakness. I couldn't be weak anymore. I couldn't be human. I was an Olympian. I yanked down the hem of my shirt.

"Got it."

My father was in his armchair when we came through the front door. The shades were drawn, casting the room in shadow despite it being late morning. My mother startled at seeing him. Her hand flew to her chest.

"Bob. What are you doing home from work? Are you sick?"

When he spoke, we saw only his profile. "Sera's school called. You forgot to let them know about her absence. So I checked Find My iPhone." His head rolled to look at us, and his eyes were drooped, like our hound Petunia's in her old age. "What were you doing in Cincinnati?"

My mother opened her mouth, but then she rerouted, and her lips spread in a smile. "Good news."

My father unwound to face straight. "I know what you were doing in Cincinnati."

"It's my best chance," I said.

He carried a glass to his lips. My stomach clenched, thinking we'd driven him to drink at eleven in the morning. But then I saw that the liquid was orange. "He's abusive, Charlene. We've heard that from multiple people."

"Sera is fierce. She can take tough love. It's not like he's sexually abusive."

He rose to his feet as if in the last agonizing pushes of a long climb. The glass dangled at his thigh and the knot of his tie hung loose. His voice seemed to come from under a pile of soil, like we'd buried him.

"This is our kid and you're throwing her to a wolf. But yes, at least he's not sexually abusive. Let us thank God for that."

CHAPTER 19

January 2017

an we meet? Coffee or something?

My phone buzzed with Lucy's text an entire year after we'd last spoken. I was sure it was a mistake. She must have sent it to the wrong person, or the message had gotten clogged in cyberspace back when we were friends and was just now spat out. I stared at it, debating whether to respond and open myself up to more rejection or to accept that it was a technological error, that she didn't really want to see me.

Hope, once again, won out.

That'd be great, I typed. And then added, Unless this went to the wrong person? That'd make for an awkward Starbucks moment, and stuck a winky face as a sloppy mask over my discomfort.

There's only one you, she wrote back. Her comment might

have been hostile, but my mind responded with the same words, and they were instilled with longing.

IF LUCY'S GAZE hadn't connected with mine, I might not have recognized her. It was as if a Snapchat filter—one of the realistic, foreboding kinds—projected a universe in which Lucy had never joined Elite Gymnastics. I too had gained weight in my time off, but hers was a more striking transformation. Her cheeks swallowed her eyes in the way they used to only when she grinned and her arms were idle battle ropes. She'd probably gained only twenty or thirty pounds, so maybe it was just the immediate juxtaposition, because I hadn't seen an image of her since last year. Or maybe my perspective was the skewed filter, imposing gymnast bodies onto the perfectly healthy.

Her blended coffee drink was crowned with whipped cream and drizzled with chocolate. That amount of calories would have sustained the old Lucy for an entire day.

By the time I returned with a green tea, she was already more recognizable. Her blaze of hair, the smattering of her freckles. Her face didn't seem quite as puffy as when I'd first arrived. This was Lucy, whose even breathing I'd listened to on nights I couldn't sleep, who didn't require names in a story to understand exactly who I was talking about, who'd drained my blisters when I was too tired and sore to hunch over my own feet. But as I settled into the seat opposite her, my familiarity was once again knocked off-balance by black script tattooed across her forearm. It said, "Still I rise."

I didn't know if it was that sentiment or the buzz of being in proximity to my friend again, but all at once I felt unsettled, like I was picking myself up from the dirt.

"So good to see you," I said.

"I saw on Instagram that you have a boyfriend," Lucy said. She smiled through what looked to be a great deal of pain.

I wished the tea had been cool enough to drink so I could occupy myself with sipping. Instead I blew through the slit in the plastic top, causing it to whistle.

"We broke up."

"Did you have sex?"

A flush worked up from my chest. I owed Lucy so much. An answer to this question was the least of it. Her eyebrows rose and the edges of her mouth were controlled into a not-smile; she seemed to enjoy making me uncomfortable.

I stammered over her forwardness. "I mean, not full-out. Just, like, other stuff."

"You should have just done it. I have." Her lips searched until they found her straw and she pulled in a gulp of cream, sugar, and caffeine.

"You have?"

One hand gripped her Starbucks cup while the other rolled a sterling ring around her thumb. "People talk about it like it's such a big deal, but it's like any other activity. Sometimes it's just easier to do something than sit around and talk, you know? It's like going for a run together or watching a movie. Sex is just another thing to do. Besides, it's not like it was my first sexual experience, right?" she asked sardonically.

I held still, though discomfort wormed through me. "Maybe next time."

"So Eddie is finally in jail," Lucy said.

This conversation was like an antique roller coaster, whipping my neck with its rickety transitions. But of course Eddie was on her mind. He was likely always occupying space, uninvited. He was on my mind too.

The previous month, just before Christmas, police went through his garbage and found a hard drive containing thirty-seven thousand images and videos of child pornography. Rumor had it the subjects of the material included his patients. Gymnasts. I couldn't let myself contemplate this—pictures of girls I'd trained alongside, videos of Lucy, perhaps. It was unthinkable. Even I couldn't deny his guilt anymore.

"Yeah. It's crazy."

"Not crazy at all. He's a monster. Jail is exactly where he belongs," she said, speaking quickly. She clasped her cup, and I imagined the plastic cracking under her hold, coffee slush spilling onto her freckled hand.

Her former effervescence had stultified into something hardier. Maybe with Eddie in prison, she was carrying the weight of incontrovertible truth—what happened had really happened. For a brief moment, a greedy moment, I wondered if life would have been easier if we never arrived at the age of knowing, if we never came into possession of the horrible truth.

"Right."

She rolled her cup around on its bottom. As she stared at it, I noticed that the inner edges of her eyebrows were sparse, like they'd been smudged out with a pencil eraser. She caught me looking, retreated into the back of her chair, and pressed her middle finger into the center of her forehead.

"The police interviewed me in the fall," she said. "USA Gymnastics called our house the day before they came. I don't know how they knew, but they did. I guess they know everything. Like God. They asked me not to say anything."

"Did you?" I asked, feeling my loyalties split, despite everything.

"Of course I did," she said, disapprovingly. "Anyway, there's this lawsuit I've been asked to join. There's already like twenty girls in the suit, but Eddie has had at least fifty complaints over the years, so I bet there'll be more."

What would my mother have said to me that night in my bedroom if it wasn't just Lucy questioning Eddie's treatments, but fifty others? How would Vanda have reacted if Lucy had had all those girls standing behind her in the gym instead of one useless friend? Rather than calling Lucy a liar, Vanda might have called her a champion, an Olympian.

"Do you think you might get money or something?" I asked.

"It isn't about that." She looked at me like I kept saying the wrong thing, and I agreed with her, but I didn't know how to make any of it right. It appeared she was going to give me another pass. "I don't know. Maybe I will get money. Anyway, Jennifer said you were training again."

"Yeah, I am. Or I will be in a few months."

"Why?"

"Lou doesn't want to train hard for longer than three years straight."

"No, why are you training at all?"

The answer was so obvious it was difficult to express; it was like asking me why I was breathing. "It's who I am."

"Why not go to college? Do NCAA?"

She must know. She'd once had the dream herself: Peanut. The happiest girl in the world. Gold.

I said, "You remember what it's like to want the Olympics."

"So you're sticking with USA Gymnastics even though they covered for him? They protected a predator because he was also a doctor who cleared girls who should have been benched. If Eddie gave the green light, they didn't care what else he did. You're sticking with those types of people?" She blinked and the curtains dropped, exposing the old Lucy, stripped of the cynicism and experience she'd caked around her eyes like too much foundation. I saw the eleven-year-old Lucy who read American Girl novels, whose teeth were fastened with patriotic-themed braces, who danced when I nailed a new skill. I saw the Lucy who had been hurt—who *I'd* hurt. The girl who couldn't believe I was still forsaking her.

I wanted to disappear. I leaned back against the chair and slid down a few inches. "Maybe they didn't know."

Lucy blinked again and restored her new persona. Her words were cold and hard, like marbles.

"They knew," she said. "Just like you knew."

PART II

CHAPTER 20

November 2017

Adderall made my world catch fire.

Images came alive in their proud new shades, from aureolin to zaffre. And I couldn't look away. It was a spectacle. It grabbed me and wouldn't let go. That's what happens during a blaze too. It's stunning, with its great reaching licks of flame, climbing to the sky inside swirling black smoke. Beautiful, even. And its cleansing renewal can be positive for growth. But fire has the equal capacity to destroy. Adderall set fire to my brain. To everything.

I'd been working with Lou for almost four months when he told me to get a prescription. He said I wasn't focused, that I was incapable of paying attention to details.

"You're distracted by the big picture, and I need you looking through a magnifying glass. It isn't anything to be ashamed of. ADD is a disease. Lots of kids get it at your age."

He referred me to a doctor his girls had seen before. The idea of seeing another medical professional, especially a gymnastics insider, set my surroundings off-kilter, like the gym was at sea.

"Shouldn't I see my regular doctor? The one who has all my records?"

"Will you listen to me for once without questioning every single thing? Just see my guy, all right? I'm telling you, sometimes it feels like I have a three-year-old again with all this 'why, why, why.'"

When I told my parents over dinner, I didn't look up from my broccoli. "Coach thinks I need Adderall."

My father was on his third glass of whiskey. When he first picked up the habit, he drank Wild Turkey. Then Jack Daniels. Then Jim Beam. Now that he was going through more bottles than ever, he'd moved on to the more affordable Old Crow. My mom told him he might as well start distilling the stuff in our bathtub.

He dabbed gravy from his mouth with a paper napkin, crumpled it in his fist, and tossed it on the table. "Charlene, you're the authority on who has a medical degree and who doesn't. Did you know that Lou was a licensed psychiatrist?"

Maybe Joe saw how I bent over my plate, how another week of training, another inevitable argument, made me wilt like a daffodil after a cold snap. He said, "So many kids at school take Adderall, they might as well put it in the vending machines."

I noticed then how handsome he was getting. His chest and shoulders were broadening, his jawline was defining itself.

My father's appearance had also changed. His mustache was flecked with silver, and his face seemed flatter somehow, like God had taken him by the cheeks and stretched. "Sera is almost eighteen and never had a problem focusing before."

My mother's face was puffy now, but while my father's seemed to have expanded, her flesh had swelled around her features, making them appear small and sunken, especially her eyes. She was still pretty, but in a softer way. She compensated for this change with more eye shadow and mascara.

She was delicate in placing her fork beside her plate. "To be fair, Sera hasn't been in school on a regular basis since puberty. Maybe she's *developed* ADD."

"Or maybe her brain is just fine."

In that moment, my desire for Adderall was a fickle feline. If Lou thought it would help me become the best, if other gymnasts took the medication to heighten their concentration, I wanted it too. No question. But beneath that, where the lamp of my ego burned beneath the bushel of my ambition, I rejected the idea that I hadn't been focused the past ten years. How much more dedicated could I have been? So while I begrudged my father's resistance, the way he dragged his feet through every leg of this Olympic course,

I was also grateful to him for his faith in my competency—for continuing to see me.

My mother tempered her tone to reason with him. "Lou is with her more than we are."

He laughed cruelly. "Oh, I'm well aware of that. Well aware."

Joe slumped in his chair. He was a senior in high school and starting to look at colleges, mostly across the country. I suspected this type of argument was at least partly why.

My father continued, "Is she even allowed to take Adderall? Stimulants are banned by the World Anti-Doping Agency."

"You can get an exemption," I mumbled. "For medical reasons."

"Medical reasons. Where have we heard that before?" He tipped his chin back to drain the last gulp of whiskey. "You're going to do what you're going to do. We all know it doesn't matter what I think."

THE DOCTOR HAD impossibly white hair. He looked like someone who should be fishing with his grandkids, not still practicing medicine. I wondered if he had an ulterior motive—if this was where he got his rocks off. Maybe all gymnastics-affiliated doctors were perverts, because perverts were the only ones who had a reason to keep quiet about their patients' malnutrition and injuries. Like Lucy said: a quiet doctor was a valuable doctor, no matter what else he was.

The exam table paper crinkled beneath me. I squeezed my thighs together even though I was fully dressed.

"What can I do you for?" he asked without looking up from his clipboard.

"I'm having trouble concentrating," I said, and then couldn't help but add, "I guess."

"I hear you. You can't focus on your schoolwork. You're distracted by irrelevant sounds and sights around you. You get bored easily. I hear you."

I wasn't sure training the same ninety-second floor routine for months could constitute becoming bored easily, but I said, "Yeah."

"You're a little thing. Maybe we should start you at five milligrams a day and see how you do," he said, and looked up at me for the first time. "How serious a problem do you think this is?"

I shrugged.

His gaze dropped down to his clipboard and he scribbled a note. "Let's say ten, then."

LOU HAD A plastic cup of water and a little blue pill waiting every morning. I dutifully drank it down, and then went into the gym to warm up: jump rope, jogging in place, head rolls, arm swings, foot stretches, and almost sixty other exercises. An hour later, once the pill had kicked in, Lou emerged from his office. Only when my neurotransmitters were available and hungry, eager to connect with norepinephrine and dopamine, so eager my brain chemistry vibrated in my fingers, was he willing to talk to me.

I felt completely turned on, like every atom in my body had switches that were flicked simultaneously, like a warehouse lighting up. I asked my mother about her day and followed up with more questions. I remembered my father's sales record each week. I had enough energy at night to flip through Joe's history flash cards. My mind was operating at full capacity, round the clock. It worked all the shifts. As I drove home from the gym, I recounted everything I'd learned, every minute way I could improve my form, my lines, my power. And when that was done, I made mental lists. Things I needed to do, things going on in the lives of those closest to me. I set goals, timelines. It was like my brain had hired a personal assistant. A personal assistant who was so jacked up on caffeine she couldn't sleep at night. Come eleven o'clock, I found myself wide-eyed. I didn't sense sleep anywhere. So I studied the routines of the Final Five in the 2016 Olympics, the one I missed by a hair—Vanda's hair, to be precise. I watched them so many times I could replay their performances behind my eyelids. And when it was one o'clock in the morning and my brain still wasn't fuzzy, my limbs still weren't sinking into the mattress, I took a dose of NyQuil. Sometimes two.

I became an enhanced version of Sera Wheeler: a better gymnast, trainee, daughter, sister—although still not a better friend.

In October, three gymnasts from the Rio Olympics accused Eddie of abusing them. Eddie had already pleaded guilty to three child pornography charges in July, and now, in November, pleaded guilty to seven counts of first-degree criminal sexual conduct. An image of him wearing an orange jumpsuit was plastered all over the internet, not just the gymternet.

I contacted Lucy a number of times, although never about Eddie. I could blindly catapult myself into the air. I could plummet and crash and get up and do it all again, but I couldn't talk to Lucy about Eddie. That would mean acknowledging how wrong I'd been, and if I gave my guilt life, it would kill me. So I commented on her Instagram posts. (She'd unblocked me after our Starbucks meeting. Maybe she figured my witnessing her life without me was a worse punishment than not seeing it at all.) When she shared a selfie clouded in smoke, a burning joint clamped between her lips, I wrote, I think I have a virtual contact high. When she posted a photo with a stripe of hair dyed sea-foam green, along with "#MermaidWarrior," I commented, So pretty! And then followed the unanswered compliment up with a text.

She ignored me, so I poured myself into gymnastics. I made it the focus of my tunnel vision so I didn't have to notice anything else.

Learning about Eddie had awakened my distrust. I was the naked emperor, suddenly self-conscious. When I first arrived at Champion Gym, I wore compression shorts over my leotard for an additional boundary between Lou and the intimate parts he'd have to handle as part of his job.

But as I pulled off my warm-ups, he saw the extra layer and said, "Will you wear shorts at the Olympics?"

"No."

"Then you won't wear shorts training for the Olympics."

The days were all the same. There was no chitchat while I stretched. No pleasantries. It was straight to work. And we worked hard, especially on floor: an Arabian double front leap combo; a roundoff into a back handspring and triple twist; a roundoff into a back handspring, double layout, and front tuck. He handed me a twenty-pound weighted vest to wear through my routines. The metal bars bruised my hips when I landed tucks. If I didn't need spotting, he studied me from a metal folding chair, where he sat holding his mouth. Only when I finished would he lower his hands to say "Clumsy," "Loose," or "Again."

Once, when he told me to redo my bars routine, I pointed to my palm blisters and said, "If I do it again, these bubbles are gonna rip."

"That's what Sting is for," he said.

The blisters tore in my next swing. When I sprayed Sting into the wound, it felt like I was soldering it closed. I grit my teeth until the burning faded and I swung again.

We broke for lunch. I ran a three-mile loop outside the gym and then came back in to shove a PowerBar down my throat and do it all again.

When we were done, Lou walked back to his office and shut the door without saying goodbye. I caught my breath, rehydrated, and stretched by myself in the dim silence.

At least I was too tired to obsess over the way Lucy had said, *Just like you knew.*

Like God, we rested on Sundays. And since Lou kept my pills, I rested sober. After church, I felt the burden of the week like so many sandbags, like the weights Lou strapped to my chest. All the practice, the precision, the sleepless nights, the lists made me heavy and pulled me down to the earth. I tried to fight off the exhaustion through brunch with my family, but I'd be cranky, snapping at Joe's dumb comment about the sermon or criticizing my mother's scrambled eggs, and someone—usually my dad—would suggest I take a nap. By then I was done fighting. I surrendered myself to bed and slept through the afternoon.

Nobody worried. I had worked so hard that week and would work hard in the week to come. A body needs its rest, after all.

CHAPTER 21

January 2018

The previous autumn, #MeToo fires blazed around the country. Harvey Weinstein was the first to go up in flames. Then Kevin Spacey. Louis C.K. Matt Lauer. Mario Batali. Women at the Golden Globes wore black to demonstrate they wouldn't stand by and let men abuse their power and privilege any longer. Time was up for unpunished harassment and assault. And in January, time was up for Edward Levett.

The man who'd given me an antihistamine when my poison ivy itched, stabilized my knee when it swelled, gifted me a 2008 Olympics water bottle, and seen me in my pajamas. The man whose voice I recognized, whom I knew as an ally among the harsh critics of my sport, had been a predator all along. By then almost three hundred girls had accused him of sexual misconduct, including one whose abuse began when she was only six years old.

The court procedures were televised. He went on trial for the world to see.

My father recorded all of it. When he returned home from work, he played the footage at a volume that was just too loud for comfort. Nobody debated the broadcast. It was a rare insistence from my father that we heard in our bones.

He looked familiar on television—Eddie, our doctor. But also foreign. The Eddie I knew wore collared sports shirts. This Eddie wore a blue prison uniform. The Eddie I knew was tidy and had round chipmunk cheeks. This Eddie's hair was unkempt and his cheeks were drawn, sallow, and shadowed with scruff. The Eddie I knew smiled. This Eddie's expression was worn, as if it was about to slide right off his face.

As part of Eddie's plea deal, every girl he'd ever harmed had the opportunity to share her experience in court. At the start of the four-day trial, there were eighty-eight women slated to speak. But fires catch. All over the country, women watched and listened as individuals just like them stood up, spoke their names into the microphone, and shared their stories. One by one, those at home stood up too. The trial was extended three days to accommodate all the other impact statements. The eighty-eight had nearly doubled.

Part of me wished I could address Eddie too, to speak the truth beating down on my shoulders: *You hurt Lucy. You destroyed what Lucy and I were. You made me into a good-for-nothing bystander. I defended you. I believed in you. I'll never trust again.* But my truth was a grass stain in his pigsty.

Aly Raisman read her statement, wearing a red blazer and a cascading ponytail, and spoke with surprising composure. I wondered how many times she'd rehearsed her speech, studying it like she would one of her routines, practicing it so that her tongue memorized the positions, like a body would a tumbling pass. Maybe she'd been preparing this speech for years, because beneath the Olympian we all claimed to know was a victim we didn't. Then again, maybe being a victim and being an Olympian had more in common than one would think.

She condemned USA Gymnastics and the United States Olympic Committee for ignoring accusations, failing to conduct investigations, and prizing Olympian success over athlete well-being. And she criticized the individuals who must have suspected the doctor's behavior. "If over these many years, just one adult listened, and had the courage and character to act, this tragedy could have been avoided."

My father sat opposite the television, and when the camera panned to the judge, it looked like my father was the man on trial, the man who knew a little and did less about it.

There had been eleven months between when my father heard about Eddie and when Eddie was arrested. How many patients had Eddie seen in that time? How many had he abused? As Aly spoke, I heard his sniff, swift and strong, as if he wanted to get it over with quickly and pretend it never happened. But, of course, it did.

My mother busied herself with other things: She clipped

coupons in the kitchen. Darned socks. Laced Joe's football cleats, though the season had ended. She climbed the stairs holding jars of Prego above her head. She had to take off her depression weight. Competition media crews liked to show-case parents in the stands before their kid's routines, and she wanted to look nervous and excited in Tokyo, but most importantly, thin.

She buzzed around the house as if preparing to host a spe-cial guest, not acknowledging that one was already there: a thirteen-thousand-pound African bush elephant sat in the corner of the living room. It plunked down back when we knew that Lucy hadn't lied for attention or the thrill of gossip, and that my mother, who was perhaps the primary reason I'd turned against my best friend, had been dead wrong. And the largest existing land mammal was going to stay between her and me, munching on twigs and fruit, until she acknowledged her mistake, and how her casual dismissal of Lucy's claim continued to affect our lives.

"Anyone need a snack?" she'd ask, and then disappear before we answered, returning with a bag of Fritos and a Twinkie before going off again.

"The next survivor you will hear from is Lucy Ford. She has decided to speak publicly."

In a pinstripe pencil skirt and matching jacket just too wide on the shoulders, Lucy looked like a child playing dress-up in her mother's work clothes. She'd rinsed out the mermaid dye and flat-ironed her fiery hair to fall straight down her shoulders, half of it pulled back with a barrette. Her face was pale, showcasing celestial freckles. And her lips were the shade of ballet slippers.

"She looks so small up there," Joe said.

My entire family gathered in the living room to hear her impact statement. Joe sat on one side of my father, wearing a hoodie with the Spartan helmet logo of his high school. My mother sat on my father's other side, clutching a glass of pinot grigio with both hands.

I wished I could reach through the television screen and touch Lucy, tell her to be strong, tell her that she *was* strong, so much stronger than me. I wanted to sink into gym face to protect myself. But I resisted. She deserved to be seen.

Lucy had always dreamed about having the world's attention. It was a shame it had to be like this.

She spoke for three minutes, the length of two floor routines, staring into the microphone all the while. Her voice wavered on the edge of crying and sometimes fell over the brink. While other statements were directed at Levett using the second person—*you* did this, *you* did that—Lucy kept hers in the third person, where it was safer.

"From the time we are little, we are taught that doctors are good. And Edward Levett was the best. Only God is a better healer, they said. But he didn't heal me. His treatments were abuse wearing a disguise I, as a child, believed. He won me over with kindness, with the authority and respect of USA Gymnastics, who called him the best gymnastics doctor in the world, and with gifts he bestowed on me every time I saw him. I trusted him—I *liked* him." She paused and wiped her finger across the bottom of her nose. "I've thought about putting an end to the pain he caused that I can't erase. But I know I won't be broken forever." Finally her stare flickered in what we knew to be Levett's direction. "And you will."

I hurried to the bathroom. My face was flushed, puffy, and damp. Maybe it was selfish to reach out to Lucy. Maybe reminding her of me over and over again was its own small abuse, and I should just let her go, allow her to move on. But I was compelled to contact her, even if one last time. I sat on the closed toilet lid, inched my phone from my pocket, and texted, You are a badass beauty.

I didn't expect to hear back from her. Her phone must have been buzzing nonstop. Besides, she'd never responded to me before. I clicked my phone to sleep, and when a text box with her name appeared on my screen, my heart opened like a birdcage, and a little canary of hope flew out.

Thanks.

Emboldened, I crept a little closer to sentiment. I hope they lock him up forever.

I stared at my phone screen until her ellipsis bloomed into words. Me too.

ON THE FIFTH day, a middle-aged man wearing a crew neck sweatshirt tucked into belted jeans stood solemnly beside his teenage daughters as they recounted what Levett did to them, as well as to a third sister. I wondered if Levett had the impulse to molest all three or if it was a strategic decision—if he knew he had to be consistent with siblings because they were likely to swap the particulars of an exam with one another, so the details had to match.

The father gripped his hands at his waist and asked the judge, "I would ask you too, as part of this sentencing, to grant me five minutes in a locked room with this demon."

The judge said, "You know I can't do that."

"Would you give me one minute?"

"That's not how our legal system—"

"Then I'm going to have to commit a crime." He lunged toward the defendant, and my legs dropped from where I was curled on the couch.

"Oh shit," Joe said.

The man reached Levett's table but was tackled by court officers. They grappled him, twisting his arms around his back and digging into the place between his shoulder blades so that his chest was pressed against the floor.

He lifted his head. "Let me have that bastard. I want one minute with that son of a bitch. Just one minute."

"Holy shit," Joe said again.

They cuffed and gathered him up, four officers surrounding him. As they led him out of the courtroom, the father turned and looked one officer in the eye.

"What if this happened to you?"

In our living room, my own father sounded like he'd been

waterboarded but was finally ready to talk. "You sure you're okay, Sera?"

My parents clasped hands. I couldn't remember the last time I'd seen such a thing. And my father's face glistened. He'd been crying soundlessly. They both searched my face for the answer they were desperate for.

I had been spared, for no good reason. I wasn't any better than those who had been hurt. Maybe I was worse. Maybe that's why Eddie had rejected me; yet another force in USA Gymnastics who didn't want me.

How could I think such a disgusting thought?

But it was true: a dark part of me wished I was part of this rally of women who could be described with Olympic-team adjectives: "magnificent," "fierce," "final." Maybe then I would feel powerful now.

Earlier that week, I was working on a double twisting double backflip into a foam pit, but I wasn't rotating fast enough to get beyond the first twist.

"You should have this by now," Lou said, running his fingers through the hair at the sides of his head. "Maybe you'd be able to if you didn't pig out over the holidays."

"I didn't," I said. The Adderall had eradicated my appetite, so I knew food wasn't to blame. I wanted a real solution.

"You don't think I see it? You've packed on some pounds." He stepped forward, tucked a finger beneath the seam of my leotard, and tugged it up my hip. "Look how that cuts into your ass. And your thighs jiggle when you run. Judges will take a point off for that flab. You've lost your discipline, and it's affecting your performance. Admit it, so we can get past it. Did you gain weight?"

My stare bored into the floor mat between my feet. "I don't know."

"Let's find out." He grabbed me by the wrist and yanked hard toward the back of the facility. I stumbled after him. When we reached the physician's scale, he released his grip. My wrist ached without his hold.

I solidified my exterior so I wouldn't betray emotion and stepped onto the metal base.

He swiped the large weight from fifty to one hundred pounds and skid the small scale hard to the right to imply he thought I was well into triple digits. When the scale clinked up in response, he ticked the small weight back pound by pound until it reached its end. Then he reluctantly shifted the bottom weight back to fifty.

By the time the scale balanced, it read ninety-four pounds. My leanest ever.

Before my triumph could swell, he bent forward and his face warped. Even though he'd been wrong, he was pleased by the results.

"So you aren't fat. You're just mediocre."

My tongue pushed into the gums below my bottom teeth. I'd heard somewhere that the tongue was one of the strongest muscles in the body, stronger than the quadriceps that launched me into a back handspring, mightier than the traps that caught the weight, even tougher than the abdominals that contracted to pull my legs over my torso. But despite its strength, my tongue collapsed against the pink tissue before it.

Back in my living room, watching the Levett trial, I answered my parents, "Nothing happened to me."

"You're lucky." My father dragged his sleeve across his damp cheeks. "I'm lucky."

The entire board of USA Gymnastics was forced to resign, and the organization ended its relationship with the Balogh Ranch. I wondered where our next training grounds would be, and how they'd protect us there, or anywhere.

Before Judge Aquilina's sentencing, she read from a letter Eddie had written the court. In it, he explained that he was a good doctor who helped many patients. The reason these women were coming forward was because the media had convinced them he'd done them wrong.

Hell hath no fury like a woman scorned, he wrote.

And there was the Eddie I never saw for myself. He wasn't our advocate. The kind presence at the ranch. The gift giver. The healer. He was a bitter, snide, and self-gratifying sadist. A condescending, perverse sociopath with no value for the life of others, especially not the lives of girls. He'd played me. He'd played us all.

CHAPTER 22

Charlene Wheeler

I dialed Lucy's mom a week after that nasty man's trial.

I spent a lot of time with Holly back when the girls were little. She was a working mom, and sometimes working moms can have an air of superiority, acting like they do my job and more when the truth might be they just do two jobs half as well. But Holly wasn't like that. She always asked about my day and was quick to laugh or offer sympathy when a story called for it. There were often circles under her eyes and her ponytail was frizzed. She was just doing her best, like the rest of us.

She wore sweat suits on a daily basis, but not ones that resembled warm-ups, like some gym moms wore, as if they might break out into a routine of their own at any moment. Hers were for comfort, with a nod to fashion. But the cuffs of her pants were often frayed from getting caught under her heels, and thick stitching signaled where she'd had to sew a burst seam back together. She was short and stout, and I thought Lucy better be careful or she could end up the same, but of course I never said so.

We'd sit and chat while our daughters practiced because the facility was too far from where we each lived to be a drop-and-go situation. We remarked on their improvement, swapped gym mom tips, and exchanged women's magazines, hers lifted from the dental office where she worked and mine brought home by Bob from the office at his car lot. We pulled the girls from school around the same time to concentrate on training, and Holly got a job in Indianapolis so she could drop Lucy off and work an eight-hour shift nearby before picking her up and driving an hour home to Kokomo. Our relationship was reduced to a passing wave and an occasional Facebook comment, still friendly in all ways but where it counted: like not mentioning when one of our daughters accused the best gymnastics doctor in the country of abuse because we assumed it just couldn't possibly be true.

Lucy's story was strange, but I just didn't have enough distrust in Eddie—in *humanity*—to believe it. If you were suspicious enough to think that a famous doctor could be capable of that level of evil, well, that's no way to live. You'd go bonkers. Everybody would be a potential criminal in your eyes: your postman, your minister, the kids' teachers, the policemen. You'd have to lock your kid in her bedroom and never leave the house. There just wasn't enough proof to contradict my benefit of the doubt, so I pushed it down. God help me, I explained it away.

When I thought of how I felt about Edward Levett before, the way I wanted to throw my arms around him when he flattered Sera and me at the Nastia Liukin Cup, and how I worshipped his experience and know-how, when I thought of him at all, this cloud of soot formed in my belly that made me want to scrub myself clean from the inside out. And when I thought about poor little Lucy, what he did to her and to so many other girls, and the way I was sure she was fabricating the whole thing because she was slacking in the gym and her routines weren't garnering the attention she wanted, or just to cause a stir, and how I advised Sera not to indulge what I called her fantasies, to ignore her friend so Sera could stay on course to what turned out be a big fat nothing . . .

Well, there was no sense crying over spilled milk.

But as I stood in the dairy section at Kroger's, staring at refrigerators stocked full of gallons and quarts and liters, I imagined all the containers exploding at once, causing the glass to shatter, drenching and slicing me in one fell swoop.

If I was dripping blood and cream, would there be sense in crying over spilled milk then?

Holly's phone kept ringing and ringing. I had no clue what I'd say in a voicemail, a recording that could live for posterity. Just as I decided I'd have to hang up and try again some other time, she answered.

I couldn't stand still, so I left my full cart by the half-and-half and paced the aisle.

"Holly. Hi there. I wasn't sure I'd reach you, but I'm glad I did. It's Charlene, by the way. Charlene Wheeler. But you know that. I'm sure my name came up on your phone. Anyway, I was just thinking of you while I'm doing a little grocery shopping here. There's that big storm coming, you know. You'll be getting it too. Over a foot, they say. Gotta get your milk and bread."

"Sure."

"They think it's going to be the biggest one of the season. But then again, they'll say anything for ratings. It's not like being wrong gets them fired, so why not make a scene of it, right?"

"You're right about that," she said.

I'd reached the other end of the store and paused before a table of freshly baked bread. I ran my fingers over a sliced loaf. Even through the plastic it felt like a pillow I wanted to rest my head on. Its softness just about broke my heart.

"Oh, Holly. I don't know what to say."

She exhaled big and full. "Nobody does. Most go with the weather, so you're right on track."

"How are you? And Lucy, of course? And Peter?"

"As well as can be, considering the circumstances." Which was a classically shapeless way for a Midwestern lady to say *We are broken.*

"I just keep going over it all in my head. Every time I saw the man, everything Sera mentioned about him."

She thinks his treatments are creepy or something. He touches down there.

I clamped my eyes closed and tried to shake the memory away. When I opened my eyes, I realized I'd squeezed the lovely shape out of the white loaf, crumpling its supple crown, ruining it. I retracted my hand into my chest.

I said, "I just had no idea. I swear to you I didn't."

"I was in the room, Charlene. I was in the room when he did it." It sounded as if her voice was being dragged over shards of glass. "If I didn't know, how could you?"

I almost confessed then and there. I nearly said, *You may have missed something, but I missed it too.* But I didn't really miss it. I saw it, and I'd just wished it away. Which was much worse.

I turned my back on the spoiled bread and started for my cart. "If it had been Sera, I wouldn't have known either."

"And are you sure?"

"Oh, sure. He fooled people way smarter than me."

"No, I meant, are you sure it wasn't Sera? I pray it wasn't, I really do, but, you know, people are still finding out he did it to their kid too."

I slowed in frozen foods. The air there was so cold and stale, it brought the very act of breathing to a person's attention. "We asked. She said no."

"You have to ask the question very specifically—that's

what they say. Because they're kids. They don't know what's right and wrong in that area. That's why so many came forward during the trial. Some were learning only at that very moment that they'd been a victim all along."

"But Sera watched the trial. She saw the whole thing. She'd know." The chill was seeping through my winter coat, so I forced myself up the aisle.

"I hope you're right. I do."

And even though I felt sorry for the woman, I resented her overreach, like she knew better. Like she knew *Sera* better. There were allegations I deserved, but neglecting my daughter wasn't one of them. And her tone was a little too familiar. We hadn't spent an hour together in the last couple years, and she wanted to imply that unspeakable things had happened to my baby?

"We should get the girls together one of these days," I said. "I know Lucy isn't interested in gymnastics anymore, but maybe they can arrange a sleepover. It's been ages."

Holly's tone pulled back too and tucked its shirt into its waist. "It has."

"Well, I better let you go. You tell me if you need anything, okay? Bye-bye, now."

I PULLED INTO the church parking lot on the way home.

I had always wanted to attend a little white clapboard church with a picturesque steeple. I got what I wanted, but it was nothing like I'd imagined. I couldn't stand the minister, whose breath was so perpetually rank he must suffer from a condition. The men sang loud and off-key. The women froze the leftover coffee to reuse the next week and put peas in their tuna noodle hotdish. Plus, they talked behind your back without the courtesy or cleverness to be discreet about it.

But the white clapboard sure did look resplendent against a bright blue sky. And God was inside those walls. Seemed to me, anyway.

I don't know what I'd been planning, going out of my way to stop at St. John's after my chat with Holly with a car full of groceries. I suppose I saw myself filing into a pew in the back of the sanctuary, which, in the middle of a weekday, would be empty and so still the dust would float inside a stream of light. Without any distractions, and under the gaze of altar Jesus, maybe I'd reflect on all that I'd done, or had left undone, as the case may be. I'd take the time to get right with myself and with the Lord. But as I eyed the double front doors, my idea of repentance seemed so silly. So stiff and sanctimonious. So . . . Catholic. I laughed at myself a bit and then started the car right back up. I'd made mistakes, to be sure. But there was no sense in self-flagellation. I just had to do better from here on out. Look forward. With that in mind, I stopped at a gas station and bought a couple Lotto tickets.

Someone had to win the jackpot. Why the heck shouldn't it be me?

CHAPTER 23

August 2018

Over the next year and a half, Tom Brokaw was accused of sexual harassment; a woman shot up YouTube headquarters; a study reported that nearly half of Americans always felt left out, calling it a loneliness epidemic; there was a school shooting in Santa Fe, Texas; Roseanne Barr's rebooted show was canceled after she posted a racist tweet; and Lucy graduated high school. In her Instagram photo, her cap tassel curtained one eye; she looked like any average teenager, and I thought, *There you go, Lucy. You've done it.* Joe graduated high school too, but, just as Lucy had fallen a year behind, I hadn't been able to complete my coursework on schedule. I prayed that greatness could offset my mistakes, so I trained and trained and trained.

MY MOTHER FLIPPED through an issue of *Good Housekeeping* with Meghan Markle on the cover, her newest celebrity icon. "She's royalty, but she came from nothing. Her mother was a yoga instructor, for cripes' sake."

Her hair was tucked into a shower cap; she was in the midst of dyeing it a color the box described as Sweet Cola, a much deeper shade than she normally chose, perhaps inspired by the Duchess of Sussex. The smell of chemicals drifted around her head, and the shoulders of my dad's old button-down were speckled with brown stains.

"Listen to this," she said. "You pick up some plastic baskets from the dollar store, wrap them in rope, and you got yourself some chic storage bins. Think I should sell them at church to raise money for Worlds?"

With her hair drawn up, exposing the expanse of her cheeks and jaw, she appeared bloated, as if she'd been crying, though I didn't think that she had been. Worse, she looked foreign; if I hadn't watched my mother squint at the directions on the box of dye earlier, I might have assumed a strange old woman had hijacked our home. It felt rude to look directly at her in this compromised state.

I was snooping on Lucy's Instagram. Encouraged by her quick responses to my texts during Eddie's trial, I had contacted her a month later during a break at Lou's gym, revising the message seven times until I struck what I thought to be the right balance of funny and confiding.

I guess it's a good thing I didn't have sex with that kid Matt.

He told everybody in town that this girl Kayla looks like a goldfish when she orgasms.

Her dots appeared and then disappeared. She was silent for three whole minutes before her bubble materialized again, and then persisted for a long time. I knew then, before I received her reply, that contacting her had been a mistake.

You can't just text me out of nowhere about your ex-boyfriend. I don't know him, and I don't care about him. You and me—we aren't friends, okay? We were just kids when Eddie abused me, and you couldn't have known better, so I don't blame you for that. But you were sixteen when you turned your back on me in front of everybody because you wanted to stay on Vanda's good side. That wasn't that young. You knew what you were doing. And you are still part of USA Gymnastics. So you are still doing it.

I slid the phone across the gym mat, shot to my feet, and alternated between three backflips and twenty push-ups until sweat dripped down my neck.

Now, at the kitchen table with my mother, I scrolled through photos of Lucy. She'd left for college, she'd left the *country,* to attend the University of British Columbia. There she was in front of a cathedral. There she was at an aquarium, imitating a walrus in the adept and goofy way only she could. There she was holding a shot glass, her arm around the neck of a pudgy brunette with square glasses. She looked happy.

"Earth to Sera," my mom prompted.

I swiped out of Instagram. It closed to reveal my phone wallpaper, a selfie I snapped in my front yard while in a handstand. Behind me, my house looked like it had been hung upside down to dry.

"Yeah," I said. "That's a good idea."

"It'll go nice with the wine cork necklace holders." She folded down the corner of the page to mark the baskets, and then scratched her head through the shower cap. "You like the necklace holders, right?"

I felt her wanting something from me, but even if I knew what it was, I wouldn't have given it to her. Ever since Eddie's trial, I'd had a nagging desire, quiet but tangible, to chasten her. I didn't know if she actually deserved reprimanding, but I thought she should have at least *acted* remorseful, instead of walking around guilt-free. It was her self-assurance, so drastically juxtaposed with my own shame, that I wanted to punish.

"Yeah," I said.

She seemed satisfied with that. "I wish Worlds wasn't in Qatar," she said, mispronouncing the country as she always did, no matter how many times I corrected her. "The most expensive flight possible."

"I know." The bulky air-conditioning unit in the window ticked to seventy-nine degrees and cranked on. I wore a spaghetti-strap tank top and shorts whose waist I'd rolled down, but my sweat still acted as an adhesive, sticking the backs of my thighs to the chair.

She flipped a magazine page, but I wasn't sure she really saw anything before she flipped again. Then she raised her voice to be heard over the thrumming of the AC. "If it was somewhere closer, like Paris or something, I'd go with you in a heartbeat." She strained to smile. "It was so fun watching you medal at the Classic. I hate to think of missing that at Worlds."

The GK U.S. Classic had been held in Ohio that year, so my whole family was there to see me take silver on bars and bronze in the all-around. Bronze was lucky; I wouldn't have medaled at all if Morgan Hurd hadn't slipped off the beam.

"Columbus was so close, but I kinda wish you did the American Classic in Salt Lake City instead. At least then I would have gotten to go somewhere special. But, you know, I should count my blessings."

"If I win Worlds, that's a fourteen-thousand-dollar prize. That'll pay for any competition you want to travel to from now until the Olympics."

Her smile softened. "I like the sound of that." She cleared her throat and directed her attention back to the magazine. "How's training going with Lou?"

"Good."

"You feel confident about your routines?"

"Pretty much."

The magazine flopped closed and she sat back in her chair. "Where do you stumble?" Her index finger scratched just above her ear and the shower cap crinkled. It must have been acting as a greenhouse for her head, because dots of perspiration sprouted beneath her hairline.

"The normal places."

My mother crossed her arms over her chest and laughed humorlessly. "I don't know what the normal places are anymore. It's been so long since I've seen you practice, now that you drive yourself."

Again I felt her want stretching its arms across the table. I was tempted to push my chair back and escape its reach. "You can always come watch, if you want."

Her eyebrows jumped, surprised by my offer. I wondered at what point her involvement became by invitation only.

"You don't think Lou would mind?"

"You're paying him, Mom. *You're* the boss."

Her lips wriggled; she liked that idea. "Maybe I will."

I remembered then what it was like to have my mother watch my sessions. Her incessant suggestions to Jennifer that sounded a lot like criticism, her play-by-play commentary of the practice during the drive home, and her obsessive analysis well into the night.

I said, "As long as you don't mind sitting around the gym for seven hours. It can get pretty boring."

"What else am I doing with my life?" she asked, sounding almost cheery.

"Crafting?" I had meant it to be a joke, but once the words existed out in the world, I recognized the sharpness of condescension around their edges and was almost ashamed of myself.

Her eyebrows fell and pulled the rest of her features down with them. She tried to force her mouth back into a smile but couldn't seem to lift it. She swallowed and leaned forward to read her phone timer. There were eight minutes remaining, but she covered the screen with her hand.

"I better go rinse this."

THE NEXT DAY, my mother listed all the things she had to do that prevented her from accompanying me to Cincinnati: laundry; grocery shopping; cooking for the week; paying bills; researching financial aid options for Joe, who planned to do a year at community college before going away. But the morning after, she met me in the kitchen with matching lunch bags.

My mother had finally updated her haircut. Now she styled it in a long bob at the front with a spiked crown at the back. Sitting on the edge of the driver's seat, as if craning to see around a corner even on a straightaway, she resembled a cockatiel on its perch.

By the time we were cruising on U.S. 31, Meghan Trainor rose up on the radio and faded away to Camila Cabello, and my mother and I still hadn't spoken. The silence felt uneasy, the kind old friends share when they haven't seen each other in years and there is so much to catch up on, they almost don't want to bother.

Burnt fields raced by my window in scorched streaks. Even Jennifer begrudged parent participation in training. What would Lou think when my mother followed me in? I had been too nervous to mention the possibility to him.

"There aren't any girl bands anymore. Have you noticed?" my mother asked, sounding like an amateur stand-up comedian. "Back in my day, it was all groups. We had the Bangles, Bananarama, the Pointer Sisters, the Go-Go's. And then later the Dixie Chicks, En Vogue, the Spice Girls, TLC, Destiny's Child. Heck, even the Pussycat Dolls. Now it's all solo artists: Taylor Swift, Katy Perry, Ariana Grande. They want the spotlight all to themselves. They should call it Generation Me, Me, Me."

Her diatribe floated uncomfortably between us. I had to say something. "If you were in Destiny's Child, who would you be?"

She snorted and tilted her head down in a way that demonstrated concession, a tip of the hat. "Queen Bey, of course."

I realized I'd made a point without meaning to. I grabbed on to the argument's tail and let it drag me along.

"Do you even remember the other girls' names?" I asked, liking the way my voice lilted when we both knew I was right.

"You got me there, smarty-pants." Even though she was admitting defeat, she appeared happier, more relaxed. She rolled her shoulders back, breathed in through her nose, and sighed. "I guess it isn't such a bad thing to be remembered, or to want that for yourself." She stole a glimpse at me. "It's too late for me to do anything worth remembering. But who knows. Maybe my singular purpose was to be your mom. Maybe it was my job to *create* someone who will be remembered."

LOU WAS IN a pissy mood. Maybe it was the weather. We were cresting a heat wave, facing down another ninety-degree day with eighty-five percent humidity. The air was almost swimmable, a hot tub you couldn't climb out of. I didn't remember Augusts being so warm, but maybe the atmosphere was changing, becoming more extreme. And though the gym had air-conditioning, Lou claimed we weren't paying him enough to afford a cool building. Besides, he said, the climate I should really be worried about was the state of our hypersensitive world, when any man alone with a girl was presumed to be getting his rocks off. I was lucky he was willing to train me privately, before he opened his gym to the public. He was putting his reputation on the line in order to give me his undivided expertise, so I'd have to be a special kind of snowflake to complain about a little clamminess.

But the thing was, I'd never complained. I was used to such a miserable environment at the Balogh Ranch, another facility that didn't invest in comfort. I knew to bring several towels to keep my skin dry and avoid slipping on my own sweat mid-routine, and to guzzle water; you only have to faint once to learn that lesson. Okay, twice. And there were benefits to heat. At least my muscles stayed warm, which meant a reduced risk of injury.

Lou's entire head was flushed, bald scalp and all, making him look like a beefsteak tomato. He wore a golf T-shirt whose cotton was already damp beneath his armpits and down the center of his back. His eyebrows were cinched at the bridge of his nose and he scowled.

"What are you doing here?" He tossed the question at my mother like change to a homeless woman. "Do I need to sign a permission form or something?"

She twirled a spike of hair around her finger. "I'd like to watch, if that's okay."

He shook his head and his eyes rolled as if the movement had jostled them loose. As my mother shrank under his disdain, I wanted to grab her hands and pull her back to her full height. I wanted to say, *Don't let him bully you. Assert your authority. We're paying him.* You're *paying him.* But she knew when she was outmatched. So did I. Lou walked the perimeter to switch on the standing fans, and I began stretching, even though the heat had already made my muscles molasses.

We were increasing the difficulty of my skills, often including an additional half or full rotation, so the equipment was swaddled in giant mats. I would begin with floor and that damn double twisting double back tuck, tumbling into the gym's foam pit.

The first run was a full twisting double back, just to orient my body to the day, marking the movement. Lou didn't even watch me; he scrolled through his cell phone.

After I landed cleanly in the foam bed, my mother clapped

across the room. Lou's gym didn't have the viewing section of Jennifer's—that's how little hospitality he demonstrated—so she sat on the floor against the wall.

"Looking good, Ser," she said.

Lou slipped his phone into his shorts pocket. "One more practice run before the real thing."

I returned to the top of the runway, exhaled, sprinted into takeoff speed, and launched. The gym whirled around me once, twice.

Again my mother clapped. "Attagirl."

Lou said, "Okay, let's enter the big leagues."

I quieted the world around me: the thrum of the fans, the oppressive heat, the attention of my mother and coach. I waited until the mat and I existed in our own universe. Then I ran. I jumped, ricocheting off my hands like a pinball. I twisted and twirled—double time. But I landed too early, on the side of my foot. The mats and foam caught my mistake, but my frustration heightened.

"Close, sweetie," my mother called. "So darn close."

I climbed out of the pit and faced Lou for evaluation. He didn't look angry anymore. His expression was focused. He too had a gym face. He just didn't always wear it.

"You need more torque. You aren't getting enough from the start and are trying to catch up in the air. But you can only catch up so much. The rest has to come from the jump. Swing your arms with more force," he said, demonstrating with his own body. "Push harder on your left foot. Set higher."

I let his advice wash over me and soak through my skin. Then I nodded and returned to the top. *Swing arms. Push left foot.* It's easy to acknowledge and accept such wisdom. It's harder to implement it in the split second between landing the back handspring and setting into the skill. Almost impossible. I just had to locate the sweet spot that made it almost.

I raced toward the pit and hurled myself forward. When I landed the back handspring, I remembered Lou's advice—just a beat too late. I threw my arms across my body to try to compensate, turned and spun, and landed almost—*almost*—right.

"Hey, that was great!" my mother cheered, her voice reaching me from across the room. "You're a rock star, Sera."

Lou appeared above me, his arms crossed over his chest. A drop of sweat fattened on his forehead and trickled down his cheek, like an off-track tear. I scrambled to my feet so it wouldn't drop on me.

"You still didn't get the twist around before landing. You're finishing the last half rotation on the floor. That's a good way to tear your meniscus. So keep it up, if that's what you want." He straightened and took a step back. "Sera's mom," he said, flicking a finger in my mother's direction. "My office. Now."

She froze for a second, as if hoping he might be referring to a different Sera's mom. But then she rose like a schoolgirl and followed him to the back of the facility.

I imagined him forcing her up onto the scale, heaving the

weight to the right, making her question everything she believed to be true about herself: *Might I look two hundred pounds?*

Or maybe, with that last run, he'd reached his quota of failed attempts and was done wasting his time. *I gave her five hundred tries. You saw her. It's hopeless. She'll never compete. You're her mother; break the news.*

I tiptoed around the corner until I was five feet from his office doorway and pressed my body against the wall; my damp skin delighted at the cool concrete.

Lou spoke at a regular volume, as if he knew I was outside and wanted me to hear. "Simone is going to roll out a triple twisting double tuck for 2020. We all know that. Worlds is in two months and Sera doesn't even have the double double. How the hell is she going to get a triple for the Olympics? At this rate, she isn't. She never will. She is not a rock star," he said, and his voice distorted the last words, mocking my mother's use of them. "Not yet, anyway. Maybe not ever. She is behind. And false compliments make her soft. So you better cut that shit out if you want to see her succeed. And tell your husband to cut it out too. Don't praise her here, don't praise her at home, don't do it anywhere. Got it?"

My mother steadied her voice. "She medaled at the Classic, in her best event and the all-around. I'd say that's something to be proud of."

"If you're happy with silver and bronze in a national

competition, keep it up. But at this rate, that's all she'll ever be. A national champion."

By the time they returned to the main area, Lou revitalized from the lambasting and my mother drained by it, I was at the head of the runway, ready to go again.

Over the next six hours, my mother didn't say another word. That was the last time she watched me train.

CHAPTER 24

November 2018

The first time I left the country I traveled thirty hours around the world and awoke in a land of sand and steel.

As the airplane descended, the sky dropped out from under us to reveal the deserts of Qatar rippling like an ocean of ground wheat. Then we approached the real sea, the Persian Gulf, and circled over it to prepare for landing. The skyscrapers of Doha stood like soldiers at attention, a metropolis army, a capital city guarding the country at its back.

At the end of our last training session, Lou had taken it upon himself to prepare me for culture shock. "We won't have much time outside the arena, but you need to bring appropriate clothes for when we walk around. It'll be ninety-five degrees, God help us, but you can't show skin from your shoulders to your knees. No shorts, skirts, tank tops, whatever. And none of that legging nonsense, the kind that goes down to your ankles but shows everything along the way. They have a saying in Qatar, 'Leggings aren't pants.' It's not very creative, but I have to say, that's one place I agree with them. I see some girls walking around Cincinnati with their rumps on display and somehow it's my fault when I look. Go figure."

I'd never spent time with Lou outside the gym. He was a hard-ass during training, sometimes downright brutal, but the last thirty some odd hours had exposed a different side of him. While I wouldn't have taken him for a bookworm, he read a paperback thriller for two hours straight. Among other movies, he watched Amy Schumer's *I Feel Pretty* and laughed in brassy bursts at the right spots. When I inhaled a piece of pretzel and was seized by coughing, he got up and returned with a glass of water. He even offered me the window seat.

Then a woman in a burka passed in the aisle and Lou leaned over to whisper in my ear. "Under Sharia law, they still punish adultery with a hundred lashes. I wouldn't wish that on anyone. Not even my ex." He sat up and added from the corner of his mouth, "Though she qualifies for it."

As the plane churned and dropped its wheels over Doha, Lou asked, "Ready?" He sat rigid with his head against its rest. His fingers gripped the armrests—he didn't like to fly. But his irises reached into the corner of his eyes to search mine.

I'd missed all the Worlds that had come before, but now I'd finally been chosen. I was there.

"Ready."

Back when Vanda was the lifeblood of USA Gymnastics, she made all the American team members, coaches, trainers, and security guards board together for a sense (or appearance) of unity. But Lou insisted we rent rooms in a completely different hotel from the rest of the team to eliminate possible distractions. Our accommodations, though cheaper, still looked like a Parisian palace, with a series of rectangular pools leading up to its front door like a water carpet.

"Holy crap," I breathed.

"Makes you feel like you've made it, doesn't it?" Lou said.

Maybe I had.

The man at the front desk printed two key cards for each room, considered me, an eighteen-year-old girl, for a moment, and then handed them all to Lou.

Lou skimmed one off the stack and passed it to me. "I'm keeping one for your room in case you sleep in. I'm not pounding on your door in the hall like an idiot. Now let's hit the sack. You snored on the plane, but I didn't sleep a wink. And tomorrow is a big day."

I'd never stayed in a hotel room by myself. This one was small but lavish, with an upholstered headboard, a gold sateen bed runner, and heavy red-and-gold curtain panels.

I wished my mom were there. She would have said she felt like Arabian royalty. Or my dad. He would have made a corny and inadvertently offensive joke about Aladdin. Joe would have slipped the complimentary robe over his clothes and ordered room service.

I kicked off my sneakers, flopped onto the bed, and stared up at the ceiling, waiting for sleep to spread, but I couldn't relax. Lou was so close. His television murmured through the wall and his faucet opened and closed. And there was that extra key card. I remembered Levett standing in our dorm doorway back at the Balogh Ranch and, later, Matt's face fixed with pleasure. Although Lou had never threatened me sexually, I reconstructed those memories until they fit his shape. I imagined his hands on my thighs, the twist of his expression, and my fingers dug into the duvet at my sides. I was in a separate building from anybody from my organization, and half a world away from those genuinely looking out for my best interests.

If Lou hurt me, I'd have to stop training with him, and there was no one else. I'd never make it to the Olympics.

I got out of bed and dragged an armchair in front of the door.

I WAS AWAKENED by a deep, melodious voice amplified through a loudspeaker outside the hotel. It flitted up and down the scale, regal, like a whale song, as pink light seeped into the sky.

It was proof of how far I'd traveled, farther from home than most people ever went. Like Lou said, I was beginning to feel like I'd made it.

Downstairs, a continental breakfast buffet of yogurt, cheese, pita, beans, olives, and a noodle omelet was spread across white linen. Lou heaped his dish in thick layers.

"Your mother spent months raising funds for this trip. Might as well get her money's worth," he said. I spooned yogurt onto my plate, but when I reached for a pita, Lou's fingers tapped my hand. "Not so fast, Carb Queen."

Lou had already fed me my Adderall along with my morning dose of six Advil, so my hunger would subside, anyway. To satisfy the ceremony of eating, I poured Arabic coffee into a white ceramic cup. It was dark and rich and spiced with cardamom.

As we headed to the arena, we passed families who'd gathered in Aspire Park to picnic and watch their children play. Women were draped in black and men were wrapped in loose white shirts, pants, and ghutras fastened by colorful rope. They mingled like black-and-white chess pieces. I wondered who were the pawns and who were the knights, if they all had personal kings to protect or if they didn't have positions of power at all.

But their game wasn't mine, and I had only enough brain space for one match.

I had two days of podium training to become acquainted with this arena's equipment. Then there were qualifications, followed by team finals, all-around finals, and apparatus finals. If I didn't screw this up, I was likely to walk away with at least a team gold medal, to be part of something exceptional on a world stage. If there wasn't a fluke in my performance, if I stayed inbounds on floor and earned credit for my connections on beam, I could also prove to be one of the best females in the world, all on my own. I could make a name for myself and pencil in a place as one of the four gymnasts competing in the 2020 Summer Olympics.

It was ninety-three degrees out before ten in the morning. By the time we arrived at the arena, I'd already begun to sweat.

GYMNASTICS ARENAS ALL smelled the same: chalk, rubber, perspiration, hair spray, and feet. The echoes of thuds and chatter were the same. The ceilings had the same sprawl. Doha's biodome of equipment, dream-seekers, and their witnesses could have been anywhere and everywhere. Arenas were a world all their own. The only signal that set this one apart was the smattering of gymnasts wearing leos cut lower on the hip.

I'd studied the footage of international competitions and recognized gymnasts warming up on the outskirts of the arena. There was Angelina Melnikova of Russia, a wispy blond star vaulter. There was Ana Padurariu of Canada, an athlete with a kind face and braces who swept Elite Canada 2017 in all-around and every individual event. There was

Chen Yile of China, whose beam performance was impressively fluid. And Liu Tingting, also of China, whose routine was riddled with mixed combinations.

And then, in their own private group on the edge of the venue floor, there were the other four young women selected from Team USA, wearing the same red-white-and-blue outfit I wore, going through the motions of our national team warm-up: Simone Biles, all four feet, eight inches of compact power that took her to heights normally fueled by an engine, the very emblem of our sport, renowned worldwide, whose acrobatics defied all reason, and who, at twenty-one, could perform movements most other gymnasts wouldn't dare attempt. Morgan Hurd, an adorable seventeen-year-old who wore thick-framed glasses, even during competitions; her strength was beam. Grace McCallum, a sixteen-year-old new to the senior team, who was consistent across all events. And Riley McCusker, a seventeen-year-old from New Jersey who must have been made of neoprene—the previous year she'd bounced back from an ankle injury, a wrist injury, and landing on her neck in an international competition. I'd met them all at the Balogh Ranch and at various championships over the years, but this was the first time we'd be in on an effort together. I walked faster, eager to join them. I was part of the team; I should be part of the team warm-up. Lou hurried to keep pace.

"Don't get too chummy," he said under his breath.

Morgan's legs were straight ahead of her in a pike stretch,

and her cheek rested on her knees so her mouth faced the other girls. "I have to get one of those bone-density tests. I'm afraid I have the mass measurement of a menopausal woman."

Simone orbited her arm to stretch her left shoulder. Her smile was straight out of a Crest whitening toothpaste commercial. I wondered if the company had approached her for sponsorship. "Fitness is bad for your health."

Riley straddled her legs and folded her upper body to wrap her hands around her left foot. "It'll be worth it when we are Playtex spokeswomen."

I stood, a bit awkwardly, over them, unsure how to meld into their group with Lou looming behind me. I thought of that moment in CVS and leapt to exchange it as common currency. "I wouldn't even know what to say about a tampon."

Simone's eyes tapered like a tiger's and glimmered with something mischievous. "Or where to put it."

I began to shrug off my warm-up jacket and debated admitting to Simone that, when I'd referred to her as the GOAT, the greatest of all time, my father had said, "Do they call her that because she's short, sturdy, and acclimated to high altitude?"

But before I could decide, Lou said, "Nice to see you ladies. Best of luck." Then he clutched my upper arm, now free of one sleeve, and steered me across the arena. He didn't stop until there were several countries between us: girls from Germany, Mexico, and Brazil.

I shrugged him off. "What the hell was that?"

"I told you not to get chummy. Sometimes I think you've got a hearing problem. Be civil all you like. Fake friendship, even. The cameras eat that crap up. But there's no point getting to know them personally. They are your opponents. The dumbest thing you could do is start to like them. You haven't worked this hard and flown across the world so you can make friends. You could have gone to summer camp for that. You're here to be a champion. Am I wrong?" I rolled my eyes in the way that comes naturally to a teenage girl. He repeated, more sternly, "Am I wrong?"

I'd already had one friend in gymnastics, and look where that got me. Maybe it was better to remain strangers until the moment we were made to look as family, all adorably biting down on gold.

"No," I said. "You aren't wrong."

"Good. So focus. Warm up here, alone, without distractions."

While I warmed up, Lou scoped out the competition. "Look there. Her form is strong but her skills are basic. And there, her skills are impressive but sloppy. She gets no height. She keeps stepping out of bounds. She just fell off the beam three times in a row. That isn't bad luck. That's just bad. I don't want you getting a big head, Sera, but looking around here, I'll just say this: keep your cool and do what you came to do."

I suppressed a smile in the midst of my jumping jacks and began the journey of sinking inside myself.

Yamilet Pena from the Dominican Republic approached the head of the vault runway. She'd been attempting the Produnova vault in world competitions for seven years. She underrotated it at the 2012 Olympics, but finally landed it—just barely—at the 2015 Pan American Games, earning the first ever medal in gymnastics for her country. Nobody had executed this skill expertly—a handspring into a tucked forward double salto—since Elena Produnova herself in 1999, the year I was born.

Yamilet sprinted toward the vault and launched into a handspring. Once her fingers touched the leather, she tucked and spun once, twice, landed with deeply bent knees, and stepped back for balance. She was twenty-five years old, ancient for the sport, and despite so many public disappointments, she was still determined to perfect this incredibly difficult skill.

Lou tapped his watch to indicate I was done with my jumping jacks. "You better hope she falls when it counts."

My coach had three goals for Worlds: for Team USA to win gold, for me to get silver or gold on the bars, and to medal on the all-around. That would require me to land the double twisting double back.

"You hungry?" he asked as I chalked my hands at the uneven bar station. I shook my head. "That's my girl."

The bar responded to my weight with more give than Lou's equipment did. I measured the bounce, dropped to my feet, calculated how this might affect my releases, and then began from the top.

My uneven bars routine incorporated several skills named after renowned gymnasts: Houry Gebeshian, an American-born gymnast who represented Armenia at the Olympics in Rio; Mohini Bhardwaj, an Indian American who competed in the 2004 Olympics in Athens; Natalia Shaposhnikova, a Soviet-era gymnast who competed in the 1980 Moscow Games; and Aliya Mustafina, a Russian who won consecutive all-around medals in the 2012 and 2016 Olympics. The routine was an homage to women before me who had worked hard and were so relentless and inventive they left their mark on the sport forever. I adopted their movements and made them my own.

I began with the Gebeshian, a flashy D-value hecht mount. I worried it was in poor taste to incorporate someone's eponymous skill so soon after they competed with it themselves, but Lou said, "There's no patent. You'll regret being so damn chivalrous when you aren't on the podium. You have this skill, and you've got to use everything in your arsenal."

So I started with fireworks: I ran toward the bars, jumped on the springboard, propelled up and over the low bar, spiraled like a football, and grabbed the high bar. Such a strong opening excited the crowd and the judges, got them sitting a little taller. And most importantly, it earned me 0.4 points, right off the bat. Then came some pirouettes for the compositional requirement. A big swooping backward giant. A stalder element, where I straddled my legs and piked my body as I swung around the bar, adding a half turn on my hands. A piked Jaeger, swinging backward into a somersault and grabbing the bar in the opposite direction. Then the Bhardwaj: from a handstand on the high bar, I swung forward, released, transitioned to the low bar, turned 360 degrees in the air, and froze into a handstand on the low bar. From the handstand, I went directly into the Shaposhnikova: I flipped my lower body down so my hip touched the bar, circled around it, pushed, and flew back to grab the high bar again. There I added a few more flights and flourishes before finishing with my big dismount—the Mustafina, or as my father and brother referred to it, the big Mufasa: a double back tucked salto with a one-and-a-half twist. It was my biggest bar skill, an E value, worth half a point on its own. I landed on the mat in chair position.

"Not bad," Lou said. "But you were cautious. You looked like you didn't trust the equipment or yourself. From the top."

Lou had me repeat the routine six times. By the end, my palms screamed, my joints ached, my muscles were fatigued—and there was a gymnast and her coach waiting on the sidelines for the apparatus, growing impatient.

Lou put his hands on my shoulders, as if to impart personal advice. "You're getting clumsy."

"Because I'm tired. And my feet hurt." Plantar fasciitis was causing stabbing pain in my heel.

"Bullshit. You're thinking about your new friends getting mad because you're making them wait. That's why I didn't want you chatting with them. Or you're thinking about lunch or the fact that this is your first international competition. I need that junk cleared. Did you take your pill this morning?"

I sighed. "Yes."

"Seems like it's time for another."

I followed him to where my gym bag was stowed. He handed me a bottle of water, which I gulped. Then he hunched over the bag, fished a pill from where we'd stored them in an Altoids case, and palmed me one. Taking prescribed Adderall was legal in podium training, and yet I faked a yawn, slipped it onto my tongue, and swallowed.

After a short break while we waited for the girl who'd hijacked the apparatus to finish, and another warm-up, we returned to the bars, and then moved onto the floor. We stayed in the dome long after the other gymnasts left to eat, rest, call home, or walk around Doha. We stayed until we were the only two remaining.

After my sixth pass on the floor—including a double twisting front layout, a double twisting double back, an Arabian double front to leap combo, and a Tsukahara—my legs trembled under the weight of my own body. I just wanted to lie down, to let my blood course horizontally for a while. I didn't trust myself to stand, never mind perform acrobatics.

I finally said the obvious. "Everyone else left. You said

yourself that I can do what I came to do, that most other girls aren't as good as me."

"You're better than other girls because you're the last in the gym. And some people work harder than you. Look at Yamilet. Still trying after all these years. If you work hard now, maybe you won't have to work as long as she has. Or are you a quitter? Jennifer thought you were. USA Gymnastics thought you were. Your daddy hoped you were. Are you?"

"No."

"So let's go. From the top."

IT TOOK ELEVEN trips to the hotel ice machine to fill the bathtub. By the last round, I seriously considered curling up in the corner of the hall closet to nap and gather energy before embarking on the long journey back to my room. The full ice bucket felt to my biceps like a boulder.

I'd gotten used to a lot of physical discomfort: blood blisters, beam crotch, bone spurs, floor burn, ingrown toenails, pulled muscles, stress fractures, shin splints, worn cartilage, torn skin. But lowering my body into frosty water never got easier. I had to amp myself up for it, and once my routine began, there was no stopping. Otherwise I would never have gone through with it. I would have quit every time.

I created a playlist titled "Ice Water of Death," featuring Eminem's "Lose Yourself," Godsmack's "I Stand Alone," and

Kanye's "Power." At home or at the gym, I turned the stereo up to full volume. I needed an overwhelming sensory experience of sound to drown out my sense of touch. At the hotel, I slipped in wireless earbuds.

As soon as the keyboard tinkered its notes, I swung my arms back and forth. When the guitar strummed its beat, I rolled my neck. While Eminem began his narration, I sucked air in and exhaled it in three spurts. By the time Eminem was rapping, I was jogging beside the tub, eyeing the floating cubes, imagining them as other gymnasts—better gymnasts. Or the Baloghs. Or Eddie. Or Lou. Or my own weakness. At the words "time's up, over," I stepped into the liquid nightmare, dropped into a sitting position, and splayed fully horizontal. I wailed as the drums kicked in. And after a beat, I began hyperventilating.

The playlist was perfectly timed. As the music faded in the last song, I scurried out of the tub and wrapped myself in a robe. More often than not, tears were streaming down my face. That evening in Qatar, after a grueling day of training, the warmth of my tears felt almost comforting.

As THE DELUXE hotel mattress lulled me to sleep, my phone dinged and the faces of my family in their respective locations—Mom at the kitchen table, Dad in his break room, Joe outside school—populated my screen.

My mother had applied makeup and positioned the phone in a complimentary downward angle. "Our Arabian princess!"

My father held the phone at his lap so we got a clear shot up his nose. "Are you having fun? What's the food like?"

Joe admired himself in his own box and steered a stray hair back into its swoop. "What are the other girls like?"

I didn't feel like a princess, I hadn't sampled much of the food, and I wasn't allowed to talk to the girls. Before I could attempt to answer their questions, my father lobbed another in my direction, this one aimed more directly.

"How are you feeling?" he asked.

My feet throbbed. My hands ached. Every movement sent a different flash of hurt down my limbs.

"Good."

I looked around my empty room and imagined how I'd feel less lonely if my mother was at the edge of my bed, rubbing my feet, or leafing through my bag, making sure I'd packed everything I'd need for the next day; if my father was in the armchair, reading a history book; if Joe was leaning against the pillow beside me, flipping through channels. I imagined how much easier it would be to face another few days of intense physical challenges, and how much more excited I'd be about the possibility of victory if I'd get to share it with them, the three people who had been there all along, who'd sacrificed, celebrated with me, and tolerated my bad behavior. The three people who mattered.

And because I wanted to say at least one true thing to them, I said, "I wish I wasn't so far away."

"Oh, honey," my father said, and my mother flicked her thumb across her nose.

Joe's attention centered back on my box. "Wait, where are you?" And before I could cry, I laughed.

WHAT DID THE best gymnast in the world look like? My mother, apparently, knew.

Each piece of makeup was fixed with a label indicating the order of application along with a helpful tip. "#3 Blush. Swipe up your cheekbones with the big brush until you look like you've finished a warm-up. If it looks like a workout, you've gone too far." And: "#5 Eyeliner. Dot between lashes to make them look fuller. You have your father's thin stubs." Then: "#7 Lipstick. Trace on, blot, and bring along for reapplication before show time."

The hair products were labeled in the same way. I tied a high ponytail using a scrunchie that matched my performance leo. With growing conviction, I pinned and clasped and sprayed. Then I creamed and powdered, penciled and dabbed. I didn't stop until I looked in the mirror and saw a world champion.

OUR HARD WORK in podium training paid off. I was performing strong in the qualification rounds. My lines were graceful, my landings were steady, my skills were clean and confident. The crowd cheered after each apparatus, and the judges smiled and nodded in my direction, betraying as much approval as they were allowed. Their deductions were fair and minimal. I held my breath while they tallied each score, and when the numbers displayed on the board, I grabbed Lou's hand and we raised it in a united fist. That demonstration of camaraderie wasn't for show. I felt close to him. We were going to make it.

With the vault, uneven bars, and balance beam behind me, I only had to perform well on floor and I'd move on to the finals. Even if I didn't make the Olympics, god forbid, at least I'd have an international medal. And maybe, just maybe, the fourteen-thousand-dollar prize that could pay down my mother's not-so-secret credit card debt.

When it was my turn, my stomach fluttered so furiously, I thought I'd either puke out winged insects or take flight myself. Before I even made my trek into the center of the arena, my heart rate was high and my breathing shallow. Lou noticed. He pointed my chin in his direction, ensuring, at least for the moment, that I saw only him—not the ten thousand fans, not the apparatuses, not the judges, not the other gymnasts, not the Jumbotron where our huddle was being captured, magnified, and illuminated—only him. His forehead dipped into mine and his voice was low but robust enough that I heard him above the clangor of the arena.

"You made it this far. You've shown that you're one of the best in this room, halfway around the globe. One of the best in the world. You've done the work. The hard part is behind you. Just finish it."

Lou wasn't a born cheerleader. He wouldn't say those things for encouragement alone. He really believed I could medal— that I was talented and capable. If he believed it, I did too.

I stepped up onto the floor and the stands swelled to welcome me. I pasted a performance smile across my face, still covered in the glitter and makeup that I'd painted on to look like a doll. The American Girl Gymnast, who was patriotic, agreeable, talented, and thrilled to be there. That was me. They couldn't see what was going on inside me: nerves, exhaustion, pressure. They couldn't see the dishonorable things I'd done.

The crowd settled as I fixed myself into position on the sideline, striking my pose, arms draped overhead, hip cocked. A marionette that came alive only at the sound of music. And I did. As the drums thumped over the sound system, I animated. My routine began with a series of ornamental dance moves. I grinned all the while, like dancing was my favorite thing rather than a means to an end. Then I stalled for a beat, took a breath, and flung myself into my first tumbling pass—the debut of my double twisting double back tuck on a world stage.

I started with a roundoff into back handspring for momentum. It all depended on how I propelled off that landing.

As my feet planted and launched me back into the air, it felt like slipping your foot into a shoe that knows your shape. I'd hit the exact degree of rotation and was careening toward the necessary height. I was going to fit the movement into my time in the air. I was going to nail this challenging skill in front of everybody. After this pass, the rest of the routine was a cakewalk.

As my feet returned to earth, relief glittered like stars on my skin. My arms flew up beside my ears to catch the landing.

My right leg gave out, as if somebody had struck my calf with a baseball bat. For a second, that's how I processed the feeling. I was convinced an angry fan or another gymnast had attacked me, a Nancy Kerrigan bashing, committed in public. I expected the crowd to react to the assault, for Lou to pounce. But no one was behind me. No one was anywhere close.

I tried to hold my smile as I proceeded, confused, with my routine. My right foot stepped aside for a dance flourish. But as my weight came down on the foot, my leg collapsed. There was no pain, no signal of my body's malfunction. I just sank.

The crowd gasped.

Lou was on the cusp of coming to the floor. His features were lifted. He was waiting for my signal. Did I need him?

I grasped my calf, my ankle, my foot, but my body didn't respond with sharpness, or even an ache. My mind scrambled to make sense of this. There was no explanation. I splayed my palms on the floor and lifted myself onto my left foot first. Fine. Everything was fine. I could still finish my routine, might even be able to manage my way into the finals. I stood tall and was met with uncertain applause. The crowd didn't understand what was going on either. I assembled my features, repositioned my smile. The music had continued on to a different part of the song. The beat wouldn't match my movement. More deductions. But I couldn't worry about that. I just had to finish.

I resumed my pose, as if I'd landed my big tumble without incident. I again stepped out with my right foot. Take two. But it was like having a cooked noodle for a leg. I crashed to my knee. The crowd expressed concern and, through tears, I lifted my head to Lou, to wordlessly tell him *Yes, yes, I need you*. But he was already on his way.

He was on all fours beside me. I smelled the false spruce of his aftershave. "What happened?"

My body had failed me, and at the worst moment. I felt betrayed, humiliated, and afraid. "I don't know."

He massaged my calf from my heel to just behind my knee, probing, tenderly at first, and then, when I didn't wince, more firmly. "Did you feel a snap? A pull?"

"I don't think so. I don't know. Maybe."

His hand stilled on my calf and his face set. He'd found something; it was a somber diagnosis. "Let's get you off the floor."

"What is it? Can I finish the routine? Can I still make the finals?"

"Let's get you off the floor," he said. Then he looped my arm around his neck and hoisted me to my good foot.

I imagined my family, under blankets on our couch in the

living room seven thousand miles away, clutching coffees because it was five in the morning their time, now on the edge of the cushions, gaping at the Worlds broadcast they'd paid extra to access, watching their daughter limp offstage, unable to help, unable even to find out what was wrong. The idea of their worry, their powerlessness, spilled my self-pity over the edge.

"You're still on camera and nobody likes a crier. They want to see a courageous athlete. Save the bellyaching for the room," Lou said through a smile that resembled a grimace.

Thousands of strangers watched my exit. Many stood to get a better look. I lifted my free hand and waved. At my gesture, others rose to their feet and cheered.

"That's better," Lou said.

But I didn't feel like a courageous athlete. A titan. A David or a Goliath. I felt like a child. Something was wrong with me. Something terrible had happened out there, and I didn't know what. I wasn't comforted by Lou and the thousands of supportive strangers who didn't speak my language. I wanted to be home, in Indiana. I wanted my mother. My father. My brother. I wanted to hear that I was okay.

We stepped carefully off the platform. The other Team USA gymnasts were waiting on the sidelines, their expressions the perfect carvings of concern and friendship. I wondered if they were sincere. They touched my back and issued words of encouragement: "You got this" and "It's going to be okay." I was sure the camera loved it. This was what a team looked like, and appearances were all that mattered.

The arena's doctor, an Arab man in a long white shirt with an identifying badge hanging from a lanyard, joined us en route to the exit. He braced my other side through a door that led to the private athletes' area, equipped with benches, massage tables, and lockers.

As they set me on a bench, the doctor lowered to a knee, reached for my leg, paused, and asked permission with his eyes, an intentional look that said, *May I?* I nodded.

"Hold it right there," Lou said, and when the doctor didn't respond fast enough, he stepped forward. "Do I need to say it in Swahili?"

The doctor lifted his palms, as if backing away from a growling animal. "I just want to take a look at the injury. Treat her, if I can."

"She ruptured her Achilles. There's nothing for you to do here."

"Would you like me to arrange transportation to a hospital?"

"I don't mean there's nothing for you to do here," he said, pointing to the floor. "I mean there's nothing for you to do here," he continued, with grand sweeping gestures. "We're flying home so she can see a qualified orthopedic surgeon. Not some towelhead who has never seen a woman's bare leg before. No thank you."

The doctor's eyes narrowed. "That is very offensive, sir."

Lou scoffed and looked to me for backup. My gaze fell to my loose calf that was no longer connected to my heel. An Achilles rupture. My dream was just given a death sentence. No, it had already died, back there on the floor. I'd just dragged its corpse off the battlefield.

Lou crossed his bulky arms over his chest. "We have an emergency here and all this guy cares about is what's politically correct. And somehow I'm the asshole?"

MY MOTHER WAS hysterical when I finally answered her call on the ride to the hotel.

"I'll never miss another competition as long as you are in this sport. You will never be alone again," she promised. And then, when I told her what Lou suspected, she said, "An Achilles rupture? Oh dear God. This doesn't change anything for 2020, does it?"

I pulled the phone away from my ear and her questions carried like tiny mouths squawking around our heads in the backseat. Lou turned away from me and peered out the window, like he was already searching for something, somebody, else. Tears clustered in a ball at the base of my throat. My ankle was propped up on the seat beside me, wrapped in an Ace bandage. My own body had become my worst enemy.

My father's voice emitted through the speaker next. "Just come home. We'll figure everything out when you're home."

Joe didn't call. He sent animal videos: a monkey sticking its finger into its rear, sniffing it, and falling off its branch; a golden retriever getting hit in the face with a series of tennis balls it failed to catch; a turtle having sex with a sneaker. Then a text that read: It's just another roadblock. You eat roadblocks for breakfast, with a side of egg whites.

By the time I left for the airport, my roadblock was swelling.

I traveled to Indiana for thirty hours knowing my Achilles tendon was coiling up inside my calf, shriveling with every passing minute, making a successful surgery more and more difficult. Last-minute flight changes cost us thousands of dollars, but the orthopedic specialist in Indianapolis said the price of waiting could be much higher.

I couldn't concentrate on the in-flight entertainment. Instead, I scrolled through Achilles tendon forums and scoured articles about the injury, surgery, and rehabilitation. Four weeks immobilized with foot elevated. No running or jumping for six months. Full recovery was likely at nine months, but not guaranteed. Some patients said it was more like a year. Some swore they were never the same.

My eyelids were fat and my nasal passages were undammed. I sniffled and hiccupped and made weak attempts to mop my wet mess. I was supposed to be a world champion, and an Olympian in a year and a half. Now I'd never be the same. Other passengers must have assumed we were on our way to a funeral. And that's just what it felt like: grief.

Lou's heavy hand moved as if to drop onto mine, but then it returned to his own lap. "You gave it your best shot. You can be proud of that."

My breath shuddered. "So it's over then? After everything?"

He sighed again and his lips thinned as he considered me. Overhead, the seatbelt light chimed and illuminated; we were heading for turbulence.

"What do you want me to say? You want me to lie to you? You'll never be in Olympic shape by the Trials. An Achilles injury is a bitch. So is life. I'm sorry this happened, but it did, and we have to accept it and move on."

Move on to what? There was only my Olympic dream and subsequent fame to get my family out of debt. There was nothing else.

He continued, "The rest of the American girls could still pull off a team medal. You'll get one for participating in prelims. So there. You'll finish your career with a Worlds medal. That ain't too shabby."

I yanked my sweatshirt sleeves over my hands and dropped forward onto the tray table to bury my face in my arms and cry in the most private way I had available.

"For Christ's sake," Lou said. "You're stronger than this. Get a grip."

But I didn't need to be strong anymore. There was no benefit to gym face. There were no judges to impress. I could just cry and cry and cry. Lou's next exhale grated over the scalloped edges of his throat.

"Miracles happen. You never know. Maybe you'll be an exception. A girl wonder."

CHAPTER 25

Mist swirled through my mind and clouds passed over my vision. Was I spinning? Maybe. I leaned into the movement; I might as well enjoy the ride. Because when it cleared, when the smog settled into the ground, it revealed a tremendous monster of pain in the distance. It had hulking muscles. A glistening flank. It panted through flared nostrils. It smelled animal. Without the haze between us, it saw me. I heard the stomping of its hooves. I watched it grow large. When it neared, it reared its ugly head and roared in my face.

Pills. Is it time for more pills?

Almost, sweetie. Hold on.

I held on by my teeth.

My lower half was pinned so I moved by clawing. I spoke in grunts and moans. My mouth was parched. The pills scraped like stones. But then red faded back into gray blue. The bed became softer; it cradled me.

His face appeared before mine and his fingers traced my hairline. His mustache moved and said, *I know you're in pain. I know you're miserable. But you're home. I'm glad you're home.*

Got to keep it elevated. She adjusted the pillow beneath my foot and peered inside my cast. *Looks clean. Shouldn't get infected. That'd be just what we need.*

Minutes lasted hours. Hours lasted days. Days lasted weeks. And I was contained within the world of my room. I grew sick of opening my eyes and seeing the same shadows play on the same walls. That shade of pink lavender. I was a prisoner of my own body. A hostage to blood flow, elevation, and tendon loading. So I closed my eyes. I slept.

When I awoke, the remaining leaves had surrendered their grip on the trees outside my window. Whether by the battering of a rainstorm or by graceful, voluntary pirouetting, I didn't know. I'd missed it. The pain had subsided—at least there was that. But one thing remained agonizingly the same: I was still in bed.

IN GREEK MYTHOLOGY, Achilles was a demigod, son of the goddess Thetis and Peleus, a mortal king. When he was a child, his mother held him by his foot and dipped him into the river Styx, causing him to be invincible everywhere but his unbaptized heel, where his mother's hand had been.

Why didn't she fully immerse him? Did she think there should always be one part of a man left defenseless? Or was she afraid that if his foot was wet, she'd lose her grip and drown her child while trying to make him invulnerable to death?

Achilles grew up to be one of the great fighters of the Trojan War. But when an arrow struck him in the only place he was susceptible, he couldn't survive the wound and died.

I too was in the midst of a Greek battle when I was struck in the heel. I too feared I might die—of boredom, as I lazily watched all the shows I'd been too busy to watch when training: *The Handmaid's Tale, This Is Us, Ozark*. I was supposed to get lost in the conflict of the characters—ceremonial rape, infertility, oppression; family drama, racial inequality, obesity; drug trafficking, murder, theft. I was supposed to care. But even though the laptop was propped on my stomach, it was hard to see beyond my own foot. Hard to see through the thickness of my own melancholy.

I feared I might die by accident, forgetting when I took my last dose of oxycodone, or by mixing it with Adderall, opiate versus stimulant. My doctor, my parents, and Lou all agreed I should lay off the Adderall. What was the point if I wasn't training? What need did I have for increased focus lounging on my bed at noon on a weekday, when my most complex task involved shifting from my mattress to my knee scooter and rolling to the bathroom? But Adderall suppressed my appetite, and if I wasn't exercising, I didn't want to eat. I didn't want to spend three months letting my ass expand around me. Because as soon as I could, I was getting back in the gym. Everyone was acting like my Olympic training was over. Like the book had closed on that story. My father was already talking about a return to school, to youth group. Suggesting other hobbies. Wondering if it wasn't too late to apply to colleges. Joe was trying to transfer to a school on the East Coast; maybe a change of scenery would do me good too. Even my mom ventured in strained optimism to ask me: "Hypothetically, if you weren't a gymnast, what would you be?"

But I couldn't let go. If I did, I feared I might die on purpose. Because if I'd spent thirteen years pursuing this one goal, sacrificing all other interests, friends, and education, if I'd kept my mouth shut about what happened to Lucy and compelled my father to drink, if I'd driven an irrevocable wedge in my parents' marriage, if I'd spent all their money, if I'd forced them to prioritize their daughter over their son, if I'd damaged my body with merciless training, if I'd stunted my own growth, if I'd squandered my childhood, all for nothing, for an injury that was arbitrary, if I'd gotten this close and lost it all by shit luck alone, then life was too painful, too unfair to bear, and I feared I'd spill a pile of oxycodone and Adderall pills into my palm, empty them into my upturned mouth, swallow them dry, and ride the swell of their high to a different place, a different story, a different me. Because if I gave up on this dream, as far as I could see, there'd be no reason to stick around. Surely I'd have to give up on everything else too.

AUTUMN WAS A memory, and still I couldn't walk. I'd spent Thanksgiving, Christmas, and New Year's stationed in different corners of my house with my foot propped on pillows and wrapped in ice. My mother was tired of waiting on me. When I asked for things—a glass of water, a magazine, the remote—she mm-hmmed in lieu of words. And I knew what that meant. But her apathy was just as well. I couldn't rely on anybody. I had to put myself back together. The clock was ticking.

My cast transitioned into a boot with lifts. Then the lifts were removed. I swung on two crutches, then hobbled on one. Then I used a cane. It took a lifetime, but now, in the beginning of January, I ditched the accessories altogether: it was just my foot and me. I'd lost muscle definition all over but especially in my injured calf, which had shriveled to the point of looking embarrassed of itself. I limped because my tendon was weak and sore and didn't remember how to support my weight. I limped because I was scared it would tear again at any moment, setting me even further back in the race for gold. But I wouldn't limp for long.

I missed the smell of the gym and the feel of leather and rubber beneath my bare feet. I missed sprinting, knowing such speed would lead to flying. I missed being upside down.

I missed the pride of new calluses—my hands were softening by the minute. I missed the adrenaline of achieving something after so much failure. I missed exhaustion. I missed knowing I was different.

And I was afraid that under all this missing was the awareness that I'd never experience the pleasures of my calling again.

"It smells like sweaty hand grips in here."

Her hair was a sandy shade of brown, a professional dye job that made it appear sun-kissed. Her sweatshirt collar was cut into a boatneck to fall around her shoulders and her jeans were ripped at the knees. She looked tan, although Vancouver wasn't known for its tropics, and healthy.

I wasn't sure I'd ever see her again, never mind have her stand in my bedroom. I nearly dropped the fifteen-pound dumbbells I was pressing over my head.

I imagined this eddy of nerves and excitement and hope was what other girls felt when they saw a boy they loved. It seemed so clear then. So clear, plaintive, and true. My friend had been the love of my life.

"Lucy." The weights thudded against the rug and I searched for follow-up words. "Hi."

"Your Instagram posts were getting pretty dark. After the fourth Inkwell filter in a row, I figured you could use some human interaction."

I had everything and nothing to say. "How's Canada?"

Her posture softened, perhaps grateful for an innocuous subject. "It's exactly what Indiana isn't, which is a lot. People have all different experiences and aren't afraid to talk about them. And really talk about them, not the whole Midwestern thing of waiting until someone leaves and just talking about them behind their backs."

Did Lucy talk about me behind my back? "That's great."

She tugged on the hem of her sweatshirt and chewed her bottom lip. "How are you?"

I tried to smile, but the effort it took made my eyes water. "Inkwell filter."

"Once you climb out of this mopey pit, you'll realize your injury is the weirdest kind of gift. Now you're free from the jaws of the Olympic industrial complex. Your filters will be vibrant in no time. Who knows, maybe even Juno."

So that's why she was here. She thought we were both former gymnasts, that we had something new in common. With her close by, I felt like a human snow globe: glitter suspended inside me like magic dust. But I couldn't bring myself to agree with her, because joining Lucy would mean giving up on me. I loved her, but there was still the Wheeler dream. And I didn't understand why I couldn't have it all, why my loves couldn't coexist. I pushed my hands into the mattress and shifted my position.

"I'll be ready for the Trials," I said, although just that

morning, when I craved a smoothie, the idea of descending the stairs was so daunting that I slurped water from the bathroom sink.

"It took me a while to accept that USA Gymnastics damaged me too," she said.

I lowered my voice and addressed my feet. "That was different."

An eyebrow jumped and she spoke like she meant to provoke me. "Because I'd been abused?"

"Well, yeah."

"A demented doctor may never have stuck his bare finger up you, but that doesn't mean you haven't been abused." She tempered the charge from her tone. "You know, all those years when he was touching me, I had phantom bone aches and irritable bowel syndrome so bad I had three different colonoscopies to test for Crohn's disease. My body was telling me something my brain didn't know yet. I can't say what your training is like with Lou Gently, but don't you think this might be your body's way of saying enough is enough?"

After three years, she was with me again; I couldn't dismiss her outright. "I don't know. Maybe."

I glanced at the trophies and medals on my dresser. Lucy had a matching set, once anyway; I didn't know where they were now that they had been tarnished by Eddie's filth and the neglect of so many USA Gymnastics officials. By my own fingerprints, even.

Somewhere downstairs, the elephant in the room was still following my mother around, scraping the walls for bark and shitting on the living room rug. It had been taking up space in our lives for years now and would stay with us until my mother acknowledged that she'd been wrong about Eddie and Lucy and named her part in what happened. At this rate, it would be with us forever, eating at our dinner table, standing in the background of Christmas photos, and cheering from the stands of gymnastics competitions.

I didn't want to become so accustomed to elephant stench that I couldn't smell it anymore. I didn't want to be like my mother.

Lucy's presence, a kindness all its own, was an opportunity I might not get again. This was my chance to plow through the thicket of guilt that had been growing wild inside me since the moment I betrayed her. This would be more difficult than any competition; the judgment of a friend was the harshest deduction. My instinct was to retreat into gym face, but she'd see that I wasn't there behind my frigid expression. She had to see me for the torn blister I was.

"While we're on the subject of Eddie and USA Gymnastics and everything, I never said what I should have said, which is that I'm really sorry. I should have heard you. I think about it almost every day and it makes me sick that I didn't believe you, or that I wanted us to keep doing what we were doing more than I wanted to believe you. You were right. I should have told Vanda that day, and anybody else you wanted me to tell. I should have been a better friend. This apology is years overdue, and I'm sorry for that too."

Lucy fixed her attention above my head, where a ten-year-old Shawn Johnson poster deteriorated on my wall. I wondered if she was remembering how we used to rehearse our Olympic interviews. I wanted to say, *We were such good friends then. I may never have another friend like that in my life. Please forgive me and let us be friends again.*

Her lips tensed. "Thanks for apologizing."

I longed for her to continue, to tell me it was okay, that she understood. There was a gaping hole where her absolution wasn't. I rushed to fill it with words. "But maybe you can start feeling better about gymnastics. The sport is moving forward. Everybody who was bad is out. Levett is in jail, the camp was shut down, the Baloghs are being investigated, the board resigned. Steve Penny was arrested. The USOC is trying to shut down USA Gymnastics. Things are different."

Her stare dropped to me, and her voice was hushed, like she was breaking bad news. "Look at you, Sera. You're lying there broken but begging for more. It isn't different. Elite gymnastics hasn't changed one bit."

CHAPTER 26

May 2019

March's days were short and dark and the nights were icy and darker. Winter's cold grip on our calendar was so tight and stubborn it delayed spring. It was almost May when the crocuses cracked through the frozen ground. And, like the blooms, my recovery was behind schedule. I was no girl wonder. Seven months out from my injury, I was jogging four miles around our neighborhood and had worked up to twenty calf raises on my injured leg, but I hesitated to jump side to side. I hesitated to jump at all, terrified my tendon might snap like an overstretched rubber band and I'd be back to where I was in November, at the beginning of winter, gaping into the mouth of darkness.

USA Gymnastics hired a new director of sports medicine to manage the team's doctors, physical therapists, and trainers. His appointment was mysteriously terminated after one day.

It was just over a year until the Trials.

I'd devoted all my free time to studying for my GED. In a month or two, I'd take the tests and be done with high school. I was in occasional, hopeful contact with Lucy. I texted her a photo of a red tulip with the color contrast turned way up, to which she replied, Oh good. You've gone from depressed to manic. She sent me an article about the NCAA gymnast who dislocated both knees during a floor routine at regionals and subsequently became a viral sensation, and was now beginning a structural analyst career at Boeing. Any interest in airplanes? she wrote.

I had to get back to the gym and ease into the movements of my craft, movements that had once felt as natural as breathing but would now be like juggling swords. I'd start small—split leap, aerial cartwheel, glide kip. Although I could handle training such basic skills at any community gym, I needed someone to oversee me who would ensure I wasn't pushing too hard too fast, or worse, succumbing to my trepidation; I needed someone to push me the way Vanda had when she forced me back on the beam after I'd crotched it.

I needed Lou.

IT WAS THE first warm day of the season when I pulled into the parking lot of Champion Gym in Cincinnati, and the sun was like an encouraging hand on my arm as I headed toward the front door. I was nervous, but I also felt more capable than I had in a long time. It was good to be at the beginning of something, to be at the starting line rather than miles behind it. Today was just a conversation, a plan. But I'd pulled my hair back and worn a practice leo underneath my warm-ups just in case he wanted to go through some motions. Thanks to a strict diet of one thousand calories per day, usually in the form of celery and arugula, my gymnastics clothes still fit, which I accepted as a small miracle. Sure, everything was softer—my thighs, my arms, my back—but muscles had memory.

Lou was running alongside a girl strapped in a harness, about to enter a tumbling pass on the floor. His eyes flicked up at my arrival and then returned to his subject, just in time for her to spring into a back layout with a one-and-a-half twist into a front layout. It hardly seemed like she needed the support. They must have been finessing form. Her small frame was encased in an emerald practice leo. I recognized her from a national competition the previous year. She was young. A junior.

When she landed, she struck a sassy pose: her arms around her ears ending in gently flicked wrists. Lou patted her upper back and headed in my direction, walking with a gait I could only describe as reluctant. I endeavored to look cheery, to construct an irresistible expression.

"What are you doing here?" he asked.

I propped my hands on my hips. "Surprised to see me?"

"Yes. That's why I asked what you're doing here."

Since his expression wasn't lifted by my girlish act, I straightened and held my hands before me, just short of supplication. "I thought we could talk about getting back to training."

His tongue bulged behind his bottom lip. When he spoke, it sounded as if he were carefully doling out his words. "You don't need me. You need a college application and an NCAA coach. Why don't you call that blond cookie you used to work with?"

"I don't want college gymnastics. I want the real thing."

His exhale was audible. "You really don't listen if someone is saying something you don't want to hear."

"You don't have to believe I can do it. I'll pay you. Consider it a job."

"Other girls pay me too. Girls who actually have a shot," he said, tilting his head back in the direction of his junior.

The girl was straddle stretching, her belly resting comfortably on the floor before her. She looked tiny, a child; even if she was going to be sixteen by the end of the following year, she wasn't Tokyo material.

I whispered, "She won't be ready for 2020."

Lou folded his arms over his thick chest and stood a little taller—he didn't like people criticizing his athletes. That was his job.

"Neither will you. And you sure as hell won't be around for 2024. She, on the other hand, still has mileage left in her."

"But I'm not ready to retire," I said.

His head angled. "You didn't retire, Sera. You expired."

I couldn't cry in front of that bastard. He didn't deserve to see how he'd destroyed my last shreds of hope, my only remaining purpose. Hell, he didn't deserve to train me.

But if he didn't, no one would. It was over. Tokyo, the Olympics, the medals. Who I was. Everything was over.

I rushed back to my car and my keys jangled as I jammed them into the ignition. Lou was standing behind the gym's glass front doors watching me, probably getting his rocks off knowing he'd caused distress in a woman. He was a pig. A sexist pig. I didn't need him.

But, of course, I did.

I wouldn't be able to stave off the tears much longer.

The car lurched forward and I peeled out of the parking lot. As soon as I veered around the building, I swerved to the side of the road and shoved the car back into park. It was a busy street with a thin shoulder. Other drivers leaned onto their horns.

I was a gymnast who'd almost made it, but who'd fizzled out. When people saw me, they wouldn't know how close I'd gotten. They wouldn't have any idea how good I once was.

I banged my fists against the steering wheel, squeezed my eyes shut, and shrieked.

As I was bent over, breathing heavy, my phone buzzed. Who would be contacting me? My family had grown sick of my bad mood. It was probably just a telemarketer. A stranger looking to scam me. I pulled the phone from my pocket, prepared to chuck it out the window.

It was Lou.

"Hello?"

CHAPTER 27

August 2019

After Lou agreed to take me on again, dumping his other protégé, I upped my Adderall dose to fifty milligrams per day—five times my original dose. The Cincinnati doctor scrawled the augmented prescription before the request finished passing my lips. The pills provided mental and physical fuel for the day, but it was too much—my gas tank was still full come nighttime. In order to sleep, I countered the effects with two doses of NyQuil and a new prescription of anxiety medication.

During a bout of insomnia, I listened to a podcast about Eddie; Lucy was one of several victims interviewed. Over the airwaves, she sounded timid and so much younger than a college student. It was like listening to twelve-year-old Lucy describe the abuse as it was happening in the dorm bed next to mine.

What at the time felt so doubtful now seemed unequivo-
cal. Levett's crimes, the way the Baloghs and USA Gymnastics
condoned his misdeeds because Levett provided results, my
mother's mistaken assurances, how my discrediting of Lucy's
story contributed to Eddie's delayed reckoning. We were all
so palpably wrong.

I navigated to Eddie's old website, where he'd demonstrated his techniques in over four hundred instructional
videos. I wanted to revisit his convincing authority, to see
again how easy it had been to be fooled. But I was redirected.
Gymnasticsdoctor.com now summoned the National Sexual
Assault Hotline. Its banner proclaimed, "We're here for you."

I bit into my pillow and cried so hard I couldn't breathe.
When I couldn't stop, even after an hour, I shocked my system by lowering myself into an ice bath.

The next morning, my father, eyeing the lineup of pill
bottles on my dresser, asked, "Do you really need all this?
I'm no biologist, but I imagine all this medication must mess
with your brain."

"My brain is fine."

"It's just that sometimes you don't seem yourself."

I didn't know who I was anymore. My personality was
set to a new default. I was angry about the injury that set me
back a year, Lou's brutal treatment, Joe traveling to a college
across the country, and that I was likely working toward
failure. I was angry that my mistakes could not be undone.
I was angry my water bottle leaked in my gym bag. Anger

was all I did. And sadness. I couldn't remember what other emotions looked like.

While I stayed home from the U.S. Gymnastics Championships, Simone Biles unveiled a triple twisting double back somersault—a stunning floor skill no other female in the world or American male could execute. Yet, on camera, she called the rest of her performance "a piece of shit." I was nowhere near competition shape, and Simone, in a league all her own, was disappointed in her history-making. That made me angry too.

The next day, in a burst of frustration while I was working on floor, I ripped kinesiology tape from my hamstring and shouted, "I'm just not happy!"

Lou replied, "Who said you should be happy?"

Sweat accumulated in salty dots that wouldn't dry. The gym door was propped open and fans spun, but such efforts were useless. Perspiration dripped from my forehead, temples, arms, and back onto the rubber floor beneath me. Lou periodically followed the slick outlines of my routine, dragging a dirty towel with his foot.

"Again," he said.

It was Friday. The end of the week for most, but I'd be back in the morning, hacking away at my limitations. Which was fine. It was what I wanted. But Joe was leaving that night for college, flying out of Indianapolis for Hartford, Connecticut. I needed to be with my brother one last time. I walked to the folding chair where I'd slung my belongings and swigged from my water bottle.

"Let's pick it back up in the morning," I said.

"Are you the coach? Here I thought that was me."

His face was oily and porous and ridiculing. Moisture stained beneath his armpits and under his man breasts. I realized suddenly that he was an oaf. Coaches didn't require certification, a license, or training to work with elite athletes. He wasn't omnipotent. His knowledge could be as extensive or as limited as my own.

I sipped again from my water bottle and spoke into its mouth. "What *you* are is an asshole."

But he heard me. His eyes narrowed and he clomped toward me, faster than I expected he could. I stood erect to defy him. He seized my biceps and wrenched.

"You're the one who wanted to train so bad. You begged me. Made me give the boot to someone with more potential. Now you got what you wanted. Do the routine again."

"Let's see your fat ass do it," I said, and my words sizzled in the hot air between us. His brows tightened and a shadow passed over his eyes. He still seized my arm in his vise, and he squeezed it so hard my muscles shifted out of his way; I felt his thumb grind against my bone. The pain made me gasp, and the rage etched in his features dislodged some of my own anger, diffusing it with uncertainty. What was Lou capable of, really? Could he hurt me? Yes. Of course he could. But would he? The gym was empty. The parking lot outside was vast. No one would hear me if I needed them. I yanked my arm back, but he didn't release me.

"Fine," I said. "I'll do it again." And only then did he toss me forward and I was free.

I proceeded to the top of the mat, fully aware of every twinge in my body—the soreness of my quads, the tightness in my calves, the dagger-like pain in my heels, the aches in every socket that allowed me to hinge, glide, and pivot. The new pulse at my biceps. This was my life now. This was how my life had always been.

Lou was stationed at the stereo system about to press play. He lifted a hand to his cheek and splayed his fingers open.

"Smile," he said.

When the drums beat, my mouth spread into a performance grin. My hip bopped with the soulful tempo, the modern-day Motown of Pharrell Williams:

Because I'm happy . . .

"TONIGHT WE'RE FEASTING on the favorite hotdish of the man of the hour," my mother said, setting a red pan at the center of the table. "Macaroni and cheese with sliced dogs." The noodles gleamed with an orange hue not found in nature, and bite-size chunks of manufactured meat were strategically positioned across the surface to spell out Joe.

"Classy choice," I said.

Joe made a show of tucking a paper napkin into the collar of his shirt. "I am who I am, and I'm not ashamed."

My mother dug a serving spoon into her mess of carbs and fat and doled a heap onto her son's plate. "What's there to be ashamed about? You're kind and funny. And so handsome."

My father swirled his whiskey glass so the melting ice mixed. "Charlene, you're embarrassing the kid."

"No, she's not," Joe insisted. "Please, go on."

The window AC unit wheezed and the ceiling fan gyrated, but their combined efforts weren't enough to combat the outdoor temperature and not-yet-cool oven, which my mother wouldn't have used in summer, but tonight was an occasion. We wore undershirts and tank tops and were still clammy.

After she served, my mother sat and folded her hands beneath her chin. We didn't normally pray before a meal, so it took a moment to even register her position. Joe and I exchanged looks across the table and then he pressed his middle fingers into his thumbs and lifted them up, as if to meditate.

My mother began, "Dear Lord. Bless this food that was so lovingly prepared by my hands."

"And the good people at Kraft and Oscar Mayer," Joe interrupted.

"We thank you for the many blessings of this life, most notably today, our dear son, Joe, who we love more than we can say." Emotion broke my mother's words, but she barreled through the shards. "Watch over him as he travels tonight and continue to protect him as he begins the next phase of his life. May he study hard, exercise good judgment in the face of temptation, and cheer those Huskies all the way to the Big East. We are so incredibly proud of our boy. Amen."

Joe's eyes were glassy. He wasn't used to being the center of attention. I wondered if he was uncomfortable or if he was savoring it, wishing he'd enjoyed the spotlight more often. He cleared his throat and nodded to my plate, which I'd prepared with four ounces of boiled chicken breast, a cup of steamed spinach, and half a microwaved sweet potato. We'd finally dropped the charade that I ate like they did.

"Sure you don't want some real food, Bugs Bunny?"

"Look," I said, tapping the skin of the potato with the tongs of my fork. "Starch. I'm celebrating."

"You're wild, all right."

Utensils clicked against chipped dishes, and as I watched my family dine, I imagined all the dinners to come, just the three of us. (Four, if you counted our pet elephant.) Joe knew how to make us laugh. Sometimes that was a phenomenon. We weren't primed for levity without his influence. I dreaded the silence. The tension nobody else was capable of diffusing.

"Why are you traveling all the way across the country just to go to a state school?" I asked.

"Nothing wrong with a state school," my father said.

I'd hoped to strike a playful note, affectionate even, but as I heard it, I realized my question sounded like I was belittling

Joe's accomplishment. My stomach turned. "I just mean we have state schools right here in Indiana. For cheaper."

Joe stuck a finger in the air. "But we don't have the ocean, do we?"

"You'll still be an hour from the ocean."

"Closer than I am now."

"Okay, but classes don't start for another two weeks. Do you really have to leave so early?"

"A lot of transfers do this program."

"Don't you want to just stay here with me?" To my relief, the lightheartedness landed this time. My mother even tilted her head approvingly, like we were adorable.

But a screw tautened in Joe's neck. "It isn't always about you, you know. I get to have a life too."

My shoulders hitched and I redirected my attention to my food. "I know that."

"Sometimes it doesn't seem like you do," Joe said. He reddened and clenched as pressure built inside him, like he was a kettle about to whistle. "In fact sometimes . . . no, not sometimes, pretty damn often . . . it feels like you use everything up—time, money, people's hopes, and dreams—and don't leave a scrap behind for anybody else. You consume everything around you but food, Sera."

My mother looked from one of us to the other, panicked. Then she clapped her hands.

"I hope everybody saved their appetites. I made puppy chow."

WE HUDDLED BEHIND Joe like a family of penguins while he printed his ticket from the kiosk. Around us, travelers squinted at flight displays, waited to check bags, pecked the screens of their phones, and sped around the glossy floor like Indiana was burning and they might miss the last plane out. The machine churned and spat out the wispy paper, and Joe slipped it into the pocket of his jeans. Tears matted his long lashes as he hugged my parents. Then he turned to me.

We'd always lived separate but adjacent lives. Now he'd sleep in a bed in a state I'd never visited. He'd have a roommate who wasn't me. We'd celebrate our shared birthday apart for the first time in twenty years. Who would tease me for sticking a candle in Greek yogurt? Would he eat an extra slice of grocery cake in my honor? Who would we be when we next met? This goodbye felt definitive. I didn't know if I'd recognize my twin brother when he came back home. I blotted my nose with the hem of my tank top.

"Jeez, Sera. Who knew you cared so much?" he said, patting my back. "Maybe you can visit some time. If Old Louie gives you furlough, that is."

Nineteen years of accumulation amounted to a single rolling suitcase and a backpack. It was like he intentionally didn't want to bring home with him.

Based on the resentment Joe had made apparent over dinner, my passion, ego, single-mindedness, and rejection of the ordinary was driving my brother away. If I'd never discovered gymnastics, maybe he would have stayed. Or maybe, if not for gymnastics, I would have found something else to feed my appetite. The hunger was a nonnegotiable void I had to fill. I was insatiable.

When we left the airport and stepped outside into an Indiana without him, I was overcome by ridiculous, ruptured-Achilles-level sobbing. My tears persisted as my father paid for parking, navigated the car out of the airport, and merged onto I-65. I cried while Jimmy Buffett sang about paradise on the radio. I cried long after my parents' emotions had steadied.

Darkness had descended around our house as we glided into the garage. There was a light on in the kitchen, but Joe would not be inside. He wouldn't be inside for a long time. My whimpering joined the orchestra of the cicadas.

My father turned off the ignition and the car rumbled to quiet around us. My parents looked to each other, communicating silently. Then my mother palmed the center console and rotated to face me.

"It's sad that your brother left. I'm sad too. But is something else going on?"

Life felt suddenly and completely irreparable, and the fact that nobody could see what I saw or feel what I felt, and that I didn't quite understand it myself, just magnified the rift. My face was sticky with salt and snot. I glared at the rakes, hedge clippers, and shovels that hung like weapons on the garage wall.

"He's my twin and he's gone. I'm allowed to be upset."

My father said, "We only ask because—"

The Adderall. I knew he'd blame the Adderall. Dopamine receptors. The whole bit. He'd said it before. But if medication made me an Olympian, I was willing to pay its other costs.

"Just leave me alone."

My mother's mouth opened, but then closed, and I was possessed by the urge to wallop the back of her seat.

Say it, Mom. Say you're sorry for insisting that Lucy was a fake. Say your shame is unbearable too.

But of course she didn't admit anything. My parents gave up on me and continued into the house, the elephant lumbering behind them.

I needed to feel less alone, less like the girl who'd sent her brother away. I reached for one last contact with Joe before his plane took off.

I want to quit gymnastics, life, everything. Can I move into your dorm room and squat there until they admit me? I typed, believing every letter.

His dots danced and sprang into words. You can't quit now. You've worked too hard. And then, just as the garage's automatic lights dropped to black: We all have.

CHAPTER 28

Charlene Wheeler

I wanted my daughter to be what I wasn't. Someone special. Someone people talked about with awe and not a small drop of envy. Someone who riveted the world.

Was that so much to hope for?

Maybe. But I like to think women's gymnastics called us, not the other way around. That YMCA brochure arrived in our mailbox. Miss Nancy urged us to enroll at Elite Gymnastics. Jennifer suggested Sera was ready for TOPs camp and Junior Olympics competitions. I didn't push for any of it. Not at first. And then suddenly it seemed like my little girl was a magnet for accolades and had the potential to thrive in one of the few arenas where women were celebrated. Even over men. (Go ahead, name all the male gymnasts you know.) And when I caught a glimpse of that possibility, of Sera being at the top of her field, male or female, well, that was a real opportunity, so sure, I nudged her toward it.

It didn't come easy for me. I had to work against all my breeding and rearing to pursue greatness inside a culture of niceness. I advocated for more money from Bob, assignment extensions from schoolteachers, and closer attention from Jennifer. Sera and I were both champions, she on her own and me on her behalf. Sometimes it felt like fighting to survive, but I got good at it. So good it was hard to stop.

I thought that's what it meant to be a mother: believing, nurturing, and encouraging. I thought by assuring my daughter she could do the impossible that I was being a better parent than my own were.

But when my daughter sobbed in a parked car in our garage, I wondered if being on the other end of the support spectrum was just as wrong. Sera looked like a feral creature cowering in a corner of a cage, snapping at any fingers that dared to poke through. She looked nuts.

Were the accomplishments of a genius worthwhile if it meant going a little crazy? What if the insanity was only temporary?

Bob followed me to our bedroom. He never could sense the difference between when I wanted company and when I needed time to myself. If I was in the mood for a married moment together, for instance, I all but had to send a flare up from my nether regions. And if I preferred to be alone with my thoughts, it'd be up to me to kick him out and padlock our door behind him. Mothers across the Midwest were so busy teaching their daughters the intricacies of the eye roll and how to slip a tome inside each and every "hmm" that they forgot to show their sons a darn thing.

"We have to do something," he said.

Bob may have been oblivious in most ways, but on this he was right. I knew he was right.

"Do something about what?"

"That." He motioned to the floorboards. "Down there. That was not a normal reaction. Something is wrong with her."

I sat on the bed and pulled off the flats I'd bought at Marshalls, whose fake leather was beginning to peel after only one summer. They were eight and a half. My shoe size kept growing over the years, first after my pregnancy and then again to accommodate orthotics. It occurred to me, if my feet ached with bunions and corns and a lifetime of just walking around, how would Sera's feet, which caught about a million extra impacts, feel at my age?

I said, "Sera was right. We don't have a twin, so we can't really know how she feels."

He waved the idea away. I always liked the size of Bob's hands. The way his fingers could span from my cheek to the back of my head, and then how lovably, laughably large they looked when he played trucks with Joe or dolls with Sera. But over the years, I stopped paying attention to the qualities that had endeared me to him at the beginning. And sometimes, like when he used his large hands to disregard me, I turned against those once-attractive traits completely.

Bob said, "This isn't just about Joe. This is about Lou, and the unreasonable dose of a medication she didn't need in the first place. It's all the hours. Too many hours. It's the lack of social interaction. She's nineteen, and she doesn't have a single friend. It's the toll on her body. It's . . ." His words trailed off and he shook his head. "It's who knows what else."

But I intuited that another item lived inside his pause, one he couldn't bear to speak out loud. *People are still finding out he did it to their kid too.* That's what Holly had said. What if he—Eddie—was the source of the pain in our baby? What if, despite all the ways I'd learned to campaign for Sera, I was still too polite to ask the necessary questions because I was afraid of the answers? My daughter was hurting, that much was clear. What if that was because she'd been hurt? *Really* hurt?

If anyone would know, it'd be Lucy. But I couldn't ask her. I'd already burned the Lucy bridge. So I made a mental note to contact Jennifer. Maybe I could bear to get specific with her.

I said, "You know, she's under a lot of pressure there, with Tokyo just around the corner."

"Come on," he said, and his head dropped back as if to appeal to God Himself. As if he were saying, *Can you believe what I'm dealing with down here?* I didn't care for that implication, like he and the Lord were just two guys exasperated by the hysterics of an irrational woman. I didn't like being the third wheel, left out of God's inner circle. Or Bob's, for that matter.

I stood back up on my bare feet and crossed my arms over my chest, trying to look as big and capable as I was. "I mean it, Bob. It isn't easy for her, so it can't be easy for us. This is what happens when you raise an Olympian."

That got his attention. His chin plunged back down to me and his expression clicked into place, feature by feature, like the gears of a lock. He saw me with clarity, maybe for the first time in a long time, and he jabbed the air with his index finger, but there was a conviction in his eyes that said it wasn't the air he wanted to be jabbing.

"Right there is exactly our problem, Charlene, and it's been our problem all these years. Because while you've been busy raising an Olympian, I've been trying my damnedest, often against your best efforts, just to raise our daughter."

"You're right. That is our problem." I stood so tall, I practically lifted onto my tiptoes. "Because all this time you've refused to see that those aren't two separate people, an Olympian and our daughter. They are one and the same, Bob. One and the same."

There we were, standing across our bedroom like two bears on hind legs, ready to pounce, and not in the good way. We held our breath and waited for the other to flinch first, to see if we were going to fight or forfeit.

Downstairs, the door to the garage slammed, and all at once we were reminded that this wasn't about our years of opposition and which one of us had been wrong all along. It was about a young girl, our girl, who had so much to lose.

Bob's shoulders softened first, but we might as well have surrendered simultaneously.

"Charlene. Our daughter is unraveling down there," he said, and now it sounded like he was pleading with me. "What are you going to do about it?"

I sank back onto the edge of the bed and listened to her snivel below us. She sounded like she was underwater. I kissed my wrists together below my chin and pressed my fingertips into my ears.

What would have become of our family if I'd just smiled graciously at Miss Nancy that evening at the YMCA? Where would we be now if my eyes had never glinted with gold, if I'd thanked the instructor for her kind words, took my kiddos—my normal kiddos—home, and later laughed with Bob about our little Mary Lou Retton? Maybe Sera still would have treated the back of our couch as a balance beam. Maybe she would have flipped on the monkey bars and cartwheeled on the church front lawn in her good Sunday dress. But she also would have had sleepovers and birthday cake, played soccer and sang in the choir. Maybe she would have broken her collarbone climbing a tree, or maybe she wouldn't have suffered a single bodily injury. She wouldn't be crying downstairs at that moment, that's for sure, because she would have been off at her sophomore year of college, studying, partying, dreaming a different kind of dream. Happy.

And if all of our income hadn't been funneled into buying equipment and paying trainers, we would have had the money to eat out at restaurants, vacation at Disney World, and send Joe to football camp.

Oh, Joe.

If I'd had the time, I would have rooted at all of his games. I'd have invited his coach to dinner and hosted cookouts for the whole team to celebrate the end of the seasons. I would have checked his homework each night, and maybe he would have gone off to Purdue or Notre Dame. Maybe he would have felt like there was room for him to stay here.

And Bob. He and I wouldn't have been bogged down by almost fifteen years of gymnastics contention, arguing over how hard to push, how much to spend, how far to take all this. We'd have been empty nesters, reacquainting ourselves with each other.

Or, I don't know, maybe we would have been bored out of our minds, having had nothing to bicker about all these years, and we'd be withdrawing into solitary silence instead. But anything would be better than this: my son on a plane, flying from me as fast as he could; my daughter downstairs inconsolable; and my husband just a few feet from me, but as stiff and separate as a stranger.

Just as I was lamenting this, lonely and sick with regret over the mess I'd made, Bob shifted. He reached forward. I was crying, but his hands were around me, and they were blessings, those hands. They were large enough to hold me up.

CHAPTER 29

January 2020

While Joe, during his first semester away from home, rode cafeteria trays downhill, painted his body blue for football games, and was tossed into the campus pond, and while other elite gymnasts attended training camps at a new facility in Sarasota, I spent four months in the same gym, with the same middle-aged man, repeating the same movements. On Halloween, I treated myself to a single peanut M&M (nine calories) and then did a minute of calf raises to burn it off. I discovered we'd experienced the first snow of the season when I left the gym at seven o'clock and found fluff on the ground, but I was too tired to appreciate its magic. I drove home and went to bed, and by the time I woke up the next morning, it had melted. I entered my twenties shivering in a tub of ice.

After three weeks home for Christmas break, mostly spent in an unwashed Huskies sweatshirt, his face lit by the screen of his iPhone, typing texts and Snaps to his college buddies and meeting high school friends out—which prompted a passive-aggressive "Going out again? You sure?" from my mother —he returned to Connecticut two weeks early to crash at the home of some kid named Coop.

I wanted to be happy for Joe. And maybe I was. I just wished, when he packed his bags again in January, he hadn't seemed so excited to leave. Or perhaps I wished I could go with him. Experience normal life, even if only for a while.

Now dinner was back to three, and one tusked mammal. Joe's chair was empty once again.

"Good meatloaf," my father said, maybe just so somebody would say something.

My mother regarded his plate. His meat was drenched in a thick layer of ketchup. "Not too dry?"

Specks of red clung to his mustache hairs. "It's fine."

The heat rattled and spat out the radiators, emitting the smell of burnt dust. The neighbor's dog barked, likely egged on by a cat. Our forks clinked lethargically. Even the utensils were bored.

My mother smiled at me with insincere cheer. "How'd training go today?"

My skills had finally progressed to where they had been in Qatar, if not quite as reliable. At the current rate of training, I could have a steady performance in June. Maybe an impressive one. But Lou's mood was darker than ever. He'd hung a countdown to the Trials on the gym wall, and every morning he made a great show of staring at it, ripping off a number, and sighing. We had 158 days.

If I stumbled on the floor, he made me repeat the movement ten times. If I was sloppy on the bars, he whacked my calf with a yardstick so I'd recognize the exact moment I was careless and tighten up. If I slipped from the beam, he pulled the mats away so I didn't have a safety net and made me do it again. He scattered obstacles around the vault so I had no choice but to stick it right; error could result in another injury.

"You think this is fun for me? You think I want to spend my days staring at a shapeless woman who makes the same mistakes over and over again? You aren't my type. Believe me. I'm doing you a favor. I work my ass off because you wanted a chance. Here it is, Sera. Here's your chance."

But his efforts weren't all for me; he'd pinned his dreams to my leotard. If I made it to the Olympics, the world would credit him for building and rebuilding a star. This would be his victory as much as mine. He pushed me because he wanted glory. He'd dropped his other trainee because he'd calculated that I was his best chance.

At the dinner table, I answered my mother by saying, "Lou is a total jackass."

My father's eyes remained focused on his food, but they expanded as if it to say, *Tell me something I don't know.* My mother's head cocked.

"He just wants what's best for you."

"He's mean. He's on me constantly. *Again, again, again,* no matter how tired I am. He's not like other coaches. He's too intense. He never lets up."

"He thinks that's what you need," she said, her voice skittering across high notes.

My fork clanged against my plate and I pressed both palms against the table. "Maybe I need a break. Ever think of that?"

My mother's chin dipped. "Sera," she said, scolding, "this is what *you* wanted."

My chair scraped against the wood plank floor that bore the scars of our family. "This is what *you* wanted. You're obsessed with the idea of a child prodigy. Everything has been Olympics, Olympics, Olympics. Joe gets to be normal, run off to college, and have a good time drinking and pulling stupid pranks with his friends, and I have to stay home and carry the dreams of the whole family on my shoulders. It isn't fair. I'm tired. But do I get to rest? No. I haven't rested in fourteen years. And I don't even get to complain about it, because 'This is what I wanted.'" I had more to say, but the words were too cruel to allow to exist outside my mind. I pushed to my feet. At the bottom of the stairs, I paused and thought, *Fuck it.* I turned and loosed what had been pressure-cooking inside me for years. "It isn't my job to make up for your failures."

I didn't watch my words detonate. Like a bomber, I kept on flying.

In my bedroom, I kneaded my muscle massager across my quads. Because it was covered in nodules, Joe called it my nipple stick. At that moment, he was probably playing pool in Coop's basement, sipping cheap beer, having no idea what was going on at home—or perhaps having a pretty good idea, but relieved that he didn't have to be here.

I expected my parents to begin their age-old fight, for my father to say, "She has a point, Charlene," and for my mother to yell back, "She loves gymnastics. I'm supporting her dream. Maybe my enthusiasm is just such a stark contrast to your heel-digging." But it was worse; they cleared the table in silence. In place of their argument was the echo of what I'd said: *It isn't my job to make up for your failures,* and the melodrama of those words stung my eyes. I had a cross to bear and wasn't carrying it with dignity. The tide of my anger was pulling in other feelings with it: guilt and regret. I plowed the nipples into my muscles despite how my legs protested.

Ten minutes later, footsteps ascended step by begrudging step. I didn't want to see the consequence of what I'd said. I locked my attention on the massager.

My mother rapped on the doorway and leaned against the jamb. She looked like she was fading away. Her eyes were red, the contours of her face had softened. She chewed her bottom lip.

"Can I come in?"

I nodded, and she sat on my bed but directed her body away from me. Neither of us said anything. I zeroed in on my massager as if stopping, even for a moment, would be disastrous.

My mother seemed to hover on the surface of the mattress without putting her weight on it, her muscles engaged, poised to bolt out the door and down the street at any moment.

"I left your father once," she said finally. The massager froze just above my knee. "We'd been married for, oh jeez, I don't know, two years? He wanted kids right out of the gate and I came up with one excuse after the other. I wasn't ready for diapers and nap schedules. Not yet, anyway. I shouldn't have gotten married so young, is the truth of it. I was only twenty, for Pete's sake. Your age. Imagine? But marriage seemed like the only way out of my parents' house, and I couldn't stand my parents." Her chin ticked in my direction. We watched each other in our peripheral vision but didn't dare venture beyond that. She turned back to the wall and continued, "Anyway, I gave myself one shot for a flashier life. I was pretty back then. I thought maybe I'd become an actress or a dancer. A model, even. If it worked out, it worked out. And if it didn't, I'd come back. I knew he'd wait for me. Your father was always dependable like that.

"The flight to New York City was at three forty-five. I still remember that, all these years later." Her voice trailed off, and for a moment I thought that was the end of the terrible story about my mother not loving my father enough, or of loving herself too much. I couldn't breathe. I certainly couldn't say anything. But I didn't have to. "I watched every other passenger board the plane. But I couldn't. I kept imagining the looks on people's faces if they didn't like my auditions. If they didn't like me." She winced, as if she were picturing those rejections again. "I told your father I'd gone to the grocery store. I didn't have any bags, but he believed me."

"Poor . . ." But I couldn't decide if she or my father deserved more sympathy.

"Yes, well, tough tomatoes, right?" She picked the pity up and placed it behind us so we could move forward without obstruction. "I'm telling you this sad story because you were right, what you said at dinner. I put my regrets on you. You are so much braver than me; I thought you could be what I never could. I wanted that for you, but I guess I wanted that for me too. I feel this rush of pride every time you walk onto the floor and the lights are shining on you and everyone is cheering, and you just nail your routines, and the crowd loves you, which means, just a little bit, that they love me too. There's no feeling like it. But that doesn't make it right."

I couldn't hold her stare now that I knew who looked back at me—a wistful girl who'd grown to be disappointed and who'd fought to prevent such a fate for her daughter, only to have her daughter throw her efforts back at her, ungratefully, spitefully. My gaze dropped to where her soft belly bulged over the waist of her jeans.

"It's okay," I said.

"It isn't, though."

She inhaled deeply, preparing herself for something, making me think, full of dread, *There's more?*

"Sera," she said. "Did Edward Levett ever touch you where he shouldn't have?"

I made it my goal to go as long as I could without thinking about that man. Sometimes it was an hour, sometimes, when I was lucky, it was more like four or five, but every day, without fail, he came into my mind, and it always felt like an intrusion. A small violation. It made me sick.

"No."

She ran her teeth over her bottom lip. It was paining her to continue. Speaking about him took concentration. "Never in your underwear region, even in a way that maybe seemed medical?"

"Never."

"You're absolutely sure? Take a minute to think about it."

"I don't want to think about it," I said. I gathered fabric from the blanket in my fist and squeezed as if to strangle it. "I'd remember."

"Okay. Because, you know . . ." She smoothed out her pant legs with two quick motions and then pressed her palms down onto her thighs. "I was wrong about him. About Lucy and him. I was very wrong. But I guess that's obvious now."

The African bush elephant paused its trunk-swinging and looked up at my mother and me, startled to be acknowledged, after years of invisibility. I froze, unsure what it would do now that it had been seen, or what I would do.

She continued, "I gave you bad advice, but I just plain didn't know better. It just goes to show that mothers are human too, experiencing things for the first time, making mistakes. And this was a big one. I still don't know what I should have done, God help me, but I do wish it had been different."

There was a vine in my throat, and it thickened by the minute. Or maybe the elephant and I were melding, becoming one, and in the transmogrification it was unfolding its trunk from my stomach up through my mouth.

"Sera, do you want to quit gymnastics?" my mother asked.

I searched her eyes for hesitation or hope, but her irises were as layered as bark.

"No," I said.

"Take me out of the picture. Don't think about Lou, Lucy, Edward Levett, Joe, your father, or anybody else. I'm talking only about you. Sera Wheeler. Is it too much? Do you want to quit?"

"No."

Her head bobbed gently, and she patted my shin. "Let me know if you change your mind."

As she passed through my doorway, I felt I owed her something for exposing herself, for all her efforts, and for my unkindness. I needed to repay some debts.

"I'm glad you fought for us," I said. "I am."

Her fingers drummed the wood frame as she looked back at me. "It's almost over, and you might find you miss all this later. The challenge, the breakthroughs, the purpose, everything. I know I will." She began to leave but stopped one last time. Our path to this reckoning had been jagged and rough, and there was still one last stone to turn. "And, Sera?" she said. "It's enough with the Adderall. Don't you think?" Then she was gone, and down the hall her door clicked as if closing it was a secret.

In my earliest memories, the world was upside down. Inside flashes of light and sound, my father's bushy mustache hung below his cooing mouth, the fan blades whirled on the floor eight feet below me, and my twin brother tottered across the ceiling.

My mother said she found me at twenty-two months in a full headstand in my crib, wearing only a diaper and a smile. My back rested against the wooden bars, my feet kicked the air, and I beamed, displaying a mountain range of teeth. Across the crib, Joe was beside himself, covering his mouth with spread fingers.

Now that reminiscence was cast in new light, and I imagined my mother crossing her arms over her chest, a smile playing at her lips as she indulged in a frivolous but by all accounts harmless fantasy that what she observed in that crib was the first taste of the extraordinary she craved but was too timid or self-doubting to seek on her own.

CHAPTER 30

March 2020

When USA Gymnastics wished Simone Biles a happy birthday on Twitter, she rejected their wishes by calling for an internal investigation of the Levett abuses. That should have been the most dramatic event of the month. But then a virus breached our cells and rewrote our entire sense of self.

COVID-19 began as an echo of something happening to someone else somewhere else. We told ourselves it was raw bats, Wuhan markets, and Hubei province—*not here*. When it eventually crossed our borders, we condescended to it, as if levelheadedness and democracy made us immune.

"I'm more worried about the flu," the president said, my mother said, Lou said.

USA Gymnastics hosted the Nastia Liukin and American Cups. Then the rest of the March calendar was cleared, followed by April, with promises that the U.S. Gymnastics Championships and the Trials would surely go on as scheduled.

Please note that the health and well-being of our athletes are our top priority.

We'd heard that before.

"Champion Gym will never close. You can count on that," Lou said, and then he spotted my next landing—exposure was a requisite between an athlete and her trainer.

College classes shifted online, but Joe remained in Connecticut, no doubt partying with Coop and the gang. Social distancing recommendations extended from three to six feet. Graphs urged us to flatten the curve. Travel from Europe was banned. Soccer games were played to empty stadiums. The NBA suspended the rest of its season. Tom Hanks got sick. Indiana suffered its first fatality, then its second. Restaurants converted to takeout only. Schools were closed across the board.

Maybe this list is out of order. Things changed so quickly, I lost sense of when and how. I know this: our confidence degraded day by day.

"The lines were crazy," my mother said as she came through the door one night, hugging a paper bag to her belly. "I barely got out of there with my life and this toilet paper four-pack. Everybody in this house better take their fiber."

My father bought Joe a seat on the next flight out of Hartford. "If you aren't on that plane, I'm coming to get you myself," he said.

As international arenas were converted into field hospitals, the floors where gymnasts used to sprint and spiral now resembled wartime triage units.

Lou began taking my temperature before training. If I ever rolled over ninety-nine degrees, he looked at me like I'd stolen something from him.

Stay-at-home orders moved in from each coast. They were closing in on us.

Lou suggested I wait out the pandemic with him so we wouldn't fall behind on workouts. "Tokyo is still on the other side of this thing, and if we're under quarantine, which of your family members is going to train you: Mustache, Stretch Pants, or Frat Boy?"

Joe was back from school, depressed to have his revelry cut short; my father was furloughed—with an inevitable recession on the horizon, who knew when people would buy cars again; and my mother's voice was pitching higher and higher as she called from the kitchen, "I stocked up on corn chips. Who's ready for a snack?" I wouldn't let those three out of my sight when shadows were creeping on the edges of my vision.

"They won't put us under quarantine," I said.

I believed I had authority over my own balance and discipline, but I was about to learn that control was an illusion. A virus would take lives. It could change the world.

USA Gymnastics surveyed its athletes about postponing the Olympics. The notion was so absurd it made me laugh, right before I cried. There'd been talk of fourteen-day self-quarantines, but was it possible this nightmare could last until July? Voices from Canada and Australia, and even our own USA Swimming peers, argued that the delay was not just about whether it would be safe to travel the week of the Games; we also needed to address the cancellation of necessary qualifiers leading up to the summer, as well as athletes being unable to access training facilities, or feeling pressure to train and therefore leaving the house, bringing the virus back to their families, and perpetuating its spread, when every Olympic effort should be made to contain the outbreak. If conducted as scheduled, the Games, which were meant to demonstrate global unity, would only work against humanity's fight for survival.

I doubted I had it in me to sustain another year, another delay, another heartbreak. My body had already been pushed too far. Surely this was beyond its limit. After all I'd been through, after all the obstacles faced and scaled, my dreams could be dashed once and for all, and by a force completely unrelated to gymnastics.

I'd once considered my Olympic ambitions to be absolutely critical, but the more the words "essential" and "nonessential" were being applied to medical workers and delivery personnel, the more my dreams felt superfluous, even to me.

Still, I closed my laptop on the Olympic survey.

As I pulled my car out of the garage to head to Cincinnati

the next morning, a U-Haul turned into our driveway, with Lou behind the wheel. I was sure he'd come to kidnap me and my belongings and stow me away in his one-bedroom apartment in Ohio so we could preserve my routines while the world beyond his bare walls spun into chaos.

My father would never allow it; even he had to draw the line at a pandemic. Any minute he'd storm from the house and wrestle my coach to the lawn, contagion be damned.

I approached the U-Haul as if it might be booby-trapped. The idea of living with Lou scared me. This insistent, forceful gesture of his scared me. *He* scared me. Or maybe fear was a preexisting condition that invaded my cells the way this virus could and likely would, infecting my heart first with Levett, and dividing and multiplying now with images of a shuttered Italy, where doctors were forced to decide who lived and who died, and the statistics rolling out as scientists and health experts conveyed the magnitude of this thing. Millions could die, they said. Hundreds of thousands, even if the United States did everything exactly right.

But when Lou hopped from the driver's seat, he said, "Tell that walking keg stand to get out here. We'll need a hand with this equipment."

When Joe stumbled out of the house, Lou shook his hand, but he wore gloves.

We carried a low beam, mats, foam blocks, a mini trampoline, and a pair of parallettes through the basement bulkhead while my father watched from the window and my mother stood on the front porch, calling nervously, "Watch it there. If you hurt yourselves, you can't go to the hospital."

Lou was winded. He held his hips as if breathing required leverage. I wondered if he was sick.

He pointed to the unfinished wood above his head. "The ceiling is too low down here. You'll have to bring the mats outside for floor and vault. Parallettes aren't the same as bars, but they're better than nothing."

We plotted the vault runway in my backyard. Lou arranged the mini trampoline, and we laid mats on cinder blocks to replicate the horse.

We went through a few runs on each event using my makeshift equipment. Before Lou left, he laid a hand on my shoulder, and it almost felt like he was saying goodbye, like his eyes were saying, *You're on your own, kid.* The next day, Champion Gym went dark.

In the casual language used by Midwesterners even in the direst situations, Hoosiers were ordered to hunker down.

My family was made to be together. For the first time since before I went elite, we were a unit, an isolated island in our living room, not knowing how long we had, how dangerous the world outside was becoming, or if that danger would find us on top of delivery boxes or during a supply run. We weren't safe, and we weren't free. We lived under house arrest. But no matter how we sacrificed and cloistered, no matter how hard we fought back, the virus was two weeks ahead. We didn't know what was to come. There could already be an infection among us, unseen. We waited for it to show itself.

While reports of people dying ticked in—and not just the old and immunosuppressant, the young and healthy too—we worried and cried, privately and openly. We slept and we couldn't sleep. We lost our appetites and we ate to feel something, anything, else. We drank. We bickered. We despaired. We dreamed vividly. But when we managed to forget our dread, we played Pictionary and watched home movies. We rummaged through storage to find puzzles. I paced like a tiger in a cage, but I also sat on the couch and let my knee fall into my brother's. We teemed with boredom and agitated inside the prison of our listless minds, but we also sang karaoke in our pajamas.

The Olympics were postponed, but by then no one was surprised. International Olympic Committee member Dick Pound leaked the announcement, which prompted Joe to say, "There's a name for the ages."

I pictured Lou's countdown calendar in my locked gym flipping backward in time.

There were decisions to be made: When would the new Olympics be? Would it be named Tokyo 2021? Would organizations that already held trials honor those who'd qualified or require athletes to try out again, possibly ripping back dreams and giving others a new shot? Would the age restrictions remain the same, or would the competition open to include younger, fresher athletes? How long should athletes rest?

Training was designed so we'd reach peak performance at the exact right moment. We were halfway through the most demanding year, leading up to the Olympics. Athletes around the world—perfectionists, artisans of their sport, control freaks—had to be asking the same question of their reflections: am I strong enough to reroute, restructure, recalculate, and do it all again?

We didn't know, but the committee hoped, when 2021 rolled around and all the arrangements had been settled, that the Games would draw people together like it never had before. The Olympic flame would be a light at the end of a global darkness, and the event would showcase athleticism, yes, but it'd also celebrate resiliency, the human spirit, and life itself.

My family ate breakfast for dinner the night of the official notice, and I indulged in pancakes along with everybody else. I likely had a year to burn them off.

"You're handling this well," my father said as he sliced off some butter from the cold stick on the table and dragged it over his stack.

Maybe I was in shock. Maybe I'd grown numb to setbacks. Maybe I was comforted that at least all the other athletes were in the same position. This wasn't having a torn Achilles while everybody else continued training strong. We were a community on hold, pausing our passion to focus on subsistence.

Or maybe I wasn't melting down because this crisis had, at least temporarily, imprinted on me a new understanding: the value of being elite paled in comparison to the value of simply *being*. It might be another year of waiting, but for perhaps the first time, I acknowledged that another year wasn't always a given, and I should accept that as a small gift in and of itself.

In the face of death, life glinted like a precious metal.

One Month Before the Olympic Trials

We convened among the ghosts of our friendship, our childhood, and our sport at a café in Indianapolis halfway between Jennifer's gym, where we trained together for so many years, and the former USA Gymnastics headquarters. We reunited at the heart of all that brought us together and all that divided us.

Venturing outside—not to go to the pharmacy or grocery store, but to follow a whim, see a friend, explore—was losing its novelty and sense of privilege. I wasn't savoring its sweetness the way I had when the virus protections were first loosened and face masks were lowered. I was once again taking liberty for granted. But maybe there was beauty in that—in the return to normalcy, when every errand didn't incite an adrenaline rush.

The door to the café chimed my entrance. My eyes met Lucy's, and her grin absorbed hers. She wore yoga pants and a sheer shirt the shade of cherry blossoms—she looked celestial; pink served her complexion, no matter what Vanda said. Lucy could have been any woman in her twenties. Only I knew she was extraordinary.

She came forward but left space between us, the way people tended to Ever Since, but the warmth in her voice crossed the distance. "I gained the COVID nineteen while you only got tinier. Let me buy you a cookie."

The reference was an extension of goodwill to put us both at ease. I felt so grateful for it I might have wept.

Her joke aside, Lucy was leaner than when I saw her last. Not as thin as she had been when she trained gymnastics, of course, but her once full cheeks were now contoured. Hungry for socialization, we'd begun video chatting during isolation, so I knew she'd been running competitively and drinking less. She was returning to a state of fitness.

As we joined the back of the line, my arm brushed hers and she didn't shrink away.

"After the Trials, I'll tear that snickerdoodle apart. Heck, I'll eat that entire display," I said, gesturing to puffs of croissants and muffin mounds. "Until then, adding cinnamon to black coffee is my sad little splurge."

"Of course. Olympic Games, take two. How does it feel?"

Since quarantine ended, Lou and I had been training feverishly. People had been sick and had died, but we were still alive. We had to make that matter, so we worked until the room whirled, until the weight of our existence was too heavy to hold up. We worked ourselves into delirium.

"I just want it to be over," I said.

A patron in the corner clacked away at his laptop. A barista set a coffee down and called the name over the gurgling of the froth machine. A woman waited for the barista to retreat before claiming her beverage. This snapshot might not look terribly different from before the virus, but we who had survived to the After knew, behind every courteous smile, every stilted wave, every exhale, people were searching for equilibrium, for a feeling of safety, unsure they'd ever find it again.

Lucy said, "I was actually thinking of getting back into gymnastics."

My eyebrows leapt up my forehead. "Really?"

She dispelled my eagerness with a quick motion. "Not competing or anything. Just, you know, doing some kips on the low bar and maybe a back handspring or two to get the feel for it again."

"You should," I said. "You were *so* good."

"Yeah?" The compliment pleased her more than I'd expected; I was glad to have said it. "I do miss it. I never thought I would, but I do. I loved gymnastics, and Levett shouldn't get to take that away from me. I shouldn't let him do that. Especially now. Who knows what will happen; you have to find joy where it is, you know? It'll be weird, but I'm tough. Probably *because* of gymnastics. There's a cycle of irony for you: gymnastics made me tough enough that gymnastics can't destroy my love for gymnastics."

"You should come to the Trials. It'd be awesome to have you there and could help you get back into the mindset." As soon as I said it, I was sure I'd overstepped into a steaming gaffe. I was part of the reason why Lucy had discarded her Olympic dream. She wouldn't want to come root me toward it. I rushed to dampen my mistake. "But if it'd be uncomfortable or if it's inconvenient, there's no pressure or anything."

Lucy's head bobbed as if to a beat only she could hear. I figured she was choosing just the right words to harangue me. *You live in your own little Olympic universe. Nothing and nobody matters outside you and your stupid goals. I hope you fall on your face.* I readied myself and began assembling a gym face to hide behind.

"You know what? Maybe I will," she said.

"Yeah?" I had to hold my expression so as not to expose my disbelief. "Well, good."

There was a time when Lucy and I were so intertwined, I thought I could keep her from unraveling by pulling her in tight. I'd just defaulted into an adjacent arrogance, casting myself not as her savior but as her chief adversary. When would I accept we were separate threads with our own unrelated design and direction? She was not mine to save or sentence, then or now.

When we stepped up to the counter, Lucy's fingertip grazed my elbow. "Sorry, Ser, but I'm not an Olympic hopeful, so I'm getting a big-ass cookie, and if you don't want any, I'm going to eat all twelve hundred calories myself."

To anybody listening, it probably sounded like we were friends.

CHAPTER 31

The Olympic Trials

Below cheering fans, I wore a sparkling red leo with long white sleeves and streaks of blue along the torso, like patriotic ribs. I'd texted Lucy a selfie that morning. She said I looked like an American orgasm, and I supposed that was about right. She drove in separately but found my family at the start of the event. Half of Joe's face was painted in our nation's colors, and the other half with my name, and I imagined he was now finding reasons to flex in Lucy's direction.

Bars was my first event. I bounded off the springboard, propelled over the low bar, and torpedo twisted to grab the high bar in the Gebeshian mount. Then I paid tribute to other great gymnasts by completing Bhardwaj's Pak with a full turn and Shaposhnikova's clear hip with backward flight to the high bar. In Qatar, I ended the routine with the Mustafina dismount, a double back tuck with a one-and-a-half twist.

But as we neared the Trials, I didn't want to end with some-body else's skill; I wanted to make a name for myself. So I added an extra full twist to make it a two-and-a-half twisting double back tuck. The blind landing made it even more dif-ficult than a triple. I could submit the element for consider-ation to the FIG technical committee and, if I performed it at the Olympic Games, have the skill named for me. Then, even after I was gone, there'd always be the Wheeler.

I landed with my chest heaving and exuberance inflating me from limb to limb. I'd shown exactly what I could do. I wouldn't spend the rest of my life agonizing over one mis-step or one overrotation, and there was immense relief in not having regret.

I stood opposite the vault like we were two gunslingers facing off in a Western. I raced, a horse out of the gate. I hurled into a roundoff, landing on the springboard into a half-turning flicflac with my hands propelling off the leather and catapulting into a stretched salto forward with a one-and-a-half twist. The Cheng, worth 6.4 points. When my feet planted, that was it. Party over. I was stationary. A statue. Like the four and a half seconds I'd lived as a whiz-zing corkscrew was a previous life, a distant memory.

Now there was only floor and beam.

Lou gripped my shoulders and spoke inches from my face. His breath smelled like Gatorade and cigarettes. He only smoked when he was panicked.

"There is only one thing standing between you and Tokyo now, and it's her," Lou said, jerking his head in the direction of Nicole Gonzalez, the gymnast he'd dismissed to train me. "The top two on the all-around will make the Olympic team and the other two they'll select based on apparatus needs. Your strength is bars. And guess what, sweetie. It's Gonzalez's too."

My attention strayed over his shoulder to where Nicole pike stretched on a mat. She didn't scare me; I'd already set into my gym persona.

"I nailed bars and vault and I'm going to nail the rest. This is why we trained so hard for so long. I can do my routines in my sleep."

"Nailing the rest won't be enough," he said.

"Not enough?" My stare flicked back to him. His forehead hooded his eyes. "What else is there?"

His feet shifted and he lowered his voice. "Gonzalez can't be an option. We have to make sure of that."

I stepped back. "What the hell are you talking about?"

His gaze floated above my head, his lips spread and parted, and he said, "Smile, we're on *Candid Camera*."

There we were on the Jumbotron. Our huddle looked conspiratorial. I nodded to appear as if Lou was offering last-minute advice. With this lightened expression, I repeated, "What are you talking about?"

Through his teeth, he said, "WADA is testing the girls picked for the team. I crushed up a couple of your little energy pills. When everyone heads to the athletes' room for break, I'll distract Gonzalez's dingbat coach while you shake your happy dust into her water. She's got a superstition with that water bottle. Drinks it half an hour before she performs, and she flavors it with some powder shit, so she won't be able to see or taste a thing."

Shock must have pulsed across my face, because Lou clamped down my shoulders to remind me that we were being watched.

"You're out of your fucking mind," I said.

"When you asked to work with me, I said you'd have to be willing to do whatever it takes. Nothing would be out of bounds. Remember that?"

"I thought you meant training hard. Sacrificing all other aspects of my life. Which I've done. But this is insane. Even for you."

"Are you confident you'll place in the top two? Because otherwise the selection committee might choose Nicole over you. And Christ knows you won't be around for 2024."

That was indisputable. The year extension hadn't been gentle on my body. I was officially in breakdown mode. As soon as one hitch was quieted, another sputtered. The newest issue was shooting pain in my back. It was so bad, Lou had a trainer inject Novocain shots that morning.

Lou continued his pitch. "The Olympics are within your grasp. Your fingers are grazing it. Do you want to walk away? If you don't do this, she might get your spot. She'll be in Tokyo. The crowd will be chanting her name while Sera Wheeler lazes on her rump on a worn couch cushion in Waynesville. This is your only chance. Are you gonna take it?"

Nicole wrapped her hands around the soles of her flexed feet. She was only seventeen. At that age, I'd missed the 2016 Olympic team. I'd learned the extent of Levett's crimes. But there was so much to come: my Achilles rupture, Joe moving across the country, training with Lou, medicating, the virus. After all that suffering, my life up to this point could finish at a dead end.

"If they think she's doping, her career will be over."

"Only if she makes the team. In that case, you'll want her career to be over. And if she doesn't, they won't test her. No harm done."

It was Nicole's turn on the uneven bars. Lou and I separated so we could watch her.

Nicole opened with the Gebeshian—the same flashy mount as me—and she hit it beautifully. But how strange that we chose the same opening skill.

The Bhardwaj salto came next. Then the Shaposhnikova. Lou must have felt me staring at him, but he didn't acknowledge it. He didn't acknowledge that in the short time he'd worked with Nicole, he'd taught her my bars routine. That before I'd interrupted his process, he'd been duplicating me.

No wonder he considered her my rival. She was my unrelated twin. The transitioning moves were a bit different, but the hallmarks were the same. We were, all in all, replicas.

She landed the Mustafina, the dismount I'd demonstrated in Worlds but had upped the ante for in the Trials. And I remembered it was Lou's suggestion that we make the skill more difficult and catered to my individuality. "If you don't get an Olympic medal, don't you at least want a movement named after you?" he'd asked. "It'd be your legacy." He'd played to my ego to right his wrongs. He'd manipulated me—and so easily too.

Lou turned to me. "Are you going to do it or not?"

Maybe a champion had to be willing to do anything.

"I can't," I said. "It's too much."

His hands dropped to his side. "Coward."

As THE GYMNASTS and their coaches filed out for the intermission, young girls and their mothers shrieked our names and flapped signs they'd painted in our honor. There was "Sera: Next Stop Tokyo" drawn in lavender crayon. And "We heart Sera" in wobbly letters surrounded by heart stickers. I thought about what my father had said about fandom. "Enjoy it, sure. But remember it won't be forever. They aren't the relationships that matter, anyway." Still, their admiration was electric. It almost felt like love.

The athletes' room was stocked with bottled water, sports drinks, fruit, and protein bars. Gymnasts chatted nervously or planted themselves while their coaches administered massage, assisted in stretching, or counseled them on their remaining routines. Still shaken by what Lou had said, I plopped onto a folding chair and twisted a cap of Poland Spring until the seal broke.

A West Coast gymnast who some commentators predicted would be the next Simone, while others argued Simone was still Simone, approached, appearing excited to see me. Her hair was pulled into a simple bun and frizzed lightly around her temples.

"You looked badass out there," she said.

I wanted to say something clever while Lou wasn't around to put the kibosh on our conversation. Maybe even something that would make her laugh.

"Thanks," I said. "You too."

"I can't believe you kept at it after your Achilles rupture, and then again with the postponement. So many deal breakers."

"It's been tough."

Her stare hovered as if waiting for me to offer more, like she'd done her part and now it was my turn. But I was a bad dance partner.

She continued, "We missed you down at the camps."

"I wanted to go, but . . ."

Lou was across the room. As soon as he caught me mingling with a so-called opponent, he'd interrupt. I wasn't there to make friends; that much he'd made clear.

What was he doing by himself over there, anyway?

"If you were worried it'd be like the ranch, it isn't," the other gymnast said. "Have they decided what they're doing with that place? I hope they burn it to the ground."

Lou turned, holding a Nalgene bottle pasted with stickers. He dropped it onto the bench and walked away. Nicole was just feet away with her coach. She reached toward the chair beside her, and when her hand came up empty, she searched. She saw her water bottle, evidently further than she remembered placing it, and her head twitched, just for a moment. Then she grabbed it.

I wanted to jump to my feet, to scream a warning across the room. But I was paralyzed.

"Sera?"

My attention snapped to the athlete in front of me. "What?"

"Do you know what they're doing to the Balogh Ranch?"

"No clue," I said. Lou was now standing on the perimeter of the room, his arms crossed over his chest, perhaps trying to look nonchalant. But he looked like a goon. A man who hurt girls. And I'd brought him into that locker room.

"Sorry, I have to . . ."

When I got close, he made a discreet downward motion to remind me to keep my voice low. Despite my anger, I obeyed.

"You have to get that bottle back before she drinks it."

"It's done."

"It isn't," I said, through clenched teeth.

If caught, she'd never compete again. We'd be robbing her, not just of the Olympic dream she'd chased all her life, but her gymnast identity. Not to mention I'd built a tolerance, having gradually increased my dose, although I'd weaned back in the last year. What if Lou had given her more than she could handle? In trying to defeat her, we could kill her.

"If you don't get that bottle back, I'm going to tell her," I said.

His eyes skid down to mine. "And get yourself disqualified?"

Nicole slipped the bottle's handle around her wrist. If she reported me, the board would assume I'd colluded with Lou and then collapsed under my guilt. He was right—I could be disqualified.

I turned back to him. "You're a real piece of shit, you know that?"

"Pieces of shit get what they want," he said, and shrugged, but the ambivalence of the gesture was juxtaposed by his mouth, which ticked up into a calculated, self-satisfied smirk. "Consider it an incentive for your performance: Gonzalez will be tested unless you make the team."

WHEN I ENTERED the arena wrapped in the colors of our nation's flag, the crowd thought they hailed an athlete who reflected hard work, commitment, and integrity—the American Dream—when really they applauded a different figure altogether. One who stepped on necks in order to climb.

First Lucy, now Nicole. I'd worked hard to get where I was, yes, but I'd had to be hard-hearted too. Maybe this—being ruthless and cutthroat—was more authentically American.

I warmed up, lying on my stomach with my arms stretched out before me, like a superhero. Lou gripped my heels and kept me from flying off.

Before I set out for the floor, my couch clasped my forearm. "Get your head out of your ass and into this routine," he said.

I had to don my most impenetrable persona yet. An iron mask. The gym face equivalent of a medieval knight's helmet. I had to recede into that dank corner of my mind, that dead place where I didn't care about Nicole, Lou, the crowd, the selection committee, or Lucy, where I didn't care about my honor, where I didn't ask myself what it meant to be a human alive in the world after the virus. There was no moral questioning inside those blank walls. There was only movement. The mission. I'd have to become my robot self. An acrobatic assassin.

When the first note played over the sound system, my face split into my performance smile, the one I'd been practicing in the mirror for over a decade. I grinned at the judges and up toward the stands. I twirled my wrists and rolled my hips. Then I spun on the ball of my foot and confronted the great expanse of blue. It eclipsed the world around me.

I sprinted with the focus and arm-pumping determination of an action hero chasing a train and I pitched forward.

I was a whirling wonder, born to move in a way no one else had. I rotated in the air like a flipped coin. The question was, would I land on heads or tails?

After my double twisting double back, the exact skill that had finished in a torn Achilles in Qatar, my feet stuck into the mat, my arms locked into place by my ears, and my wrists flicked.

My heart beat in my ears. I was alive. I was meant for this. The skills were the stars of this narrative and my body knew the script by heart. But Nicole and Lucy peered around the corners of my tumbling passes. They watched me while I pirouetted. They joined me in the air. And they were with me when I stuck my final landing.

Applause thundered around me. I was a triumphant gladiator, and this my Colosseum. The question remained: Was I their Olympian, or was there a more worthy champion?

Nicole would drink her poison any second. She'd be out of the competition. Then I was as good as gold.

But our world still shivered from the shock of the pandemic, and our sport still reverberated with Levett's crimes. Gymnastics shouldn't be further discolored; it should serve as a spot of brilliance in a sometimes muddled landscape. Our athletes—our people—deserved the chance to feel safe again.

I needed to be better than Vanda and the other coaches who condoned abuse because it optimized their success. I needed to be better than the version of me who didn't stand with Lucy. I needed to hold on to the perspective gained after the entire world was ravaged by a coronavirus. Otherwise, this whole experience would have been for nothing.

Nothing, of course, except everything I ever wanted.

I looked to where Lucy cheered with my family. Her hips rocked and her fists punched the air. It wasn't the same innocent celebration from our youth. It wasn't as jubilant. This version was laden by experience. But still, Lucy was dancing.

I jogged over to where Nicole stretched with her coach. Lou stepped forward, but realizing he didn't have time to intercept, he retreated and lowered into a chair, watching, warning.

Nicole's Nalgene bottle balanced beside her. It was still full.

The cameras followed as I dropped to my knees and spoke close enough for Nicole to hear me. At first she flinched, uncertain and put off by my sudden and assertive presence. But then her head drifted closer to mine.

"Don't drink your water," I said between breaths. "Lou put something in it."

My confession was projected onto the Jumbotron, and likely broadcasted. Millions watched a magnified Nicole smile strangely, assuming this was some weird joke. She checked my face for the punch line, but when she found none, her lips bowed and her eyes enlarged. She knew Lou; if anyone was capable of something so terrible, it was him.

I nodded to reinforce her realization and squeezed her foot. "You didn't drink. You're still okay. Good luck."

Lou didn't say anything when I sat down beside him. He didn't even look at me. Maybe he couldn't put his disgust into words, or maybe he was saving his words for when we weren't in the public eye, and he could use them as daggers.

Nicole whispered to her coach. His horror focused into rage. He snatched the Nalgene bottle from Nicole and hastened around the center floor to the selection committee's table.

This was it. They would hear what Lou did. They would pull me from the competition. He would go to jail. *I* could go to jail. And in twenty years, they'd make a movie about me. I'd be depicted as the gymnast who was willing to do anything—abandon a friend, poison a colleague—until she had a last-minute crisis of conscience. *I, Sera: the cold-blooded coward.*

The coach's features were drawn in brusque lines as he bent over the committee members and gesticulated toward us. I clenched my glute muscles and attempted to look as far apart as anybody could from the man she was sitting beside.

The committee member at the center was a middle-aged man in a suit with a sculpted hairstyle. He reached for the bottle and, for a moment, both men palmed their half, but then Nicole's coach released his. The male judge conferred with his female colleagues and, when they reached an agreement, he tucked the bottle beneath their table. He communicated evenly and nodded to the coach, as if to thank him, and more importantly, to dismiss him. The coach waffled.

Then he reluctantly rejoined Nicole. As the two scanned the arena, presumably expecting the consequences to initiate—the event to be paused, police to escort Lou out in handcuffs, *something*—the next gymnast was called to the floor. Their outrage deflated into bewilderment. The arena was proceeding as if the last five minutes—my confession and the coach's whistleblowing—had never happened.

Perhaps the officials would wait until after the event to involve law enforcement, test the bottle, interview bystanders, investigate. But it was also possible that, though I had grown, though I hadn't been silent about Lou the way I'd been silent about Levett, the organization remained much the same. The Trials were watched by the world, and it was too soon after Levett's controversy to allow this new scandal to be available for public consumption. They had appearances to reconstruct.

Like Lucy said: elite gymnastics hadn't changed one bit.

"Now what?" The question escaped before I remembered that my coach and I weren't speaking.

To my surprise, Lou answered, and sounded almost upbeat. "Now nothing."

His nonchalance revolted me. "You can still get in serious trouble, you know."

"If they ask, I'll deny it."

Now I spoke like he wasn't just a monster, but a stupid monster. "They have the water. They can test it."

"I hope they do. It's clean. I wouldn't drug a girl. I'm not crazy."

The swinging brass of a gymnast's floor music blared over the loudspeakers, too loud to ask questions and demand answers. Lou's smug face quivered in its efforts to hold itself together. He was one snicker away from disintegrating into delight.

He was either bluffing now, or this had all been a ploy to motivate me. Or worse, he'd predicted that I would rat him out to Nicole, unsettling her before she performed. In trying to save Nicole, I might have sabotaged her.

Words sat like gym chalk on my tongue. I prayed Lou's plan wouldn't work, that Nicole would be able to retreat into the mind space that protected her from emotion—we all cultivated one. And yet, to my disdain, I also hoped she wouldn't.

When Nicole approached the beam, she rolled her shoulders back and cupped her chin, using it as a leverage to crack her neck. Her routine was nimble, solid, unfaltering—until she dismounted. Then one foot was pulled from the soil of her landing, and her other followed. Her moorings came uprooted while she still carried the momentum of her movement. Nicole stumbled back and the crowd groaned the inevitable. Her arms dropped from around her ears and flapped at her sides. She searched for balance. And it was as if she found it, as if she grasped something invisible in the air and took hold. Her feet stilled. She steadied and carried her arms, uncertainly, back to their place, pointing toward the rafters. The crowd clapped appreciatively. She'd saved herself from disaster, but not from deductions.

WHILE THE SELECTION committee deliberated, we were shepherded to the athletes' room, and Lou was audacious enough to stick around in the faces of his former gymnast and her coach, who wore an expression of bafflement that said he didn't recognize anything or anyone around him. I wondered if he was still expecting due process to play out or if he'd resigned himself to injustice, and was hoping, at least, to be comforted by a dream realized. I knew the feeling.

Lou paced in front of me, the athlete he'd counted on to betray him. He was a fiend and I his fool. But he'd also gotten me this far. The chill of the chair cooled my sweat, my blood. I pumped a heel and concentrated on not vomiting.

Noise drifted into our room as dancers, singers, and an MC entertained the crowd overhead and the viewers at home. They needed to keep their enthusiasm up in order to welcome the new Team USA. The First Four.

At the last Trials, the selection committee had debated for an eternity. This time, I was surprised when they filed in so soon. The decision must have been easy. My stomach pitched.

The new high-performance team coordinator spoke about the caliber of talent, and the way in which we'd faced challenges that no athletes had faced before. His voice droned like a cloud of wasps. I waited for names to be read—I waited for a sting.

He named the winner of the Trials and the runner-up. Two spots remained, and then the alternates. My eyes flashed around the room; I calculated consistency, flare, skills, health, showmanship, image, and personal bias. There were at least five arguments to be made. This wasn't a no-brainer.

When the first letter of the next name wasn't an S, I turned off my ears and guarded myself. *That's it. It's over.*

"Sera Wheeler."

My name. He said my name. I was the last member of Team USA. Sponsorships. Name recognition. Medals. Press tours. Glory. I'd gone from wanting so fiercely for a small lifetime, to suddenly having, being. I was an Olympian.

Then I was inside Lou's embrace. He squeezed so hard he lifted me off the chair. His biceps muffled my ears, but through them I heard his whisper.

"You did it, girlie. You did it."

Whenever I'd been in the gym, so had he. He had watched and rewatched my routines and scrutinized footage. He'd sacrificed social obligations for training hours, just as I had. He'd bet all he had on me. He'd been unethical, yes, absolutely, but wasn't that also for me?

From inside Lou's hold, I watched Nicole lean against her coach. She hadn't made it.

But didn't it make sense that I was chosen above her? Her bars routine was a less challenging version of mine. Her floor routine wasn't faultless. And she'd made an error on the beam. Unless that error was because she'd been distracted by what I'd claimed Lou had done—falsely, as it turned out.

Every gymnast had her off days; this sort of error happened all the time. But not every gymnast thought someone she once trusted had drugged her, and that the organization she'd committed her young life to didn't care.

I pushed myself free of Lou's hold. His leather cheeks were streaked. I searched for any sign of conflict, for any emotion besides elation. I found none.

The committee distributed royal blue warm-ups embossed with "TEAM USA." Other girls—my teammates—clung to my arms and squealed their congratulations. Their faces and their words are streaked in my memory, like passing scenery.

We were steered like prizewinning champion cattle to the double doors that led back into the arena. On the other side, the audience chanted "U-S-A, U-S-A." They chanted for us. They just didn't know who we were yet.

"Are you ready to meet your Olympic team?" the MC said. "I am proud to introduce you to your first team member."

The door opened and cheers swelled and rushed through it. Phones glowed in the stands, Jumbotron animation flashed, and spotlights panned. The first girl was swallowed by madness and the door closed.

With the next two names, I imagined my mother biting

her nails, Joe pulling the collar of his shirt over his nose, my father practicing calming breaths, Lucy praying that I got what I wanted, or perhaps praying that I didn't.

An event coordinator tugged me forward. "Are you all right? You look like you might faint." Then, inside the arena, my name boomed through the sound system. There wasn't time for an answer. The coordinator lowered her face in front of mine. Her mouth was as wide as a bridge. "Smile."

The door opened and I was pulled by the rip current of sound, a physical feeling, like a tide ebbing against my ears.

The other girls waited at the center of the arena, their arms around one another's waists. They were bouncing and their mouths were open, although I couldn't hear them.

I saw myself on the Jumbotron, first as a graphic performing the two-and-a-half twisting double back tuck, and then in real time. I looked stunned. Maybe even a little scared. This was my moment. The highlight of my life, only to be topped, perhaps, by what was to come. I was an Olympian. I better start acting like it.

My face burst into a grin and my hand shot in the air. The cheers amplified. Beneath blaring techno music was a throbbing beat. It took a moment to realize that the audience was chanting my name: "Sera, Sera, Sera." I was their victor. Their Greek goddess. I floated in on their esteem. When I reached the center, I threw my arm around the shoulders nearest to me.

The First Four. Fans admired our clean lines, sparkling

leos, painted faces, and yes, our skills—we were badass bal-
lerinas. But we, these smiling jewels, had also been berated
by coaches. Our bodies hadn't known a day without pain
since we were children. We thought of quitting but were in
too deep. We'd starved off the instincts of our female bodies.
We were gemmed roses, but we hid thorns. There were scars
beneath our spandex.

The MC would call the name of the first alternate next,
and my moment would end. So I breathed it in, slow and
steady. As I panned the view, the Jumbotron no longer illuminated my image. Now it featured my family. Most notably, my mother, who had forgotten the proud but dignified
persona she'd rehearsed over the years, and appeared to be
screaming out all her oxygen, like a roaring gorilla.

A fellow Olympian leaned in to my ear and said, "Your
mom is crazy."

I nodded vigorously. Yes, she was crazy, delirious, because
she'd gotten exactly what she'd wanted. We all had, hadn't
we? We'd finally realized this dream that began back when
two girls sat in the shadows of a gym, all elbows and knees
and bobby-pinned hair, gold glittering in their minds.

Lucy's hairbrush was aimed at my mouth. "What's it like
to be Shawn Johnson right now?" she asked, and then broke
from her journalist persona. "You know what? This is going
to be you someday. You should get used to hearing your real
name." She deepened her timbre again. "What's it like to be
Sera Wheeler right now?"

"It's amazing," I said. "I feel like the happiest girl in the world."

All those years ago, if I had just taken a moment to look around me—at Lucy, our unscathed bodies, our love of gymnastics, so simple and pure—I would have seen that heaven wasn't some faraway place I was hoping to visit. I'd already arrived; it was the here and now. That moment in time, when we didn't know how deeply we could be disappointed, violated, or betrayed, when we believed in movement, possibility, and the power of each other, was as sweet as life was ever going to get.

Fifteen years later, as part of the next Olympic team, I coursed with pride and relief and adrenaline. But there were other sensations too, ones I'd never factored into the rehearsals of my girlhood: lightning in my spine, igniting my back like an old tree stump; stone bruises on the pads of my feet that made it feel like I was standing on pebbles; wrist and ankle aches; muscle strains; and calcifying weariness—physical, mental, and emotional. I carried the weight of knowing what arriving at this moment had siphoned from my family, that Lous and Eddies existed in the world, and that they'd existed in mine. Then there was fresh guilt: I'd never know if I'd honestly earned my spot or if I'd inadvertently kneecapped my opponent. I'd carry that wondering far longer than any gratification.

If I could bring this insight back in time, would I admit to that young gymnast playing make-believe that this—tired, bitter, and sorry—was what it would feel like to become the happiest girl in the world? Would I keep quiet and let her dream free as long as time would allow, or would I grab her by her small frame and shake, saying, "If you can do anything else, be anything else, by God, do that thing, be that thing. Because this will bruise and break you. And it'll bruise and break everyone around you."

No, I probably wouldn't, because I suspected there was a greater truth: that little dreamer had no choice but to see this thing through, because some desires aren't an entity that you chase, an external object that you can keep at arm's length. They are born from within, proliferating from organ to organ, bone to bone, metastasizing like a cancer, and you can't escape what lives inside you.

In the coming days, there'd be flashing cameras and microphones. There'd be an Olympic Village grouped by country of origin with flags in windows. There'd be piles of condoms embossed with the Olympic logo stationed throughout every housing complex, because nothing is sexier than being the best. There'd be the opening ceremonies—the most spectacular event I'd ever witness, with bright lights and deafening noise, parades, bands, dance performers, and fireworks. There'd be the torch and the Olympic rings. There'd be Novocain shots to keep my back quiet when it counted. There'd be the podium and those medals that hung heavy against my chest. There'd be people stopping me on the street, waving to me from cars, requesting autographs in restaurants, coffee shops, and gas stations.

There'd be Lou, now an Olympic-medal-winning coach, taking on another girl to train, his eye set on 2024, with no consequences or visible regrets smudging his rearview mirror.

Back home, I'd pack up my trophies and medals, sit down, and wander the halls of my life, searching for something, somebody, anybody else. Who else lived inside me, without my ever knowing? An architect, artist, engineer? I was committed; that much I knew. If someone was there, I'd find her.

I'd leave gymnastics behind. I wouldn't even talk about it much, except when my mother interviewed me for her new business, a consulting service for parents with children on the elite track. But gymnastics wouldn't leave me. There'd be Adderall withdrawal. My left wrist would never bend without soreness. There'd be lifelong shin splints, kidney disease from Advil overuse, and arthritis.

There'd be a series of dysfunctional relationships. I'd become so accustomed to mistreatment, abuse of all kinds felt ordinary. Comfortable, even. Or maybe I would continue seeking punishment as recompense for having escaped Edward Levett. When I finally found someone tender and respectful, I'd cling to him for the rest of my life like he was a high bar.

There'd be our two daughters, through whom I'd experience childhood for the first time. We'd lick ice-cream cones, ride merry-go-rounds, and tumble into ball pits. We'd pump our legs on swings, comb the grass for ladybugs, play hide-and-seek with Grandpa and Uncle Joe, and ride bikes in the driveway.

They'd run in circles in the backyard, shrieking at the top of their lungs with their arms flung wide, and I'd want to call to them, "Yes. Yell until your voice wears out. It's yours. Use it." But I didn't need to; they already knew. Or at least they knew for the moment, and if they ever forgot, I'd remind them.

My daughters and I would giggle at one another from headstands, our hair spilling onto the carpet, our smiles inverted but bright. They'd beg me to show off moves on the playground monkey bars, doing things other mothers couldn't. But when they'd ask me to enroll them in gymnastics classes, the back of my neck would prickle with heat.

"How about karate?" I'd ask. "Soccer? Tap?"

I'd remind myself that there was joy in the movements, in wagging your tongue at gravity, in exploring your body's abilities, in the meditative focus required of discipline. And so I'd relent, but I'd never leave a practice. I'd eye their instructors like they were in a police lineup. And for every hour spent in the gym, my girls would have to devote another to something else.

One day, Grandma would bring a poster from my Summer Olympics to hang in their bedroom. "They should know what their mama accomplished," she'd say, and I'd stuff the poster down in the storage box beside my medals.

It would take years, but my relationship with my family would be restored. Sometimes, as with an old piece of furniture, you had to dig in—tear off the upholstery, rip out the stuffing, and remake it. We'd rebuild from a composite of materials: memories, love, loyalty, and resentment. Our history would be there, but we'd look like new.

All that, and so many delightfully ordinary moments, was to come. For now, there was only the arena.

The Jumbotron swept from my frenzied mother, whose inner compass had locked onto this moment as due north since that day at the YMCA; to my father, who had worried that all our sacrifices and discord would never be worthwhile, and who may have been right; to my brother, who had quietly, obediently, drifted into my background; and to Lucy, who was supposed to be sharing this spotlight, but whose dream had been infected by a sick healer and her fickle friend. They were all clapping, dancing, and hollering so hard their vocal cords bulged from their necks. They were celebrating the success whose cost they'd each paid in part.

Confetti and streamers dropped from the ceiling, and there, on the big screen, forty feet across, was me, Sera Wheeler, the happiest girl in the world, beaming her open-mouthed smile, shedding tears of a complicated joy. This was her moment, the culmination of so many layers of purpose, pride, and pain.

Outside, the sun was setting, and the clouds were burning into something gilded.

ACKNOWLEDGMENTS

Writing is a solitary act, but building a book requires a village, and I am endlessly grateful for mine.

Thank you to my agent, Nicki Richesin, who went back and forth with me on drafts until the words began to spin. Thank you to Wendy Sherman for her advocacy and Lindsay Quackenbush for her feedback. Thank you to my editor, Lucia Macro, who believed in my project (and me) once again, and coaxed Charlene's voice to life. Thank you to the entire team at William Morrow for their support, efforts, and enthusiasm, especially Asanté Simons, Jessica Lyons, Amelia Wood, Jennifer Hart, Lainey Mays, and Iris McElroy. I'm sure I am failing to name other crucial contributors, inside William Morrow and beyond, and to all those: thank you. Thank you to Hope Breeman, whose meticulous copyediting expertise saved me from embarrassment. Thank you to the Book Club Girls for being so fun and welcoming. Thank you to Katrina Escudero and Jason Richman for their behind-the-scenes magic.

Thank you to Peter Nelson, whose comments helped to reveal the heart of this story; to Julia Maggiola, whom I badger for opinions I so value; and to Elizabeth Matelski and Courtney Lentz, for hot tips on Midwest life—most notably the concrete goose.

Thank you to Blythe Lawrence for being so incredibly generous and thorough with her gymnastics prowess, participating in the interview at the back of the book, and letting me pepper her with innumerable questions along the way. (She knows so much!)

Thank you to my parents for providing childcare that allowed me to carve out time for this novel (and for so many other things). Thank you to my husband for protecting and honoring my identity as a writer, and for being a sounding board and steadfast partner in all things.

This novel was written while we were hoping for my son, throughout my pregnancy with him, and from when he was eight weeks to fourteen months old, so thank you to Rowen for sharing from the start.

About the author

About the book

Insights,
Interviews
& More . . .

Meet Alena Dillon

Debasmit Banerjee

ALENA DILLON is the author of *Mercy House*, which is in development as a CBS All Access television series. Her work has appeared in publications including Lit Hub, *River Teeth, Slice* magazine, The Rumpus, and Bustle. She teaches creative writing and lives on the North Shore of Boston with her husband, son, and dog. ᕃ

Behind the Book

I began mapping this story on the second day of Larry Nassar's trial.

Before that, gymnastics only crossed my radar every four years. Along with much of the world, I was swept up by the thrill of the Olympic Games and made a special effort to tune in for the U.S. gymnastics team (and volleyball), hungry to catch up on all I'd missed since the last cycle. I was moved by curated backstories and what was at stake for these girls I suddenly referred to by first name. And then, after the closing ceremonies, the athletes moved on with their medals or disappointments, and so did I.

In January 2018, though, we began to hear about what so many of these young women suffered when we weren't paying attention. And it seemed like we'd been reckless; because we'd been entertained by their ambition and talents, it almost felt like we were complicit in what these girls endured to achieve their heights.

It got me thinking: If someone who wasn't involved felt this way, how did the parents feel? How did the coaches feel? How did the athletes feel? How did it feel for those who knew everything? How did it feel for those who knew something, but not quite enough to interfere—especially when those individuals were generally well meaning? And most significantly, what sort of culture allowed abuse to propagate uninterrupted, contributing ▸

Behind the Book *(continued)*

to a world in which someone like Nassar could slink below the surface?

Those wonderings sparked this narrative.

I am a novelist, so my plot and characters would be fictional, but I wanted them to reflect true conditions and experiences to the best of my ability. I wanted to take truth and spin it into a story, but first I had to gather the threads, so I began to research.

Memoirs, podcasts, documentaries, competitions, YouTube videos, official materials, social media accounts, and gymnastics blogs all revealed that gymnasts often operated inside a realm of imperatives: obedience, pain, and victory above all, even physical well-being. They worked *hard*. Extreme commitment, sacrifice, and rigor were normalized. Such a stifling biosphere was bound to suffocate the ordinariness of a young life, I thought, and affect the air of those around that individual as well.

An overarching question beat beneath my research and ruminations. It compelled me to create this fiction, and its urgency stayed with me through the research, character building, drafts, and various plot re-envisionings. That question was: What did greatness cost, and who paid its price?

There are as many answers to that question as there are dreamers. *The Happiest Girl in the World* is a story that illustrates one possibility. ◠

Interview with Blythe Lawrence, Gymnastics Expert

Blythe Lawrence is a gymnastics journalist, an analyst at RockerGymnastics.com, and the coauthor of Aly Raisman's memoir, *Fierce: How Competing for Myself Changed Everything*. She was gracious enough to read two versions of the manuscript for *The Happiest Girl in the World* to check for accuracy and authenticity. Since I had no firsthand experience with the sport, the insight she provided was invaluable. I was so impressed with the nuance of her knowledge, and so thankful, after all she'd already contributed, that she was also willing to participate in this interview.

Alena Dillon: *You were a gymnast yourself. What drew you to the sport?*

Blythe Lawrence: Watching the U.S. Olympic Trials on TV one Saturday afternoon in 1992. I remember being absolutely transfixed and thinking that it was the coolest thing I'd ever seen. I was eight years old and had been taking ballet. Afterward I begged my parents to let me switch to gymnastics. ▶

Interview with Blythe Lawrence, Gymnastics Expert *(continued)*

Alena: *What was your favorite part about training?*

Blythe: I loved almost everything, but especially training on balance beam. There's something about the zone you can get into on beam—the world falls away, everything goes quiet. It can be very peaceful.

Alena: *Why did you stop?*

Blythe: Adult gymnastics was far less popular and accessible in the early 2000s than it is today, so like a lot of teenagers I all but stopped after graduating from high school. But when I got a job in Switzerland at age twenty-nine, I joined an adult gymnastics team there and even competed for a few years. It was a wonderful and unexpected epilogue to my career!

Alena: *Do you think your experience in gymnastics has affected other aspects of your life, outside of work?*

Blythe: Certainly the discipline I learned in the sport has carried over to other areas. Some of the mentality too. While not a perfectionist, I can be quite self-critical. Maybe that has something to do with the sport, but maybe not. I didn't have mean coaches or traumatizing experiences, nor did I ever get close to the elite level. But even so, gymnastics is a hard sport, and you definitely leave it tougher than when you came in.

Alena: *How did you become a gymnastics journalist?*

Blythe: I studied journalism and got a reporting job at a small weekly paper out of college. Because the paper was located in a maritime community, I covered marine trades, and it was a subject with a steep learning curve. When I came home at night I wanted to write about something I felt I had more mastery over, and wound up starting a blog about gymnastics. The blog got some traction during the next few years, and I got some freelance writing jobs because of it. Things kind of snowballed from there.

Alena: *What was it like for you when the Larry Nassar story broke?*

Blythe: At events leading up to the 2012 Olympics, I distinctly remember people raving about what a class act Larry Nassar was, so it came as a shock to learn what had been going on. Then working on *Fierce* with Aly and hearing her stories, and hearing and reading the stories of survivors as they came forward ... "heartbreaking" and "infuriating" are two words that come to mind. ▶

**Interview with Blythe Lawrence,
Gymnastics Expert** *(continued)*

Alena: *You travel to competitions and qualifiers. Do you have preferred events to attend? Can you tell us a little about the atmosphere?*

Blythe: The World Championships are always spectacular. There are a lot of different styles of gymnastics, and they're all on display, and watching the history unfold is incredibly special. During the past few years, Worlds organizers have also made the event a lot more dramatic and entertaining. Athletes are introduced like rock stars, entering the arena by walking across a stage with jets of flame shooting up around it and a 3-D image of them doing a jump or flip displayed on an enormous screen behind them. In addition to being a serious athletic competition, the whole thing is more of a show, and it's really exciting. I hope it's fun for the gymnasts as well!

Alena: *Do you have preferred apparatuses to watch?*

Blythe: Perhaps women's floor exercise, because it incorporates music and choreography. The best floor routines tell stories; they're theater as much as sport.

Alena: *How do you think the sport will be different in five years? Ten?*

Blythe: It's hard to say. Different skills and combinations come into vogue or fall out of favor depending on how the code of points changes with each new Olympic cycle. Simone Biles has brought skills that only existed in people's imaginations to life, and I suspect that we'll see the sport continue to reward very high-difficulty routines. But one of the nice things about gymnastics is its variety; there are different ways to achieve a really high score. Hopefully that doesn't change.

Alena: *What was it like working with Aly Raisman?*

Blythe: Aly was an absolute pleasure to work with! She brought the mentality of an Olympic athlete to the writing process: she was focused and meticulous, and paid so much attention to detail. She took ownership of the stories she wanted in the book and was a very thoughtful collaborator.

Alena: *If you weren't a gymnastics nerd, what sport would you follow, or would you have a completely different career?*

Blythe: I love sports that have a big performance art component to them, so figure skating would probably be one main occupation. Even if gymnastics didn't exist, I'd still be a journalist, and probably still write about the Olympics. There are so many fascinating stories to be told there. ▶

**Interview with Blythe Lawrence,
Gymnastics Expert** *(continued)*

Alena: *Do you still handstand or
cartwheel every once in a while, just
to be upside down?*

Blythe: Every day! ∿

Reading Group Guide

1. This novel is narrated in the first person, largely from Sera's perspective, but with regular insertions from her mother. Did you find them to be reliable narrators? Were there moments in which you questioned their points of view?

2. How did the relationship between Sera's parents affect the life trajectory of their children?

3. Which characters contributed to a culture of abuse? Were any blameless?

4. At what point did you expect Sera or Lucy to speak out about their doctor?

5. The moment when Sera betrays Lucy is a turning point for their friendship. Under what conditions is it possible for relationships to survive betrayals?

6. Can a young person ever pursue extraordinary ambitions in a healthy way?

7. What is your level of attachment to Olympic sports? Did you find that attachment influencing your experience as you read this novel? ▶

Reading Group Guide *(continued)*

8. What sort of life sacrifices can be justified if greatness is achieved? Is the *quest* for greatness enough to justify those same sacrifices if the dreamer falls short of her goal?

9. What are the consequences of affording those who interact with children the benefit of the doubt? What are the consequences of always suspecting the worst?

10. How did the setting influence the plot and characters of this novel? How might the story have changed if set in a different part of the country or world?

11. How do you think Olympic organizations should be amended moving forward to avoid endangering and/or commodifying their athletes?

12. In what ways were the topics of substance abuse addressed in the novel? ∽